PRAISE FOR
MANDASUE HELLER

'Mandasue Heller never disappoints!'
Roberta Kray

'One of the bad girls of gritty crime'
Daily Mirror

'Mandasue Heller's at the top of her game'
Heather Atkinson

'One of the country's top crime novelists'
Great British Life

'Her storytelling is unmatched with characters so vivid they leap off the page'
D.S. Butler

'Mandasue Heller knows the world she writes about'
The Herald

MANDASUE HELLER is a million-copy bestselling Queen of Manchester Gangland crime. She was born in Warrington, Cheshire and has worked as a professional singer and full-time writer, with various other jobs in between: TV extra, barmaid, waitress, pharmacy assistant, phone-line tarot card reader, to name just a few.

Connect with her here:

𝕏 @MandasueHeller
@mandasueheller
http://mandasueheller.com/

Also by Mandasue Heller

The Family
Running Scared
Witness
Brutal
Save Me
Run
Afraid
Respect
Broke
Lost Angel
The Driver
Two-Faced
Snatched
Shafted
The Club
The Charmer
The Game
Tainted Lives
Forget Me Not
The Front

THE CHILD

MANDASUE HELLER

ORION

First published in Great Britain in 2026 by Orion Fiction,
an imprint of The Orion Publishing Group Ltd.
Carmelite House, 50 Victoria Embankment
London EC4Y 0DZ

An Hachette UK Company

The authorised representative in the EEA is Hachette Ireland,
8 Castlecourt Centre, Dublin 15, D15 XTP3,
Ireland (email: info@hbgi.ie)

1 3 5 7 9 10 8 6 4 2

A CIP catalogue record for this book is
available from the British Library.

ISBN (Hardback) 9781 3987 1342 0
ISBN (Ebook) 9781 3987 1345 1
ISBN (Audio) 9781 3987 1346 8

Typeset at The Spartan Press Ltd,
Lymington, Hants

Printed and bound in Great Britain by Clays Ltd,
Elcograf S.p.A.

MIX
Paper | Supporting
responsible forestry
FSC® C104740

www.orionbooks.co.uk

For my beautiful mum, always xx

Prologue

It was 9 p.m. and pitch-dark when the door suddenly opened and voices and light from within spilled out onto the pavement. Huddled in the doorway directly opposite the unmarked building, a woman squinted at the silhouettes of the men who came out. Her stomach did a little flip when she saw the one she was looking for. When, at last, the group dispersed and the door had closed, plunging the deserted road back into darkness, she took a deep breath and stepped out of the shadows. Then, head down, her frozen hands stuffed into her pockets, she followed the man down the road to where she'd spotted his parked car earlier that evening.

As he turned the corner, the man heard her heels clipping on the concrete behind him and snapped his head round. At first, there was no hint of recognition in his eyes. But that quickly changed and a deep crease formed between his eyebrows.

'What are you doing here?' he demanded, casting a glance around to check that no one was watching.

'I need to talk to you,' she replied quietly.

'About what?'

'I've got a problem,' she murmured, shivering when she saw the ice in his eyes. 'And it's too big for me to handle on my own, so I need—'

'Let me stop you right there,' he interrupted, giving her a knowing look. 'Whatever you're after, you can forget it. We had a good time, but that's all it was. And I paid you, so that's the end of it.'

'I'm pregnant,' she said. 'And you're the only one I've slept with in months, so it's yours.'

'Nice try,' he scoffed. 'I wore a condom, in case you've forgotten, so go find yourself another mug to hang this on.'

He turned away from her at that and walked briskly to his car. Angered by his dismissive words and the scornful way he'd looked at her, she went after him and stepped in front of the car to prevent him from opening his door.

'This is *your* child,' she hissed. 'And it's as much your responsibility as mine, so you don't get to walk away scot-free and leave me to struggle with it.'

'I wore a *condom*,' he repeated through gritted teeth. 'Now quit trying to pin another man's bastard on me and move, or I'll move you myself.'

'It's yours,' she reiterated. 'But if *you* won't step up, maybe I should talk to your wife instead?'

His reaction was swift and brutal, and she cried out in fear when he seized her by the throat and slammed her up against the car.

'You open your filthy whore mouth about me and it'll be the last thing you ever fucking do,' he warned. 'I'll make you disappear so fast, you won't know what's hit you. Understood?'

Unable to breathe, she desperately clawed at his hand. But he increased the pressure and stared down into her eyes, hissing, 'I said do you understand?'

Too weak to do anything but give a tiny nod, her face crumpled when he drove his fist into her stomach.

'Hopefully that'll solve your problem,' he spat, letting her go and watching, coldly, as she slid to the floor. 'Now stay the fuck away from me and my family.'

In agony, she clutched her stomach and curled into a ball as, seemingly satisfied that she'd got the message, he tugged his cuffs back into place and smoothed his jacket down before climbing into his car and driving away.

Chapter 1

Isla Hanson could hear the drone of her husband, Jerry's, ride-on lawnmower as she typed her credit card details into the booking form on her laptop. He'd been going out into the garden so often lately, she was starting to wonder if he was actually mowing or just riding around to make himself feel busy. Retirement clearly wasn't suiting him as much as he'd expected it would, and Isla wished he had thought things over a bit more thoroughly before selling his half of the company he'd co-owned with his old friend and business partner, Peter Jenkins. If he'd retained his shares, he could have taken the break he'd claimed he needed and then gone back to work. But he'd been adamant that he wanted all the way out, and Peter wasn't the type to relinquish control now he had it. So Jerry was now rattling around the house like a lost soul; bored, irritable and driving Isla crazy.

Finished with the form, Isla waited until she received the email confirmation of her booking and then closed the laptop.

She had an appointment at the hair salon in half an hour, so she made a sandwich for Jerry's lunch and left it on the counter, along with a note telling him that she would be back in a few hours.

As she waited for the electric gate to open a few minutes later,

Isla's phone started ringing. She quickly answered it when she saw that it was her best friend, Tia.

'Hey, I thought you were supposed to be working today?'

'I am,' Tia replied quietly. 'But my bride's turning into the Zilla from hell, so I've left her and her mother squabbling over the brunch menu and snuck out for a vape break. It was either that or deck the pair of them. Which, obviously, I *can't*, 'cos I need the money. But, my God, they're doing my head in.'

'That bad?' Isla asked, using the fob to close the gate behind her before driving out onto the road.

'Worse,' said Tia. 'But never mind me. Did you manage to book your tickets?'

'I sure did,' Isla affirmed. 'It cost way more than our actual honeymoon, but it's our fifteenth anniversary *and* Jerry's sixtieth, so it was worth it. And it'll be my thirty-sixth soon, so I thought I might as well roll it all into one big celebration. I'm just hoping he cheers up before the day, or I might have to leave him at home and go by myself.'

'Is he still struggling?'

'Yep. And so am I now he's under my feet all the time.'

'Well, this break should do you both good,' Tia said. 'And it might even pep Jerry up in other ways, as well,' she added with a chuckle. 'If not, I'm sure there'll be plenty of sexy waiters to keep you occu—'

'Excuse me. What the hell do you think you're doing?' a woman at Tia's end barked before she could finish. 'Why are you out here yapping on your phone while I'm in there doing your job for you?'

'Sorry, I had a family emergency,' Tia lied. 'I'll be back with you in a moment.'

'Make sure you are, because I'm seriously close to exploding,' the woman snapped. 'I'm under so much stress right now and you don't seem to give a damn. I wouldn't mind, but you're supposed to be the wedding planner and I've practically done all this by myself so far. It's an absolute joke!'

Isla's eyebrows shot up as she waited for her friend to clap back at the rude woman. But Tia merely reiterated, politely, that she would only be a moment. The woman muttered something under her breath and stomped away, and Isla heard Tia blow out a loud breath when a door squealed open and then slammed shut again.

'Did you hear that?' Tia came back on the line. 'Now do you see the kind of shit I've been dealing with?'

'Yeah, I heard,' Isla replied indignantly. 'What a bitch.'

'I reckon she's trying to make me quit so she can get out of paying me,' said Tia. 'But she can fuck off if she thinks I'm walking away at this late stage. And if she tries to sack me, I'll have her in court so fast, her head will spin.'

'Too right,' Isla agreed.

'Oh, well, I've only got to put up with her for a couple more days,' Tia sighed. 'If I make it that far without getting arrested, I might book myself a ticket and join you and Jerry on the beach to decompress.'

'You will not,' Isla protested, amused by the thought of Jerry's reaction if her friend gate-crashed their second honeymoon.

'Don't worry, I was joking,' Tia assured her. 'Right, I'd best get back in there before bitchy-poo kicks off again. Thanks for letting me vent.'

'Any time,' said Isla. 'And if she goes off on you again, give me a shout. You might not be able to deck her, but I certainly can.'

'I might just hold you to that,' Tia laughed. 'Speak later. Love you.'

'Love you, too,' Isla said, smiling as she cut the call.

*

Isla felt like a million dollars when she left the salon later that afternoon. Her long auburn hair had been subtly highlighted, and the stylist had taken off a couple of inches, so it now felt lighter and healthier. She had also decided to treat herself to a spray tan while she was there, to give herself a head-start before she and Jerry arrived in Almeira for the joint anniversary and birthday trip.

Excited by the thought of revisiting the place where she and Jerry had honeymooned, and praying that it would snap him out of the funk he'd fallen into since retiring, Isla stopped off at the butcher's in the village to pick up a couple of steaks for dinner before heading home.

When she entered the kitchen, the note and sandwich were still sitting on the ledge where she'd left them. Guessing that Jerry must still be outside, Isla looked out through the window. She knew he hadn't left the house because his car was still on the driveway, but the lawnmower was now parked up and there was no sign of him in the garden. He didn't answer when she called his name, so she put away the shopping and then picked up the sandwich and went to look for him.

The summer house and shed were both empty, but the gate at the rear of the garden was standing slightly ajar. The land beyond the gate sloped steeply down to a stream that ran past the backs of the houses on their block, and Isla knew that Jerry sometimes went down there to smoke a cigar when he thought she wasn't looking. That, along with forgetting to eat if Isla wasn't there to remind him, was the cause of most of their arguments of late. He wasn't getting any younger, and his GP had already warned him that he needed to start taking better care of himself. But Jerry had never taken kindly to people telling him what to do – least of all his wife.

It was a sunny day, but the dense undergrowth and trees that lined the banks of the stream made it impossible for Isla to see anything clearly. After calling Jerry's name several times to no avail, she was about to head back into the garden when she noticed two deep grooves in the mud to her left. They looked fresh and a feeling of unease stirred in her gut when it occurred to her that Jerry might have slipped down the slope and could be lying injured in the thickets below. She pulled her phone out of her pocket and was relieved to hear the faint sound of his ringtone coming from the garden behind her. Turning, she followed the sound across the lawn. It grew louder the closer she got to the lawnmower, and her heart lurched in her chest when she spotted the toe of one of Jerry's gardening shoes poking out from behind it.

Jerry was lying on his side between the hedge and the machine. At first glance, he appeared to be sleeping, so Isla reached down and gently touched his shoulder to wake him. She cried out in alarm when she saw that there was no sign of life in his partially open eyes.

Chapter 2

It was a bright day, but Isla felt like a dark cloud was hovering over her head as the hearse pulled up outside the crematorium doors. Tia, who was sitting beside her in the back of the limousine behind the hearse, reached for her hand and gave it a gentle squeeze.

'Are you OK?'

Isla nodded, but it was a lie. It had been almost five weeks since Jerry had died, but it still felt unreal, and she prayed that her legs wouldn't give way as she climbed out of the car. Tears blurred her vision as she watched the pallbearers slide Jerry's casket out from the back of the hearse and hoist it onto their shoulders. She determinedly blinked them away and raised her chin as she and Tia slowly followed them inside.

Several neighbours and a handful of villagers were seated at the rear of the small chapel, and the rest of the seats were occupied by Jerry's old friends, clients, co-workers and their spouses. There were no family members present, because the ones Jerry had been close to had already passed away. He'd had no contact with his more distant relatives in years, so Isla hadn't been able to personally notify them. She had hoped that one of them might spot his obituary in the paper and reach out, but none had. Still, Jerry had always insisted that she and his friends were the family he had chosen, so she was glad that the people who had been the most important to him in life had come along to pay their respects.

The service was mercifully short, as per Jerry's wishes on the one and only occasion he and Isla had ever discussed what to do in the event of the other's death. That conversation had taken place early in their marriage, and Isla had been horrified when Jerry had told her to bung him in a box, chuck him on a bonfire and scatter his ashes into the stream. She wouldn't have dreamed of doing that even if she'd been allowed to, but Jerry had made it very clear that he didn't want her to waste money on an extravagant funeral. She hoped he would have approved of the choices she had made.

As the curtains began to slide shut around the coffin, Isla and Tia rose to their feet. An usher led them out through a side door into a small, enclosed yard at the rear of the building. The funeral directors had already placed the mourners' flowers out there, along with the small spray of lilies Isla had bought.

'Who's that?' Tia asked, nodding towards a blonde woman who was squatting down at the far end of the row of flowers, reading the cards attached to them.

'No idea,' Isla shrugged. 'She was probably passing and stopped to admire the flowers.'

'More like planning to nick them,' Tia said loudly. 'Yeah, *you*,' she went on when the woman snapped her head round. 'I'm watching you.'

A blush seared the woman's cheeks and she quickly stood up and grabbed the handles of a bright yellow pushchair that was parked behind her.

'That stopped her game,' Tia sneered, watching as the woman wheeled the pushchair out through the gate at the rear of the yard. 'They're so cheeky, these people.'

'I'm not taking them home, so she'd have been welcome to them,' Isla said, gazing down at the cellophane-wrapped blooms, some of which were already wilting. 'It's hard enough getting used to Jerry not being around without these reminding me that he's as dead as they soon will be.'

'It'll get easier,' Tia said, stroking her arm when she saw the tears in her eyes. 'You're doing really well.'

Isla nodded and blinked the tears away when she heard the other mourners coming out of the chapel. Peter Jenkins was leading the way, and Tia pulled a face when his booming voice ricocheted off the walls enclosing the yard.

'Christ, he's loud. I wish you'd let me hire a venue for the wake instead of doing it at the house. At least that way we could have escaped when we'd had enough. I don't know about you, but he gets on my last nerve.'

'It wouldn't have felt right,' Isla replied quietly. 'You know how much Jerry liked having them over, so he'd have wanted me to do it at home – even if he won't be there to enjoy it.'

'Trust me, he'll be there, watching over you,' Tia said.

'I hope so,' Isla said, comforted by the thought, even if she didn't quite believe it, given how sceptical Jerry had been about that kind of thing.

'I *know* so,' Tia said, reaching into her handbag when she felt her phone vibrate. 'It's Sam. I'll tell him to call back.'

'No, go and speak to him,' Isla insisted. 'He's hardly seen you in weeks; he must be missing you.'

'Is he hell,' Tia snorted. 'He'll have been having the time of his life without me there to boss him around. God only knows what state the flat'll be in when I get home.'

'It'll be fine,' Isla said, glancing at her watch. 'I think we should head back to the house, so you go and talk to Sam while I thank the vicar. I'll meet you out front.'

Tia nodded her agreement and stepped out through the gate to answer her boyfriend's call.

'Hi, babe. Is everything OK? I was trying to get hold of you earlier, but your phone kept going to voicemail.'

'Yeah, sorry about that,' Sam said. 'We've had wall-to-wall meetings all morning, so I had to keep it switched off. How's it going?'

'Just finished,' Tia told him. 'We'll be heading back to Isla's in a minute. What time do you think you'll get there?'

'Actually, I had a bit of an accident on the way to work and had to get my car towed, so I was going to ask if you could pick me up?'

'An accident?' Tia was alarmed. 'What happened? You're not hurt, are you?'

'No, I'm fine,' Sam assured her. 'But it turns out the car's not too keen on potholes,' he added sheepishly. 'So the suspension's a bit knackered.'

'Are you kidding me?' Tia spluttered. 'How many times have I warned you about those damn holes? And you've got the nerve to call *me* a bad driver.'

'I never said you were bad, just too fast,' Sam countered. 'So can you pick me up, or should I book an Uber?'

'I'll come for you. But only if you promise not to cling to the sides of your seat and squeal like a little girl.'

'Don't drive like a maniac and I swear I won't make a sound.'

'Touché,' Tia laughed. Then, glancing in through the gate and seeing that the mourners were no longer in the yard, she said, 'I'd best get going. I'll ring you when I'm on my way, but please be ready. I don't want to leave Isla on her own with this lot for too long.'

'No worries,' Sam said. 'Can't wait to see you.'

'Me too,' Tia replied, smiling as she cut the call and slotted the phone back into her bag. She had been staying at Isla's place since Jerry had died and had only seen Sam for the odd hour here and there, so she really couldn't wait to see her boy.

About to walk around to the limo, Tia hesitated when she spotted the blonde woman with the pram sitting on a bench in the graveyard on the other side of a low wall. She looked like she had the weight of the world on her shoulders. Remembering what Isla had said about the woman being welcome to the flowers, Tia walked over to the wall and called out to her.

'Excuse me, love … can I have a word?'

Bemused when the woman flashed a guilty look her way before jumping to her feet, Tia shook her head as she watched her push the pram away.

'Oh, well; your loss,' she murmured, shrugging it off as she walked around the building to join Isla in the limo.

Chapter 3

Rain had been forecast for that afternoon, but it had turned out to be a warm, bright day, so Isla had asked the caterers to serve the food outside. Jerry had loved his garden and had always been at his happiest when his friends gathered there for summer parties. He would man the fancy built-in barbeque on those days, tossing burgers and sausages, while the men stood around swilling whisky and continuing whatever discussions they had been having in the boardroom during the week. Their wives, in the meantime, would congregate on the patio, where they chugged wine and gossiped about whichever one of them was absent that day. Jerry had known them all before he'd met Isla, so she had never felt that she knew the women well enough to join in on those gossip-fests. But she had always been happy to play hostess; making sure that everybody was comfortable and had enough to eat and drink.

Today, without Jerry's presence to bolster her confidence, and with Tia on her way back to Manchester to pick up her boyfriend, Isla felt more like a waitress than the lady of the house as she wandered around with trays of drinks and sandwiches. The women seemed to stop talking whenever she went near, so she didn't feel able to join them. And Peter Jenkins was holding court in the barbeque pit surrounded by the men, so she couldn't join them, either. The invisible divide made Jerry's absence weigh all the more heavily on her heart, and she found herself checking the time every few minutes; praying that Tia would come back soon so she wouldn't feel so alone.

The caterers left at 6 p.m., and the few neighbours who had attended quickly followed suit. It was getting dark by then and the temperature had plummeted, but Jerry's friends seemed in no hurry to leave, so Isla switched on the garden lights and the patio heater, then poured another round of drinks. As she was making her way over to the group by the barbeque, she heard a commotion on the patio behind her. Shocked to see that Tia was back and appeared to be having a heated argument with Peter's wife, Felicity, Isla put the tray down on a table and rushed over to them.

'What's going on?' she asked. 'Has something happened?'

'Yeah, I've just walked in and caught this bitch mouthing off about you,' Tia explained. 'And *that* lot were smirking their fake little heads off,' she added, glaring at the other women, who collectively shrank back in their seats.

'Nonsense,' Felicity scoffed, the venom in her eyes at odds with the smile on her lips. 'We weren't even talking about Isla, so whatever you *think* you heard, you're barking up the wrong tree, my dear.'

'Oh really?' Tia shot back. 'Let's take a listen then, shall we?'

She held up her mobile phone and pressed *Play* on the audio clip she had recorded. Isla felt sick when Felicity's voice hissed out through the speaker.

'*Look at her, sashaying around like a bitch on heat. We all know the gold-digging whore used the oldest trick in the book to get her claws into Jerry, but if she thinks any of* our *men would touch her, she's even more stupid than she looks!*'

Tia switched the recording off at that and gave Felicity a challenging look. 'So, tell me again how I'm barking up the wrong tree and you weren't speaking about Isla.'

Caught out, Felicity's mouth flapped open and a deep blush seared her cheeks. Then, raising her chin defiantly, she said, 'How dare you record my private conversation with my friends.'

'Are you serious?' Isla stared at the woman in disbelief. 'How could you say something like that? It's my husband's wake!'

'It wasn't about you,' Felicity replied smoothly. 'Your friend was eavesdropping and obviously got hold of the wrong end of the stick.'

'No I didn't,' Tia shot back. 'I knew exactly who you were talking about. And I recorded you because Isla's *my* friend, and she's got a right to know what you lot are saying about her while she's bending over backwards to make you feel welcome. You should be ashamed of yourselves.'

'Oh, do go away,' Felicity drawled, flapping her hand dismissively. 'Don't you have glasses to wash or plates to collect?'

'You'd better watch your mouth, lady,' Tia warned.

'What on earth is going on over here?' Peter demanded, marching over to the women.

'This creature is attacking me,' Felicity told him. 'She illegally recorded me and then somehow managed to edit it to make it look as if I had said something that I absolutely hadn't.'

'Liar!' spat Tia. 'You know what you said, and so does everyone else.'

'She's going to hit me,' Felicity squawked, darting behind her husband. 'Do something, Peter.'

'That's enough!' Isla yelled. 'You need to leave.'

'Allow me to do the honours,' Peter said, puffing up his chest as he turned to Tia and reached for her arm. 'Come along, young lady. It's time for you to—'

'Not her, *you*.' Isla stepped between them. 'The party's over and I want you all to go.'

'Oh, come now...' Peter gave her a patronising smile. 'You've been through a lot and you're obviously tired, but the night's still young and Jerry's parties never finished before midnight. Why don't you take yourself off to bed and get some rest. We can see ourselves out.'

'I *said* the party is over,' Isla repeated firmly. 'Now please leave.'

'What did I tell you?' Felicity sniped to Peter as she snatched her handbag up off the floor. 'She was trash when he met her, and no amount of *his* money was ever going to change that.'

'Lady, you've got exactly two seconds to get out of here before I *put* you out,' Tia hissed. Then, turning to the other women, she clapped her hands together sharply, saying, 'And you lot can move it, as well. Chop-chop.'

Angry and upset that the day had ended so badly, Isla left Tia to it and rushed into the house. In the living room, she grabbed a bottle of wine off the liquor cabinet and poured a large glassful. The guests began to traipse past the door a few seconds later, and she clenched her teeth when she heard them grumbling about the disgraceful way they were being treated as Tia loudly hurried them along.

The door creaked open and Tia's boyfriend, Sam, popped his head inside.

'Is it safe to come in?

'Of course,' Isla said, waving for him to join her. 'Thanks so much for coming, and I'm really sorry you had to witness that.'

'I didn't catch it all,' he said, looking a little disappointed about that as he sat beside her on the sofa. 'The front door was locked when we got here, so Tia walked down the side of the house while I was getting our bags out of the boot. I missed the start, but what I did hear was pretty nasty.'

'I just can't believe she did that, today of all days,' Isla said, her jaw clenching as she recalled Felicity's vicious words. 'They're Jerry's friends, and they were supposed to be celebrating his life, so how could they behave like that?'

'Because they're arrogant, stuck-up bastards with no manners,' Tia said, walking in at that moment and taking a seat on the other side of Isla. 'I'm sorry you had to hear what she said, babe. But I couldn't let her get away with talking about you like that.'

'I'm glad you recorded it,' Isla sighed, resting her head back against the cushions. 'At least now I know what they really think of me.'

'They're jealous as hell,' Tia said. 'They can't stand that the best-looking guy in their group fell in love with someone who's so much younger and prettier than them. And I guarantee the men envied Jerry, as well; because he got to wake up next to *you* while they're saddled with those leather-faced old trouts.'

'You have such a way with words,' Sam chuckled.

'I'm not wrong, though, am I?'

'Nope. I'd say you summed it up pretty well.'

'I'm not sure about the women being jealous of me, but you're right about Jerry being the most handsome one,' Isla said, gazing at the framed photograph of him on the mantelpiece. It had been taken at a charity gala they had attended the previous year, and he'd looked so tanned and healthy, with his silver hair gleaming in the sunlight and his eyes crinkled at the corners as he smiled at whoever was behind the camera.

'Hey, come on.' Tia gently touched her hand. 'He might be gone, but you've still got your lovely house and all the beautiful memories you've made here. No one can ever take those away from you.'

Isla nodded her agreement, but, secretly, she wasn't actually sure that the house *was* hers. Jerry had bought it shortly before he married his first wife, Belinda; and he'd kept it when the pair divorced a few years later. Isla didn't know much about that part of his life, because he hadn't liked to talk about his past. He also hadn't liked to think too far into the future, preferring to live in the present. So, aside from that one glib conversation they'd had about funerals, they had never actually discussed what would happen to his estate when he died. She hadn't even known that he'd made a will until his solicitor, Marcus Bennett, rang her a couple of days after he died to set a date for the reading of it. That had really thrown her, and she was terrified that it was going to turn out to be an old one that he'd made while he was still married to Belinda, leaving everything to her.

'Are you OK?' Tia asked.

Isla snapped out of her thoughts and nodded before downing the rest of her wine.

'You look as wiped as I feel,' Tia said, taking the empty glass from her. 'So how about I pour us all a nightcap before we go to bed?'

'You don't need to stay,' Isla said. 'Sam's got work in the morning and the traffic will be horrendous.'

'He's got the day off, so we're good,' Tia assured her. 'And I don't think you should be alone after the day you've had.'

'Honestly, I'll be fine,' Isla insisted.

Tia argued for a few more minutes, but eventually gave in when she realised that Isla wasn't going to back down.

'All right, we'll go,' she conceded, pushing herself up to her feet. 'But you know where I am if you change your mind. It doesn't matter what time it is. If you need me, call me. OK?'

'I will,' Isla agreed, getting up to hug her. 'Thanks for everything you've done. You've been amazing.' Then, turning to hug Sam, she said, 'Thank you, too. I know you must have missed her like crazy, but I don't think I could have got through this without her, so I really appreciate you letting her stay.'

'Hey, don't thank me, it's been heaven being able to play on my Xbox without her nagging me to pay attention to her instead,' Sam grinned. 'She's a terrible cook, so it's been great not having to eat the slop she forces on me when she's home,' he went on conspiratorially, as if Tia wasn't standing right there. 'And don't even get me started on the booze, drugs and prostitutes.'

'Excuse me?' Tia drew her head back. 'So I'm a terrible cook, am I?'

'Seriously?' He laughed. '*That's* the bit that offended you?'

'Get out of here.' She shoved him towards the door playfully. 'I'll deal with you when I get you home.'

Isla was smiling as she showed them out, but it slid off her lips as soon as she stepped back into the hallway. It was the first time she had been truly alone since Jerry died, and the silence was deafening as she made her way around the house, checking that all the doors and windows were locked.

Isla noticed that the garden lights and patio heater were still on when she walked into the kitchen, and she sighed when she looked out through the window and saw the mess. Discarded paper plates littered the decking and the lawn; the patio tables were heaving with empty wine bottles and lipstick-smeared glasses; and numerous whisky glasses lined the wall surrounding the barbeque pit.

A vision of Peter holding court in Jerry's spot by the barbeque caused Isla's jaw to clench. She'd been too busy serving everyone to notice at the time, but it was almost as if he had taken it upon himself to assume Jerry's role as host. And Felicity, in turn, had assumed hers; acting as if *she* were the hostess, while Isla was relegated to the role of waitress.

Angered all over again when she recalled Felicity's words on Tia's recording, Isla switched off the lights and the heater and then poured a large glass of wine before heading up to bed.

Chapter 4

Isla's head was banging when she woke up the following morning, and her tongue was so dry, it felt like it was superglued to the roof of her mouth. The wine hadn't been enough to knock her out, so she'd opened the half-full bottle of whisky Jerry had kept on his bedside table and poured herself a shot. And she realised she must have poured a few more after that, when she opened her eyes and saw the now-empty bottle on the pillow beside her head.

Nauseated by the smell coming from the bottle, Isla rolled onto her back and threw her arm over her eyes to block out the sunlight that was leaking in through the partially open curtains. Almost on the verge of falling asleep again, she heard what sounded like footsteps in the hallway below.

'Hello?' a man called out. 'Anybody home?'

Heart pounding when she realised who it was, Isla jumped out of bed and snatched her dressing gown off the hook on the back of the door.

'Ah, there you are.' Peter beamed at her from the foot of the stairs when she came out onto the landing. 'I did ring the bell, but there was no answer, so I thought you—'

'How the hell did you get in?' Isla cut him off as she marched down the steps.

'Jerry left these in the safe when he vacated his office.' Peter held up a keyring on which two keys and a gate fob were hanging. 'I found them a few weeks ago; kept meaning to drop them off.'

'Have you used them before?' Isla snatched them out of his hand and dropped them into her pocket.

'No.'

'And you haven't made any copies?'

Peter's smile slipped and he drew his head back and gave her a hurt look. 'Of course not. I wouldn't have even used them today if you'd answered the door. But you were in such a state last night, I was concerned about you.'

'How kind.' Isla flashed him a cold smile.

'I brought coffee.' Peter held up two lidded cups in a cardboard holder. 'Let's go and sit down so we can chat in comfort.'

'I'm not dressed.'

'Well, run along and do whatever you need to do. I'll wait in here.'

Irritated when Peter turned and strode into the kitchen, Isla went after him and stopped in the doorway.

'I really don't have time for this,' she said, folding her arms.

'Nonsense,' Peter said, sitting at the table and patting the chair beside his. 'Everyone has time for coffee with friends.'

'We're not friends,' she replied frostily. 'And I'd really like you to leave.'

'Ouch!' Peter grimaced. Then, sighing, he said, 'You know, I've always been rather fond of you, and I'd hate for what happened last night to come between us. I appreciate that things became a little heated between Felicity and your friend, which must have been upsetting for you. But I spoke with her on the way home and she assured me that she hadn't said whatever she was accused of, so—'

'Oh, please!' Isla cut him off. 'I heard exactly what she said, so don't try to turn this on Tia. To be honest, it only confirmed what I already knew. Felicity has never thought I was good enough for Jerry. And the rest of you obviously feel the same.'

'Come now, that's not true,' Peter protested. 'I've always held you in the highest regard, and if lucky old Jezza hadn't bagged you, I'd have been tempted to take you out myself.'

'Excuse me?' Isla frowned.

'Don't look so surprised,' Peter said, smiling as he got up and walked towards her. 'You must know I've always found you attractive.'

'You're a married man,' Isla said, darting past him when he reached out to embrace her.

'Felicity will never find out, if that's what you're worried about,' Peter crooned, going after her when she backed further into the room. 'You're a beautiful woman and any man would be lucky to call you his own.'

'Have you lost your mind?' Isla gasped, wincing when her back hit the sharp edge of the counter.

'No, I'm perfectly sane,' he said, wrapping an arm around her waist. 'Now Jerry's gone, you need a strong man to take care of you. And I would like to *be* that man.'

'Stop it!' Isla squawked when she felt his erection pressing into her thigh. 'You're disgusting!'

'You don't mean that,' he said huskily, sliding a hand over her breast. 'You want this as much as I do.'

'No, I don't,' she protested, grimacing when she got a blast of his coffee-and-stale-cigar-smoke breath.

The front door suddenly opened and Isla almost fainted with relief when Tia called out her name.

'In here!' she yelled.

'Sorry I didn't call first,' Tia said as her heels clicked over the hallway tiles. 'Sam's gone to the gym, so I thought I might as well come and spend the morning with my bestie. Did you know the gate was ope—' She abruptly stopped speaking when she reached the kitchen doorway and saw Peter adjusting his trousers as he backed away from Isla. 'What's going on?' She switched her gaze to Isla. 'Are you OK?'

'I will be when he's gone,' Isla said, putting more distance between herself and Peter.

'I'll, um, call you,' he murmured, straightening his jacket.

'No, you won't,' she replied coolly. 'You've said more than enough already, and I'm sure Felicity will think the same when I tell her.'

'Please don't do that,' Peter implored. 'I obviously misread the situation and I wholeheartedly apologise if I've upset you. But, please, I'm begging you, don't tell Felicity. This would end us.'

Isla saw the fear in his eyes and shook her head. She knew Felicity well enough to know that the woman would make his life a living hell if she found out about this. She also knew that the bitch was just as likely to twist it around and accuse Isla of trying to seduce *him*. And, given that the other wives all already thought that she'd only married Jerry for his money, they were bound to believe her.

'Just go,' she sighed. 'I won't say anything.'

Peter opened his mouth to speak but seemed to think better of it and quickly snapped it shut again. Then, nodding goodbye, he walked out, avoiding Tia's accusing glare as he went.

'What the hell was that about?' Tia asked when he'd gone.

'Oh God, don't even ask.' Isla sank down onto a chair and rubbed her pounding temples with her fingertips. 'I was in bed and heard noises in the hall; came down to find *him* standing there.'

'What?' Tia was alarmed. 'Did you forget to lock up after we left? I know you were tired, but that's so dangerous.'

'He had Jerry's spare keys,' Isla told her. 'Reckons he found them in the safe at work and had been meaning to bring them back.'

'That doesn't give him the right to *use* them,' Tia huffed. 'Cheeky bastard. He'd better not try that again, or he'll have me to deal with.'

'I took the keys off him, so he won't be able to,' Isla assured her. 'I just dread to think how far he might have gone if you hadn't walked in.'

'What exactly happened?' Tia asked, sitting beside her when she saw her shudder. 'Did he touch you?'

'He had me up against the counter, trying to grope me,' Isla said, grimacing as the words left her mouth. 'He said he's always been attracted to me and wants to look after me now Jerry's gone.'

'What an absolute snake,' Tia said, shaking her head in disgust. 'Now you know what I meant last night about the men envying Jerry. I bet that creep's been lusting after you for years, just waiting for a chance to make his move.'

'You don't think I could have done something to give him the impression that I was interested, do you?' Isla asked. 'I honestly don't think I have, but he was convinced that I wanted him.'

'You can stop that right now,' Tia scolded her. 'You've done nothing wrong and he's disgusting for doing this the day after Jerry's funeral. He's got zero shame.'

'Well, I doubt he'll dare try anything like that again after I threatened to tell Felicity,' Isla said, reaching for one of the coffees.

'Don't touch that!' Tia jumped to her feet and snatched the cups up off the table. 'I'm guessing *he* bought them if you were in bed when he got here. He could have spiked one of them.'

'Oh, come on; there's no way he'd know how to get hold of that sort of stuff,' Isla argued. 'They've got the logo of the village deli on them, so he must have called in there on the way over here.'

'Do you really want to chance it?' Tia arched an eyebrow as she tipped the coffees into the sink. 'He was obviously planning to have his wicked way with you, whether you wanted it or not. Personally, I wouldn't put anything past him.'

Isla shuddered at the thought and got up to put the kettle on.

'Leave it,' Tia said, wiping her hands on a tea towel after dropping the empty cups into the bin. 'Let's go out and get something to eat, then hit the shops.'

'I need to deal with that first.' Isla nodded to the window, through which the debris in the garden looked even worse in the cold light of day.

Tia took a look and reached into her bag for her phone.

'What are you doing?' Isla asked.

'Calling the caterers,' Tia said. 'They were supposed to clean up before they left, so they can damn well come back and finish the job.'

'No, it's OK,' Isla said before Tia could make the call. 'They offered to do it last night, but Peter and the others were still here, so I told them I'd do it in the morning. It shouldn't take too long, but I need to do it before it gets warm or the rats will come up from the stream. I couldn't go outside for weeks last time we left food outside.'

'Yeah, I remember.' Tia grimaced. 'OK, I'll make a brew while you get dressed, then we'll do it together before we go out.'

Grateful that she wouldn't have to tackle the mess on her own, Isla swallowed a couple of painkillers to ease the throbbing in her head and then went back to her bedroom. Nauseated by the cloying scent of Peter's aftershave on her dressing gown, she took the keys out of the pocket and shoved the gown into the laundry basket in the bathroom. She instantly recognised her front door key, but the other key was smaller and had an unfamiliar shape. Guessing that it probably belonged to Jerry's office, she slid it off the ring and dropped it into her dressing-table drawer. At some point she would return it to Peter, but there was no way she wanted to see or speak to the man right now, so it could wait until she was ready.

The clean-up didn't take as long as Isla had feared and the garden was soon tidy again. She left Tia loading the glasses they had collected into the dishwasher and carried the rubbish bags out to the bin. As she was dropping them in, she heard the crunch of gravel by the gate. She had closed it after Peter left and a woman was now standing on the other side looking in through the bars. Her face looked vaguely familiar and Isla wondered if she was one of the waitresses from the catering company who had been there the previous day.

'Hello,' she called out, wiping her hands on her jeans as she walked over to her. 'If you've come to help clean up, it's all taken care of.'

The woman had been gazing up at the house, but she snapped her head round at the sound of Isla's voice and stared at her like a deer caught in headlights. Able to see her more clearly now, Isla frowned. Her blonde hair was limp and quite greasy-looking, and her face was gaunt, with deep hollows under her pale blue eyes. But it was the yellow pushchair standing beside her that reminded Isla exactly where she had seen her before.

'Hey, you were at the crematorium, weren't you?' she said.

The woman didn't answer, and Isla's frown deepened when she turned and grabbed the handles of the pushchair before walking away.

'How did you know where I live?' Isla called after her. 'Hey… I'm talking to you!'

Again, no answer came, so Isla pressed the fob to open the gate and went after her. Almost running to catch up with her, she stepped in front of the pushchair to force her to stop.

'Just tell me who you are and why you're here,' she demanded. 'Did you follow me home from the funeral?'

The woman shook her head and dipped her gaze.

'Why were you even there?' Isla persisted. 'Did you know my husband?'

'I'm sorry,' the woman murmured. 'I just…'

'Just what?' Isla snapped when she tailed off.

The woman physically jerked back from her and Isla, aware that she probably sounded aggressive, held up her hands.

'Look, I'm sorry if I scared you, but this is the second time you've bolted at the sight of me and I need to know why. Did you know my husband? Is that why you were at the crematorium?'

Irritated when the woman bit her lip and, again, didn't answer, Isla said, 'You'd better start talking, or I'm going to call the police. This is really creepy and it's starting to feel like you're stalking me.'

'I'm not stalking you,' the woman said, meeting Isla's gaze at last. 'I-I did know Jerry,' she went on nervously. 'And I was shocked when I heard he'd died, so I went to the funeral to say goodbye. But I stayed outside because I didn't want to upset you.'

'If you knew him, you'd have been welcome to come in,' Isla said. 'But that still doesn't explain why you're here now.'

'Isla?' Tia called out. 'Where are you?'

Isla turned her head and waved when Tia walked out through the gate. Seizing the opportunity to escape, the woman swerved the pushchair around her and took off. Frustrated, Isla contemplated going after her. But she doubted she'd get anything further, so she walked back to Tia.

'Who was that?' Tia asked, watching as the woman disappeared around the corner at the end of the road.

'The woman who was looking at Jerry's flowers after the funeral,' Isla said. 'I caught her staring through the gate when I brought the rubbish out. I asked her what she was doing here, but it was like trying to get blood out of a stone until I threatened to call the police and report her for stalking.'

'What did she say?'

'Apparently, she knew Jerry and went to his funeral to say goodbye. But she stayed outside because she didn't want to upset me.'

'Why would that upset you?'

'No idea.' Isla shrugged, heading back to the house. 'Maybe she dated him before he met me and felt awkward.'

'I'm not being funny, but there's no way Jerry would ever have been interested in her,' Tia said with certainty. 'She wasn't his type at all. If I had to guess, I'd say she was probably one of the temps he took on after he fired you.'

'He didn't *fire* me,' Isla protested. 'He just didn't think it was appropriate for his wife to work for him.'

'Nah, he totally fired you, and then he hired that scruffy mare so you wouldn't get jealous,' Tia teased.

'Whatever.' Isla rolled her eyes.

'Joking aside,' Tia said as they walked into the kitchen. 'Even if she did know Jerry, she doesn't know *you*, so why come here? That's weird.'

'Yeah, it is,' Isla agreed, frowning as she recalled the woman's cagey behaviour.

'Right, enough about Scary Mary,' Tia said, pulling her jacket on and reaching for her handbag. 'We're done here and I'm starving, so let's go grab some lunch in the village.'

'As long as it's a pub lunch,' Isla said. 'After the morning I've had, I need a stiff one.'

'So do I,' Tia grinned. 'But Sam's at the gym, so I'll have to settle for a drink.'

'You're disgusting,' Isla laughed, pushing her out through the door.

Chapter 5

The pub lunch turned into an all-day booze-up, and Isla quickly forgot about Peter and the strange woman as they lazed on the grass in the pub garden watching the barges drift by on the river.

Tia started work on her new client's wedding the next morning, so Isla knew she wouldn't be seeing her for a while. But she wasn't prepared for how rudderless she suddenly felt when she was alone again. Tia had moved in to look after her after Jerry died, and there had been a steady stream of neighbours popping in with food and condolences right up until the funeral. These neighbours weren't like the ones she'd grown up around on the Grange estate, where everybody had known each other's business and somebody's kettle was always on the boil. Here, they were mostly elderly and tended to keep themselves to themselves, so she hadn't been surprised when their visits stopped and they went back to simply waving hello in passing.

Bored and lonely, Isla started to reminisce about the past as the days dragged by. She'd had lots of friends before she met Jerry, but Tia was the only one she had stayed in regular touch with. It hadn't been a deliberate cutting of ties with the others, but more of a natural drifting apart as their paths branched off in different directions. Isla had married Jerry, moved into his house and immersed herself in his already established circle of friends. And she had never regretted that decision, because they had been happy together. But now he was gone, she realised how empty her life was without him – and how much she had given up for him. Not least, her mum.

It still hurt that her mum had issued a '*him or us*' ultimatum after meeting Jerry for the first – and only – time. Isla got that most parents might be concerned if their twenty-year-old daughter started dating her forty-five-year-old boss. But her mum hadn't even given Jerry a chance. She had labelled him a pervert on sight and had warned Isla that he would dump her for a younger model as soon as she got her first wrinkle. Jerry had been a great husband, and Isla had been tempted to visit her mum many times to show her how well they were doing. She'd never had the courage to actually do it; too scared of being rejected again. But now Jerry was gone and her mum had no reason to keep the war going, she decided that she would take the plunge and go to see her after the meeting with Jerry's solicitor, Marcus Bennett, at the end of the week.

Isla was nervous as she drove into Manchester on Friday morning. As hard as she had tried not to let it play on her mind, the thought of losing everything and starting over from scratch was terrifying. She had confided her fears about Jerry's will leaving everything to his ex-wife to Tia over the phone a few nights earlier, and her friend had insisted that she had nothing to worry about; that Jerry would have taken steps to ensure that she would be OK. Tia often had strong feelings about people and situations, and she was usually right. But Isla was convinced that she'd got it wrong this time, and she was shaking as she walked into Marcus's office.

The solicitor was sitting at his desk going over some paperwork, but he jumped up when she entered and walked around his desk to give her a hug. Thrown by the gesture, because she and Marcus had never really spoken beyond polite hellos and goodbyes whenever he'd visited Jerry at the house, Isla wondered if he was being nice in order to soften the blow that he knew was coming.

'How are you?' he asked, pulling out a chair for her when he'd released her. 'I'm so sorry I couldn't make the funeral, but I had to go to court that day and couldn't find anyone to replace me at short notice.'

'I'm OK,' she said, perching on the chair. 'Just taking each day as it comes.'

'That's the best way; slow and steady,' Marcus said approvingly. 'Now, before we start, is there anything I can get for you? Tea, coffee, water?'

Isla shook her head. Her stomach was already upset with nerves and she just wanted to get this over with as quickly as possible.

'Let's get to it, then,' Marcus said, going back to his seat.

Isla clutched her handbag tightly on her lap when he pulled an envelope out of his drawer. He opened it and took out the enclosed will, and she listened intently as he began to read it out loud. It started with Jerry's name and his declaration that he had been of sound mind at the time of writing it, then went on to name Marcus as the executor of his estate, and Isla as the sole beneficiary. More followed, but Isla barely heard a word of it as an intense wave of relief washed over her and drowned out his voice.

'So there we have it,' Marcus said when he reached the end. 'As short and sweet as one would expect of a man of few words like Jerry.'

Isla didn't reply, and Marcus tipped his head to one side when he noticed her dazed expression.

'You seem confused. Is something wrong?'

'No.' Isla smiled and sat up a little straighter. 'Sorry, I just wasn't expecting that. I know it'll probably sound stupid, but Jerry never mentioned that he'd made a will. So when you told me about it, I was terrified it might be an old one he'd made when he was with his first wife and forgotten about.'

'Believe me, he ended *that* chapter of his life long before he met you,' said Marcus. 'Belinda received a very generous settlement at the time, and Jerry made a new will straight after the divorce was finalised to ensure that she wouldn't get a single penny more in the future. *This* will was written when he paid me a visit a few weeks before he passed away, so I can assure you it's the final one.'

'I didn't know he'd been to see you.' Isla frowned. 'Do you mind if I ask why? Only, it seems a bit of a coincidence that he should suddenly decide to write a will a few weeks before dying. Am I missing something?'

Marcus pursed his lips and gazed at her in silence for several long moments, as if trying to decide how to answer the question. Then, sitting back in his seat, he said, 'Jerry spoke to me in confidence and asked me not to discuss the details of our conversation with anybody – particularly *you*, because he hadn't wanted to worry you. But now he's no longer with us, I'm sure he wouldn't mind.'

'Please just tell me,' Isla urged.

'He said he'd been experiencing chest pains and stomach issues, and that was why he'd decided to sell his half of the business,' Marcus said. 'So that he could spend whatever time he had left with you, instead of – as *he* put it – rotting away behind his desk.'

'I don't understand,' Isla murmured. 'He never told me he was in pain. If I'd known he wasn't feeling well, I would have made him get checked over.'

'I guess he thought he was protecting you.'

'By dying unnecessarily and leaving me widowed?' Isla blurted out. Then, tempering her tone when she saw that Marcus looked uncomfortable, she said, 'I'm sorry if that sounded harsh, but I don't understand why he'd tell you something as important as that and keep it from me. I'm his wife. I should have been the first person he spoke to if he was worried.'

'I'm sure I'd feel the same if I were in your position. And if it's any consolation, I did urge Jerry to tell you. I also advised him to consult with a specialist, but he was convinced that he would make a full recovery once he was free of the toxic atmosphere in the office.'

'What do you mean by toxic? Jerry loved his company.'

'In the early days, yes; but not so much by the end,' said Marcus. 'Between you and I, he and Peter didn't appear to be on the best of terms when they terminated their partnership. Jerry didn't tell me why and I didn't feel it my place to ask, but I could see he was under a lot of pressure. In hindsight, I wish I'd tried harder to persuade him to see a specialist. But there was only so far you could push a man like Jerry. He was a law unto himself.'

'Yes, he was,' Isla agreed. 'But he still should have told me and given me the chance to help him.'

Marcus gave her a sympathetic smile. Then, glancing at his watch, he said, 'My next client is due at any moment, so I'm afraid we're going to have to wrap this up. I'll be in touch shortly when I've started the process of transferring Jerry's assets into your name, but please feel free to reach out if there's anything you need in the meantime.'

Still reeling, Isla thanked him and said goodbye and then

quickly left the office. She was upset that Jerry had chosen to confide in Marcus instead of her, when she was the one who could have made him seek treatment before it was too late. And she was also angry that Peter had play-acted the part of the grieving best mate at the funeral, when, in reality, they hadn't been getting along before Jerry died. And then, to add insult to injury, the bastard had let himself into her house and tried it on with her, as if Jerry had meant nothing to either of them.

When she reached her car, Isla gripped the steering wheel tightly with both hands and breathed deeply for several moments to calm the storm that was raging inside her mind. She was sorely tempted to drive over to Jerry's old company to have it out with Peter. But she had a feeling that he would deny it and make himself the victim, as he'd effectively done when she had rebuffed his advances. And what was she supposed to do then? She couldn't prove anything, because Marcus had already admitted that Jerry hadn't told him anything specific. So all she really had to go on was Marcus's opinion that all hadn't been quite right between Jerry and Peter.

Frustrated, but in no mood to confront Peter and make herself look like an idiot, Isla decided to concentrate on the more positive aspects of the meeting. She was still angry that she'd been kept in the dark, but the relief of knowing that she wasn't about to lose her home was huge, and she silently thanked Jerry as she set off to visit her mother.

Chapter 6

Four blocks of flats stood like sentries on each corner of the Grange estate. It was the first time Isla had gone near the place in years and the sight of them made her both nostalgic and nervous. That feeling intensified when she drove into the estate, and long-forgotten memories began to resurface as she passed all the landmarks of her youth. The dirty alleyways behind the terraced houses, where she, Tia and their small group of friends had played hide-and-seek among the stinking wheelie bins, discarded mattresses and sofas. The open garages beneath the flats, where, in their teens, they had congregated to share cigarettes and cider. The abandoned caretaker's house on the corner of the park where Isla had shared her first ever kiss with a boy called Kyle McAvoy.

That last memory made Isla smile when she recalled the fall-out it had caused with Tia. She hadn't known at the time that her friend had developed a crush on the boy, so she'd been devastated when Tia had stopped talking to her for three long weeks. When Tia had eventually confessed that she'd acted out of jealousy, Isla had promised never to talk to Kyle again. And she had stuck to her word, despite really liking him. That had proved her loyalty to Tia, and their friendship had been cemented from that day on. Tia had, in turn, been Isla's rock during the difficult times that lay ahead. When her mum kicked her out, Tia had picked up her things and brought them over to Jerry's house. She had later helped Isla organise her wedding – and had dropped everything to support her through her first miscarriage a few short months later. And she'd done the same the next two times it happened, before Isla and Jerry decided to stop trying for children. And, true to form, it was Tia who had rushed straight over when Jerry died.

Truly grateful to have such an amazing friend, Isla was still smiling as she turned onto her mother's road. The smile slipped when she pulled up outside the rusted gate of her childhood home, and she felt the sting of tears behind her eyes as she gazed up at the window above the front door. That had been her bedroom and she could still vividly recall every inch of the space in her mind's eye. The narrow bed with its flowery duvet cover and dodgy headboard; the tiny dressing table with its cracked mirror; the threadbare brown carpet that had always looked dirty no matter how often she swept it. She'd hated it all at the time, wishing that her mum would invest in new, matching furniture, like Tia's house-proud mum had done for her kids. But now, she would give anything to see, touch and even smell it all again.

She had tried to call her mum the previous day to let her know that she was planning to visit, but her calls had gone unanswered. Unsure if her mum had recognised her number and deliberately ignored the calls, she braced herself for an awkward, if not outright frosty, greeting as she unclipped her seatbelt and climbed out of the car. As she reached the gate, the front door of the house suddenly opened, and a large, angry-looking woman came out and strode down the path.

'Why are you parked in my space?' the woman barked. 'If you're from TV licensing, I already told the last guy we don't need one. My son only uses the telly to play his games on, and that ain't illegal, so if you think I'm letting you in to nosy around, you can—'

'I'm not from TV licensing,' Isla interrupted, shocked by the woman's aggressive tone. 'I'm actually looking for my mum. This is her house.'

'No it ain't, it's mine,' the woman shot back. 'And you're in my space, so shift it before I get you towed.'

Isla opened her mouth to ask if her mum had left a forwarding address, but the woman turned and stalked back into the house before she had the chance to speak. Surprised by how deflated she felt at learning that her mum had moved, she got back into the car. She knew it was her own fault for not trying to keep in touch, but it was a shock nonetheless that her mum hadn't even bothered to tell her that she'd left her childhood home, and she gazed sadly up at the house one last time before driving away.

Almost at the end of the road, her heart leapt when she spotted a familiar face in one of the tiny front gardens, and she quickly pulled over and rolled down her window.

'Hello, stranger. Fancy seeing you here.'

The man looked back at her over his shoulder and frowned. 'You talking to me?'

'Well, I can't see anyone else out here,' Isla said. 'So, how's it going, Mr Big Shot? Or are you too important to talk to the likes of me nowadays?'

'Excuse me?' The man turned fully around and gave her a look, as if to say *who the fuck are you*?

'It's Isla,' she said.

'Isla,' he repeated, pursing his lips thoughtfully. Then, shaking his head, he said, 'Nope. Not ringing any bells.'

'Are you being serious?' She peered at his face to see if he was joking. 'You honestly don't remember me?'

'Should I?' He arched an eyebrow. Then, laughing when her face fell, he walked out through the gate and opened her door, 'Of course I remember you. How are you? It's been years.'

'I know,' Isla said, climbing out and giving him a hug. 'It's so good to see you.'

Benny Valdez and his family had moved onto the estate when Isla was fourteen, and she, Tia, and every other girl in the area had immediately fallen in love with him. He'd stood out from all the other boys because of his glossy black hair, which he'd worn in a ponytail. And he'd had the most beautiful brown eyes, and a smile that could melt an iceberg. His hair was now short, but that was all that had changed. If anything, he was even more handsome than she had remembered. Isla and Tia had decided that he was gay long before he moved to London to pursue a career in musical theatre, so it hadn't been a surprise that he hadn't been interested in them, or any other girl.

'It's great to see you, too,' he said, stepping back to look her over. 'You look amazing, as always.'

'Oh, I don't know about that,' she laughed. 'But never mind me, tell me what you've been up to?' she went on, excited to hear about his career. 'I heard you'd got a part in a film?'

'That was years ago,' Benny said dismissively. 'And it was more of a blink-and-you'll-miss-me kind of thing than an actual part.'

'It's still a massive achievement,' Isla said. 'So what are you doing now? Are you back in Manchester working on something, or just visiting?'

'I actually moved back last year,' Benny told her. 'I won't bore you with the details, but I'd hit a bit of a rough patch and my mum asked me to come home so she could take care of me while I got back on my feet. My dad had already died by then, and she was diagnosed with cancer shortly after, so I stayed to look after her.'

'Oh no.' Isla's face fell. 'Is she doing OK?'

'She passed away a few months ago,' Benny said.

'I'm so sorry,' Isla murmured, reaching out to touch his arm when she saw the sadness in his eyes.

'It's OK,' he said. 'She went pretty fast, so at least she didn't suffer too much.' Then, shaking it off, he smiled, and said, 'But that's enough of my woes. What's been happening with you? Last I heard, you'd married some rich dude and moved into a mansion out in the sticks.'

'Not quite.' Isla smiled. 'I did get married, and he was pretty well off. But I wouldn't say he was rich.'

'Was?' Benny gave her a questioning look.

'He died last month,' Isla said. 'Heart attack.'

'Oh no.' Benny touched her arm. 'I'm so sorry, darling. I had no idea.'

'It's OK.' Isla sighed. 'It's been tough, but I'm getting there.'

'You always were the strong one,' Benny said. 'That's why we all used to turn to you whenever we had a problem. It was like, where's Isla? She'll know what to do.'

'Really?' Isla was surprised by that.

'Hell, yeah. You were the only one of us who had any sense back then,' Benny said. 'What are you doing now? Have you got time for a brew?'

'Yeah, that'd be lovely,' Isla said, using her fob to lock the car door before following him up the path.

His house had the same layout as her mum's, with a short, narrow hallway that led to the kitchen at the back. The steep staircase rose to a tiny landing, in the middle of which was the bathroom, with a bedroom on either side. The tiny, square front room still had its original gas fire, and Isla smiled when she saw that he'd kept his mum's chintzy sofa and flowery carpet.

'Oh wow, this takes me back,' she said. 'I feel like a teenager again.'

'It's not really my taste, but it reminds me of my mum, so I can't bring myself to change anything yet,' Benny said, leading her into the kitchen. 'Coffee, tea or something stronger?' He pointed to a ledge on which numerous bottles of spirits and wine were standing.

'It's a bit early for me, so I'll just have tea,' Isla said.

'The time never stopped us in the past,' Benny grinned. 'We had to take any chance we could get when we were in the *Grangers*.'

'Oh Christ, I'd forgotten we called ourselves that.' Isla grimaced. 'We thought we were so cool having a gang name.'

'We *were* cool. Until we got home and had to try to act sober. My mum saw through it every time and whacked that cool right out of my arse with the yard brush.'

'Mine too,' said Isla. 'But while we're on the subject, I don't suppose you know where my mum moved to? I called round there before I saw you and a rather *charming* woman told me it was her house now.'

'Charming ain't the word I'd use for that gobby bitch,' Benny snorted. 'And you should see the state of her old man and their goon of a son. I used to think it was rough when we were kids, but it's way worse now all the old neighbours have gone and this new lot have taken over.'

'This is the first time I've been here in years, and I've got to admit it does look a bit dingy,' Isla said. 'The houses look a lot smaller than I remembered, as well.'

'That's what living in a mansion does for you,' Benny quipped. 'And here's me, back where I started.'

'How come you didn't move back to London after your mum

died?' Isla asked. 'I would have thought that was more your kind of scene.'

'It was, for a while,' Benny said as he switched the kettle on and dropped teabags into two cups. 'But things got a bit difficult when I lost my other half. Me and Vic weren't married, so I know it's not the same as you losing your hubby. But it really makes you re-evaluate your life when they're gone.'

'It really does,' Isla agreed, leaning back against the counter. 'Do you mind if I ask what happened?'

'Car crash. It's been a couple of years, so it's not as raw now. But it shattered me at the time, so I know how you must be feeling.'

'Yeah, it is pretty shattering. One minute everything's going perfectly, then bam! You've lost the one person who made life worth living.'

'Tell me about it,' Benny sighed. 'But, hey... life goes on, and here we both are.'

Teas made, they went back to the living room, where Isla took a seat on the sofa and Benny sat on the armchair by the fire.

'So has everyone from the gang left?' Isla asked.

'Kayla and Mikey still live fairly close, but the others are long gone,' Benny said. 'I bumped into Tia a few years back when I was making a flying visit, but I don't think she lives round here now.'

'No, she's got a place in town with her boyfriend,' Isla told him. 'They're doing really well for themselves. Sam's an accountant, and she's a wedding planner.'

'I always knew she'd make something of her life.' Benny smiled. 'She was another strong one, like you.'

'She's far stronger than me,' said Isla. 'I honestly couldn't have coped without her after losing Jerry. She was amazing.'

'Tell me about Jerry,' Benny urged. 'I've heard bits and pieces over the years, but no one seemed to know too much about him. Forgive me if I'm crossing the line, but wasn't there some sort of controversy around him? Was he married when you met him, or something?'

'He had been married before, but he was already divorced when we got together,' Isla said. 'The controversy was that he was my boss and he was twenty-five years older than me. My mum was disgusted and forced me to choose between them. Obviously, I chose him, and we were really happy. But I haven't seen my mum since.'

'Wow,' Benny murmured, shaking his head. 'Well, I guess that explains why she slammed the door in my face when I called round there looking for you after I came home.'

'I wouldn't take that personally,' Isla said. 'She was always funny like that. If she fell out with someone and another friend carried on talking to them, she'd fall out with them as well.'

'Yeah, I think my mum might have been one of her victims,' Benny chuckled. 'But if it's been that long since you've seen her, what made you decide to come over today?'

'I've been meaning to for ages, but never got around to it. Losing Jerry made me realise how short life is, so I wanted to try to mend some fences before it was too late.'

'If there's one thing I've learned, it's that the most important fence to mend is the one between your head and your heart,' Benny mused. 'Like you said, life is short, and if you waste it trying to please everyone else at the expense of your own happiness, it usually leads to misery, loneliness and disappointment.'

'Whoa.' Isla drew her head back and stared at him. 'When did you get all philosophical on us?'

'When I realised that I'd wasted years of my life trying to fit in with people who didn't give a shit about me,' Benny replied bluntly. 'I had a great group of mates in London, but when I lost Vic and needed a shoulder to cry on, every last one of them suddenly had more important things to deal with. *Man*, that was tough.'

Isla nodded her agreement, thinking that his experience echoed her own situation with Felicity and the other wives. Given how long they had known her, and how regularly they had all met up for lunches and dinners while their men were working, she had expected at least *one* of them to message or call to ask if she was OK after the wake. But there had absolute silence from them all.

'Well, I'm back on my feet, and you'll get there in time,' Benny went on. 'I know you've probably got tons of posh mates now, but I'm always here if you need to talk to someone who knew you when you were slumming it.'

Isla laughed and thanked him, but pride prevented her from admitting that, Tia aside, she no longer had any real friends. Luckily, she was still young enough to rectify that. And reconnecting with Benny again, despite living in different cities for the majority of their adult lives, was a great start.

Chapter 7

It was late afternoon and starting to get dark by the time Isla left Benny's house. He had always been funny and, once they'd got the more serious stuff out of the way, he'd had her crying with laughter at his stories about life in London. Some of it clearly hadn't been fun for him at the time, and she had been saddened to hear that he'd more or less given up on his dreams of becoming a West End star. But when she heard how hard it was to get into the business, and how many rejections he'd faced along the way, she didn't blame him for wanting out. The time he'd spent travelling to auditions that invariably came to nothing, added to the cost of the train fares which had often left him with no money to eat for the rest of the week, was shocking. He had persisted for far longer than Isla herself would have; convinced that the next audition would change his fortunes and rocket him to international stardom. But he claimed that he'd now accepted that, in London, he was never going to be anything other than a tiny fish in a huge, shark-filled pond. And he was at peace with that.

Still thinking about Benny when she reached the road that led off the estate, Isla caught a flash of white in the corner of her eye and slammed her brakes on. Somebody had stepped out in front of her, but they had their hood up so she couldn't see if it was a man or a woman. Shocked, she unclipped her seatbelt and jumped out.

'Are you OK? I didn't hit you, did I?'

The person raised their head at the sound of her voice, and Isla's mouth dropped open when she saw that it was the woman from the crematorium.

'My God, have you been following me again?' she demanded. 'What the hell kind of game are you playing? This is downright weird!'

The woman turned and scuttled away, but Isla wanted answers, so she climbed back into the car and went after her.

As she drew alongside her, she rolled down the passenger-side window, and said, 'Stop running away and talk to me. I need to know who you are and why you're doing this?'

The woman walked on for a few seconds, but eventually stopped when Isla carried on driving alongside her. Shoulders hunched, she nervously glanced both ways along the road and then leaned down and looked into the car.

'OK, I'll talk to you. But I don't have long.'

'Get in.' Isla flicked the switch to unlock the doors. Then, determinedly keeping her voice even so she didn't spook the woman when she climbed in, she said, 'I won't keep you long, but this needs sorting out. I'm Isla, by the way. But I'm guessing you already know that?'

The woman nodded but didn't offer her own name in return.

Sighing, Isla said, 'It would be kind of helpful if I knew who I was talking to.'

'Melanie,' the woman said quietly.

'OK, Melanie, so you said you knew my husband, but you didn't tell me how.' Isla got straight to the point. 'At first, I thought you might have dated him before he met me. But that was almost sixteen years ago, and now I can see you properly, you don't look old enough. What are you … twenty-five, twenty-six?'

'Twenty-eight.'

'As I thought; way too young,' said Isla. 'So did you work for him, or was he a friend of your parents, or something?'

Melanie shook her head and slotted her hands between her skinny thighs. 'I, um, met him at the bar where I was working,' she said after a moment. 'He used to come in for his lunch.'

'Really?' Isla frowned. 'As far as I knew, he always ate lunch at his desk. I made it for him every morning, and the box was always empty when he got home. Are you telling me he threw it away and ate at your place instead?'

Melanie gave a tiny shrug in reply.

'If that's true and he was just a customer, why on earth would you go to his funeral?' Isla asked. 'And, more importantly, how did you know my address? Because there's no way Jerry would have given it to a waitress.'

'I need to go,' Melanie mumbled, reaching for the door handle.

'Not until you tell me what's really going on,' Isla said, hitting the switch to lock the doors. 'You're the one who started this, and I need answers, so talk.'

Melanie squeezed her eyes shut and bit her lip. Then, releasing a heavy breath, she said, 'Are you sure you want to know?'

Stomach churning, because she sensed that she wasn't going to like what she heard, Isla nodded and steeled herself for whatever was about to come.

'I did meet Jerry at the bar,' Melanie said. 'But he didn't come in for lunch. He came to see me dance.'

'Sorry, *what*?' Isla squinted at her in confusion.

'They had booths where the men could pay for private dances and Jerry always asked for me,' Melanie went on. 'After a couple of times, he asked if he could take me out for dinner. He was wearing a wedding ring, so I said no, but he told me you were separated. Things weren't going too well with my boyfriend at the time, and Jerry was really nice to me, so I agreed to go out with him. It started from there.'

'Bullshit!' Isla spluttered. 'Jerry would *never* have done something like that.'

'I'm sorry,' Melanie apologised. 'I know it isn't what you wanted to hear, but it's the truth. He said he wanted to start a new life with me after his divorce came through, and I believed him. But then I saw you and him together and realised he'd been lying.'

'What do you mean you saw us together?' Isla demanded, struggling to contain her anger. 'Where?'

'In town last year,' said Melanie. 'I was walking home after work and saw his car pulling in behind a restaurant he used to take me to. He knew what time my shift ended, so I thought he'd come to surprise me. But then I saw you getting out of the car and I could tell by the way you were looking at each other that you were still together. He rang me the next day and tried to act like nothing was wrong, but when I told him I'd seen you, he eventually admitted that he'd lied about being separated. But he swore it was just a convenience thing; to stop you getting his money if he divorced you.'

'Do you seriously expect me to believe that?' Isla asked when she'd finished. 'We were married for fifteen years and Jerry never *once* said he wanted a divorce. And he always came straight home from work, so how would he have had time to be seeing you behind my back?'

'We always met up in the day when you thought he was at work,' Melanie explained. 'He'd take me out for lunch and then we'd go to the hotel round the corner from his office.'

'That doesn't sound quite like the love story you're trying to pass it off as,' Isla snapped, angered that Melanie was trying to paint Jerry as the kind of man who'd frequented sleazy strip clubs. 'That sounds more like a prostitute and a punter, if you ask me.'

'Jerry never paid me,' Melanie insisted. 'Not outside the club, anyway. That was personal, so it wouldn't have felt right. If I'd known he was lying about being separated from you, it would never have gone that far. But it did, and I can't change that.'

'Supposing any of this is true, which I absolutely don't believe it is,' Isla said. 'How do you explain not seeing him after he retired if you were so *in love*? And don't say you did see him, because he didn't leave my side for two whole months before he died.'

'I'd already finished with him by then,' Melanie replied sadly. 'He said he loved me, and I really wanted to believe him. But I couldn't get that image of you out of my head, so I ended it last year.'

'Then why turn up at his funeral and come to my house?

Melanie shifted in her seat and plucked at a loose thread on her leggings. 'I didn't do that for myself, I did it for my son. I know he won't remember, but I wanted him to see where Jerry had lived.'

The hairs on the back of Isla's neck bristled and she narrowed her eyes. 'You'd better not be saying what I think you're saying. It's one thing to claim that you had an affair with a man who's not here to defend himself, but I will *not* have you implying that my husband fathered your child.'

'I didn't say that,' Melanie said, leaning closer to the door when she saw the anger in Isla's eyes. 'I just…'

'Just *what*?' Isla demanded. 'Just thought you'd try to scam a grieving widow? Because that's obviously what this is. I reckon you saw his obituary in the paper and looked him up, then came up with this bullshit story in the hope that I'd pay you off to stop you from ruining his reputation. Well, you've picked the wrong mark this time, because I grew up on the Grange and I can spot a con artist from a mile away. So if you think you're getting a single penny from me, you can think again.'

'I don't want your money,' Melanie insisted. 'I wouldn't take any from Jerry when he offered, and I definitely wouldn't expect you to—'

She abruptly stopped talking and Isla was confused when her eyes widened and she slid down in her seat. Curious to know what – or who – had caused her to react in such a way, Isla turned and looked out through the window. Several people were milling around outside the shops on the opposite side of the road, but her attention was immediately drawn to a tall, dark-haired man who was pushing a pram – the same grubby yellow one she had seen Melanie pushing on the previous occasions they'd met. He was walking fast; his head swivelling from side to side as if looking for somebody. He suddenly stopped and appeared to yell at the child in the pram before moving on again, and a chill ran down Isla's spine when she saw the rage on his face.

'I take it that was your boyfriend?' she asked, turning back to Melanie, who was almost lying flat in her seat by then.

'He didn't see me, did he?' Melanie whimpered.

'I don't think so,' Isla said, taking another look. 'He's gone now.'

Melanie slowly sat up and released a tense breath.

'What was that about?' Isla asked.

'I'm late home and he'll be looking for me,' Melanie said.

Isla heard the tremor in her voice and felt guilty for forcing her to stay in the car for so long. She was still furious with her for trying to sully Jerry's memory, but she was shocked by how terrified the woman had become at the mere sight of her own boyfriend.

'Will you be OK?'

'I should be, as long as I get back before him,' Melanie replied. Then, making an effort to pull herself together, she said, 'Sorry for freaking out. I was just scared he'd come over and have a go at you if he saw us together. He gets really paranoid if he sees me talking to people he doesn't know.'

'I wonder why,' Isla murmured sarcastically. Then, sighing when she saw that Melanie was still shaking, she released the door locks, and said, 'Go on. Get yourself home.'

Melanie quickly opened the door and climbed out. Then, leaning back in, she said, 'I know you won't believe me, but I really am sorry about Jerry.'

Isla didn't answer. Done with talking, she stared straight ahead until Melanie closed the door and walked away.

Chapter 8

The house was in darkness when Isla pulled onto the driveway, but the security lights came on as she parked up alongside Jerry's car. It was a beautiful, detached house, and Isla remembered how impressed she had been the first time Jerry brought her there. She'd loved the bay windows and deep porch; all prettily decorated by ivy, which made it blend seamlessly into the mature bushes and trees lining the perimeter. She remembered being in awe of the double garage attached to the house, which Jerry had converted into a home gym when he'd gone on a fitness kick a few years earlier. He had used it for precisely one month before abandoning it forever.

She had grown used to the large house over time and no longer really saw it. But now, after revisiting the Grange, she could see how grand it really was. She recalled how relieved and overjoyed she had been a few short hours earlier when Marcus had read the will and she'd learned that it now belonged to her. But, as she gazed at it, she couldn't help but wonder if Jerry had ever brought Melanie here. How else could the woman have known the address, unless Jerry had told her? And why would she have wanted her child to see it?

Isla's jaw clenched in anger at that last thought, and she mentally replayed the conversation she'd had with Melanie as she climbed out of the car and let herself into the house. In the whole time they had been married, she had never once suspected that Jerry might be cheating on her. And God knew he'd had ample opportunity given the way his friends' wives had behaved around him. He'd been a handsome, charming, self-made man who possessed the ability to make people feel relaxed and comfortable in his presence. A little *too* comfortable, Isla had sometimes thought, when she'd observed the wives batting their eyelashes at him and 'accidentally' brushing up against him. She'd always felt confident that he wasn't interested; that he was just an old-school gentleman who treated women with respect. And that was *all* women, from the wives, to the women who worked in the village shops, to the waitresses who served them in restaurants…

That last thought reminded Isla of Melanie's claim that she'd met Jerry when he went to the strip club where she danced for lunch. After which he had supposedly asked her out before starting an affair with her. As plausible as Melanie had made it sound, something about the story didn't quite ring true to Isla. Despite their age gap, she and Jerry had enjoyed an active sex life. It had slowed down a bit in the latter months of his life, but that was understandable if he'd been worrying about his health. Prior to that, however, they had still been making love quite regularly, and she truly believed that she would have noticed a change in his behaviour if he'd been seeing another woman.

Sex aside, Tia had been absolutely right when she'd pointed out that Melanie wasn't Jerry's type. Not only was she blonde, whereas Isla, his previous wife and girlfriends were all brunettes; she was also too skinny and – loath as Isla was to even think it – *scruffy*. Jerry hadn't been a snob by any means, but he had always taken great care of his appearance, and Isla didn't believe that he would have looked twice at a woman like Melanie.

But what if he *had* looked at her, precisely *because* she was so different from Isla and the other women he'd dated? She didn't want to believe it, but now the seed had been planted, she could feel its evil tendrils snaking their way into her brain; making her doubt everything she'd thought she knew about her husband.

Sickened to think that Jerry could have been living a double life and she had been too trusting to see the signs, Isla poured a large glass of wine and gulped half of it down before heading up to the bedroom.

Jerry's phone was still sitting on the dressing table where she'd placed it on the day he died. They had known each other's passcodes, but she had never used his before. She'd never had a reason to. As she tapped in the numbers now, she felt as if she were somehow betraying him. But she brushed the feeling aside and sank down onto the edge of the bed when the phone unlocked.

There was nobody named Melanie in Jerry's contact list, but Isla figured that he wouldn't have been stupid enough to use her real name if they had been having an affair, so she scrolled through the list to look for names that she didn't recognise. She knew them all, so she switched to his call log; looking for numbers which didn't have names attached that he might have made regular calls to. Nothing unusual jumped out at her, but he had made quite a lot of calls to, and exchanged a number of messages with, Marcus in the weeks leading up to his death.

She went into the messages and saw that the last thread had been initiated by Jerry; asking if they could meet up to discuss something in private. They had gone on to set a couple of dates, which Marcus had subsequently cancelled and rearranged due to work commitments. But they had obviously managed to get together at some point after that, because the last two messages were from Marcus, asking how Jerry was feeling and if he had managed to consult with a specialist yet.

Remembering what Marcus had said about Jerry and Peter not being on the best of terms when they ended their business partnership, she opened their messages next. It was immediately apparent that there had been a significant shift in tone shortly before Jerry had sold his shares in the company. Prior to that, the messages had been jocular and familiar, which was exactly as Isla would have expected given their long-standing friendship. The later ones, however, were abrupt and businesslike, which seemed to confirm what Marcus had said. Curious to pinpoint when and why that shift had occurred, she scrolled through their earlier messages again to look for clues. But she couldn't see anything that explained the sudden cooling between them. One day they had been fine, the next they hadn't. It was all very odd, but Jerry was no longer around to explain it, and there was no way she wanted to ask Peter. So she switched the phone off, picked up her now-empty wine glass and left the room.

It was 9 p.m. by then and she hadn't eaten since that morning. Too tired to cook, she decided to order a pizza from the village takeaway and then get an early night to sleep away the stresses of the day. About to head down the stairs to get her phone, she hesitated when her gaze was drawn to the closed door of Jerry's study at the other end of the landing. Certain now that he had done nothing wrong, and feeling guilty for letting Melanie get into her head and make her doubt him, she walked to the door and slowly pushed it open.

Jerry had jokingly called this room his man-cave, even though all he'd ever done in there was work, often late into the night. He hadn't gone in there as much after retiring, and nor had Isla, so everything was exactly as he had left it.

The air smelled musty and a thick layer of dust coated the top of the antique desk. But it was the sight of the old leather chair behind the desk that brought a lump to Isla's throat. She had only ever gone into the office to take Jerry food or drinks when he'd been working. He had always been sitting in that chair on those occasions, but now it was empty and she felt the weight of his loss press down on her all over again.

Heart aching, she walked over to the chair and sat down. Dust rose into the air before quickly settling again, and she squeezed her eyes shut and inhaled deeply when she picked up the faint scent of Jerry's aftershave embedded in the soft leather. Comforted by the aroma, she stroked the arms of the chair before reaching out to touch the wood of the desk. There were four drawers, the first of which was full of pens, pencils and notepads. The second drawer was deeper and, at first glance, she thought it was empty. About to close it again, she hesitated when she saw something dark at the very back. It was a small metal money-tin, and she felt something shift inside when she lifted it out.

The tin didn't open when she pressed the release button and she realised it was locked when she spotted a small keyhole beneath the button. Her eyes narrowed thoughtfully when she remembered the unfamiliar key Peter had brought round the morning after the funeral, and she quickly got up and went to the bedroom, taking the tin with her.

The key was still in the drawer of her dressing table, so she grabbed it and inserted it into the lock. It fit and the lid clicked open, and Isla's eyes widened when she saw that it contained six bundles of twenty-pound notes; each bound by a bank-strap on which £1000 was printed. She thought it odd that Jerry had decided to keep that amount of money in his drawer instead of his safe, and she wondered why he had withdrawn it in the first place, when he had always used his debit and credit cards. But, right then, she honestly didn't care why. It was just a relief to know that she had a solid chunk of money to live on until Marcus transferred the rest over to her.

Elated, but also exhausted and hungry, she stashed the box in her bedside cabinet. Then, heading downstairs, she ordered her pizza and poured herself another drink.

Chapter 9

In her nightclothes and on her third glass of wine when the bell rang half an hour later, Isla went to the front door and pressed the fob to open the gate. It was almost 10 p.m. and pitch-dark by then, so she stood in the porch and waited for the delivery driver to bring the food to her. The man was in shadow as he crossed the driveway, but when he reached the halfway point and activated the security lights, she was shocked to see that it wasn't a man at all. It was Melanie, and she had the child with her.

'What the hell . . . ?' She stared at the woman in disbelief. 'Why are you here again? Haven't you done enough damage?'

'I'm sorry,' Melanie mumbled. 'I know I'm probably the last person you wanted to see again, but I needed to see you.'

Isla caught the hitch in Melanie's voice and sensed that something was wrong even before she spotted what looked like dried blood on the young woman's lip. A closer look revealed that one of her eyes was swollen, and her cheek also appeared to be bruised.

'I take it *he* did that?' she asked.

Melanie nodded and visibly gulped, and Isla could see that she was struggling to keep from crying, when she said, 'He was mad because I made him miss his appointment at the job centre.'

'It was gone five when I saw you,' Isla reminded her. 'How could he have had an appointment at that time?'

'He was supposed to be there at four, but I got held up,' Melanie said, dabbing at her tears with the sleeve of her jacket. 'And then I saw you and was even later.'

'Where is he now?' Isla peered out over Melanie's head to check if the man was loitering by the gate. 'If you've brought him here, I'll call the police.'

'He's not here,' Melanie assured her. 'He doesn't know where I am.'

'So what do you want?' Isla folded her arms. 'Obviously, it isn't nice that he's done this to you, but I'm not sure what you're expecting me to do about it. Haven't you got family or friends you could have gone to?'

'No.' Melanie shook her head. 'My family live in Devon and I've got no way of getting to them. They haven't spoken to me since I got with him, so there'd be no point. And he won't let me have friends, so there's no one.'

Isla knew first-hand how isolating it was to be disowned for falling in love with a man her family disapproved of, but that didn't make her feel any less angry about the grief Melanie had caused her. If any other woman had turned up on her doorstep injured and in distress, she wouldn't have hesitated to invite her in. But she was sorely tempted to slam the door in this one's face.

That last thought evaporated when a small white car pulled up outside the still-open gate. All too aware that she would be the talk of the village by morning if the delivery man clocked the state of Melanie's face, she made a snap decision and told her to come inside.

'No, it's OK,' Melanie said. 'I'm not expecting you to put yourself out for me. I just wanted to tell you—'

'That you're sorry... yeah, you've already said,' Isla cut in. 'But you're about to cause a scene I don't need, so just hurry up and get inside. You can go as soon as he's gone.'

Melanie glanced behind her and saw the car. Then, seeming to understand, she turned and pulled the pushchair backwards over the step.

Eager to get to the delivery man before he came too close, Isla brushed past her and met him halfway. Then, pressing the fob to close the gate behind him in case Melanie had lied and her violent boyfriend *was* out there, she went back into the house.

Melanie was standing in the hallway and Isla could see that she was shivering and cradling her ribs. Unsure what she was meant to do or say, Isla looked down at the child when she heard a noise coming from the pushchair. He was small and fair-haired, like his mother, and had the same dark hollows under his tired eyes. He'd been so quiet until then, she had assumed he must be sleeping. But he was now staring at the pizza box, and she guessed he must have smelled the contents when he started to thrash his legs beneath the thin blanket.

'Has he eaten?' she asked.

'I gave him his breakfast before I went out this morning, but I'm not sure if Carl gave him any dinner,' Melanie replied quietly. 'There was a bit of milk in his bottle when we left, but he finished that on the bus.'

'Is he OK with pizza?'

'Yeah, but it's all right. I'll get him something when we leave.'

'I ordered this just before the takeaway closed, and you'll be lucky to find anywhere else open at this time,' Isla said. 'I'm only offering because he's a baby and he's clearly hungry. But it's up to you if you'd rather take him back out into the cold with an empty belly.'

Melanie looked guiltily down at the child and then nodded. 'OK, thanks. But only if you don't mind.'

'I wouldn't have offered if I did,' Isla said, leading her into the kitchen and gesturing for her to take a seat at the table.

'You don't have to give me any,' Melanie said when Isla took three plates out of the cupboard. 'I'm all right.'

'Are you sure about that?' Isla arched an eyebrow when the woman's stomach rumbled loudly. She rolled her eyes when Melanie blushed, and placed a couple of slices onto each of the plates before carrying them to the table.

'Do you mind if I take him out?' Melanie asked when the child started to strain against his restraints.

'He's yours; you can do whatever you like with him,' Isla said, taking the seat facing hers.

Melanie thanked her and unstrapped the boy, then lifted him out and placed him on her lap. He immediately made a grab for the food, so she moved the plate out of his reach and broke off a little piece of pizza. She blew on to cool it down and then popped it into his mouth, and Isla watched as he hungrily swallowed it and reached out for more.

'How old is he?' Isla asked, assessing that he was around the one-year mark, given his small size and the fact that he was being hand-fed.

'Nearly two,' Melanie said. 'He's a slow starter,' she added defensively. 'But the doctor said he'll catch up when he's ready, so I'm not worried.'

'I'm sure he'll be fine,' Isla said, sensing her embarrassment. 'So, Carl – is that what you said his name was? Won't he be wondering where you are?'

'He will when he wakes up,' Melanie murmured, guiltily dipping her gaze as she added, 'I put a couple of sleepers in his brew when he stopped hitting me, so he was out of it when I left. I know it was wrong, but something snapped and I couldn't take it anymore.'

Isla was a little shocked to hear that Melanie had drugged the man, but she couldn't honestly say that she wouldn't be tempted to do the same if she were being attacked and it was her only chance to escape.

'I'm not judging you,' she said. 'But won't that make him even more angry?'

'Probably, but I'll stay out of his way till he calms down,' Melanie said, wiping her hand on her thigh and slotting the child back into the pushchair when he started rubbing his eyes. 'Thanks for that. He should sleep better now.'

'There's more in the box if you want to take it with you,' Isla offered, conscious that Melanie had barely eaten any.

'No, we're OK,' Melanie said. 'But he could probably do with a bottle to get him to sleep, if you have a bit of milk I could borrow?'

'Help yourself.' Isla pointed her in the direction of the fridge. 'The microwave's in the cupboard next to the cooker if you want to warm it up.'

Melanie leaned forward to get the boy's empty bottle out from under the blanket, and Isla saw her wince and clutch at her ribs again.

'Are you in pain?' she asked.

'A bit,' Melanie replied. 'I took a couple of Paracetamol earlier, but they've worn off.'

'Right, stay there. I'll do it.'

'It's fine. I can manage.'

'Carry on like this and you won't be fit to do *anything*,' Isla chided when Melanie tried to stand up and winced again. 'I'll do the bottle. Then I'll get you some painkillers and make you a brew while you get him to sleep. OK?'

Melanie nodded her agreement and Isla took the bottle from her. She filled it with milk and warmed it, then took a packet of Paracetamol caplets out of the cupboard and passed them to Melanie before switching the kettle on.

The child had fallen asleep by the time Isla had finished making the tea. Melanie gently covered him with the blanket and then popped two caplets out of the strip.

'Thanks,' she murmured, reaching for the cup Isla had placed on the table in front of her. 'I'll have this and get going.'

'The last bus will probably have gone by now,' Isla told her. 'And I had a few glasses of wine before you got here, so I can't give you a lift.'

'I wouldn't have expected you to,' Melanie said. 'We'll wait at the bus station till they start running again.'

'That won't be till six in the morning,' said Isla. 'You can't sit on a bench all night in this weather. I'll call an Uber for you.'

'No, don't; I can't afford it,' Melanie protested. 'All I've got is my bus pass.'

'I'll pay,' Isla said. 'But they'll ask for an address when I book it, so is there somewhere safe you can stay until your boyfriend calms down?'

Melanie shook her head and gazed at the sleeping boy. 'I'd best just take him home.'

'Really?' Isla frowned. 'You want to take him back there, knowing that his dad's probably going to attack you again? And what if he hurts him as well?'

'That won't happen. I would never let him touch Jacob.'

'Sorry to be cynical, but how would you stop him when you can't even stop him from hitting you?'

'I just will.'

'I think you're fooling yourself,' Isla said bluntly. 'I've already seen him yelling at the boy, and we both know that's likely to progress into something worse as time goes on. The fact that he's done this to you tonight, because you were late home, tells me exactly what kind of man he is.'

'I know you're trying to help, but you don't know what he's going through,' Melanie said. 'It's been really hard for us these last couple of years. You live in this lovely house, so you don't know how it feels to have to choose between eating and paying bills. But we're not that lucky. I lost my job when I got pregnant, and Carl's been struggling with his mental health, so it's not all his fault.'

'You're wrong about me not understanding,' said Isla. 'I told you earlier that I grew up on the Grange, so I know *exactly* how it feels to go without. My mum tried her best, but there were plenty of times when we didn't eat. The difference is, she never took it out on me.'

'It's not that easy to walk away when you love someone and know they're struggling,' Melanie replied defensively. 'Carl only gets angry because he can't look after us the way he wants to.'

'So he wants to take care of you, but then he beats you up if things don't go his way,' Isla shot back. 'Do you hear how ridiculous that sounds?'

Melanie's chin wobbled and a teardrop slid down her cheek. 'I've literally got nothing,' she croaked. 'Our benefits go into Carl's account, so I can't get any money without asking him. And the tenancy of our flat is in his name, so I can't even ask the council for a place of my own. I'm totally trapped.'

Isla felt a little uncomfortable at the mention of Carl controlling their finances. Her situation wasn't comparable, because Jerry had given her a credit card to buy whatever she wanted or needed. But, like Melanie, she'd had no access to his actual money. And she hadn't had any of her own, because Jerry had insisted that she stop working when they got married. Thankfully, he had left her well provided for, but it could have turned out very differently if he hadn't made that new will before he died, and she could now be homeless and as broke and desperate as Melanie clearly was.

'I'm sorry,' Melanie sniffed. 'This isn't your problem, and I didn't mean to put it on you. You'd have had every right to tear me to pieces after what I said about Jerry. But when you saw how scared I was when I saw Carl earlier, it felt like you actually cared. Nobody's treated me like that in years and it did something to me. In *here*.' She touched her chest. 'That's why I came tonight; because I need to tell you the truth.'

'And what *is* the truth?' Isla asked, bracing herself for more salacious revelations about her husband.

Melanie bit her lip and stared down into her cup. Then, quietly, she said, 'You're probably going to hate me for this, and I honestly don't blame you. But you were right. I *was* lying about the affair. I did meet Jerry at the club, but he only came once and he never asked me out. To be honest, I don't even think he knew it was a strip club until he got there. He was with some other men and they were really loud and rude, but he stared at his phone the whole time. One of them started trying to grope me while I was dancing and Jerry told him to pack it in. Then, when they were leaving, he took me aside and gave me some money; told me to stop wasting my life and find a better job.'

Isla stared at her in disbelief. 'If that's true, why tell me all that other stuff about meeting up in hotels and him wanting to divorce me to be with you?'

'Because that's what I *wished* had happened,' Melanie said sheepishly. 'No man had ever been that nice to me before and I couldn't stop thinking about him, so I found out his name and googled him. Loads of photos came up of him at charity events, and what have you, and he was so handsome and had such a lovely smile, I started fantasising what it would be like to be with someone like him instead of Carl. I guess it was my way of escaping when things were bad at home, and it started to feel real. I know this will probably sound crazy to you, but when he died, it felt like I'd lost *my* husband. And that's why I went to the funeral and then came here: because I wanted to be near him.'

'Yeah, you're right; it does sound crazy,' Isla said. 'But I'm glad you told me.'

'So am I,' said Melanie. 'And I'm really, really sorry for putting you through that. I honestly don't know why I did it, and I hope you can forgive me.'

Isla was still trying to process what she'd heard and didn't immediately answer. She couldn't believe that anyone could let their imagination run away with them to the extent that they would create a fictitious life with a man they had only met once. And, worse, get so invested in the lie that they would tell his grieving widow that they'd had an affair, knowing full well that nothing had ever happened. Fortunately for Melanie, Isla's anger was dampened by the relief of knowing that Jerry hadn't cheated on her, and she now felt only pity for the woman.

'I can't say I totally understand why you did it,' she said after a moment. 'But you're obviously going through a rough time, so I get why you'd want to want to imagine a better life for yourself and your boy.'

'He's my world,' Melanie said, gazing at the child.

'Then sort yourself out before it's too late,' Isla said. 'You're his mother and it's your job to keep him safe.'

Before Melanie could respond to that, Isla's phone started ringing, and she excused herself when she saw Tia's name on the screen.

'Sorry, I need to take this. We'll talk more when I get back.'

Isla left Melanie in the kitchen and went to the living room to take the call.

'Sorry for ringing so late,' Tia apologised when she answered. 'My bride's grandmother had a fall, so they decided to move the wedding to London to be closer to her. I've been running round all day trying to secure another venue. But I'm back at the hotel now, so I thought I'd give you a quick call to ask how things went with the reading of the will.'

'Better than I expected,' Isla said. 'He left everything to me.'

'See!' Tia exclaimed. 'Didn't I tell you he'd look after you?'

'Yeah, I know,' Isla smiled. 'But I'd kept the fear to myself for so long, I thought you were just trying to cheer me up.'

'I *felt* it,' said Tia. 'And now Jerry's proved me right, you can relax and stop worrying. Just tell me you went straight to a bar and had a glass of champers to celebrate?'

'No, I went home,' Isla said. 'To my mum's,' she elaborated, conscious that Tia would probably think that she meant she'd come back to her own home.

'Wow. So you finally plucked up the courage to do it. Good for you, girl.'

'Well, it would have been good if she'd actually been there. Turns out she's moved and some gobby bitch is living there now.'

'Oh no. I'm so sorry, babe.'

'It's OK,' Isla said. 'I was upset at the time, but I ran into Benny straight after and he cheered me up. Did you know he'd moved back to Manchester?'

'No, I didn't,' Tia said. 'I bumped into him a couple of years back when he was visiting his mum, but I'm sure he said he was still in London. How is he?'

Isla relayed what Benny had told her about losing his partner and his mum. Then, lowering her voice, she said, 'But you'll never guess what happened when I left his place…'

*

Melanie was slumped at the table with her head resting on her arms when Isla had finished talking to Tia and went back to the kitchen. Her eyes were closed and Isla could see that the bruises had already darkened in the short time she had been there. She still had her phone in her hand, so she opened the camera and zoomed in on the injuries before taking a quick snap. The photo highlighted the damage more starkly and she saw that the bruise on Melanie's cheek was forming a distinctive knuckle-shaped pattern, indicating that a solid punch had landed there. Isla and Jerry had argued many times throughout their marriage, but he had never once raised his hand to her, and she could only imagine how terrified Melanie must have been while Carl was beating her.

As if sensing that she was being watched, Melanie suddenly stirred, and panic flared in her eyes when she looked up and saw Isla standing over her.

'It's OK; it's only me,' Isla said, guessing that Melanie must have thought she was Carl. Then, speaking before she'd had a chance to think about her next words, she said, 'Look, it's late and you're obviously exhausted, so why don't you stay here tonight.'

'Thanks, that's really kind,' Melanie said politely. 'But I've caused enough stress for you today.'

'Yeah, you have,' Isla agreed. 'But you came out of your way to put it right, and I really appreciate that. If you don't want to do it for yourself, do it for your son. I'm sure he'd rather be sleeping in a nice, warm bed than freezing in his pram.'

'He doesn't deserve any of this,' Melanie replied, releasing a heavy sigh as she gazed at her son. Then, looking up at Isla, she said, 'I hope you don't think I came this late on purpose so you'd let us stay? I wasn't thinking about the time when I left, and

I honestly didn't expect you to let me through the door. I just wanted to tell you the truth, because I felt so guilty.'

'It's done now, so stop worrying about it,' Isla said. 'Just get him out of the pram and I'll show you to your room.'

'Thank you so much,' Melanie said tearfully as she gently picked up the sleeping child.

Isla nodded and led her up the stairs to the guest bedroom. She said good night and left her to settle in, then went back downstairs to turn off the lights and check that the doors and windows were locked before heading to her own bed.

Tia had been furious when she'd heard about Melanie claiming to have had an affair with Jerry – and even more so when she learned that Melanie had subsequently turned up at the house. Tia had told Isla to kick her out and warn her she'd better not ever dare show her lying face around there again, and Isla knew that she'd be horrified when she found out that she had, instead, invited her to stay the night. In truth, Isla knew that Tia was right. She didn't know Melanie from Adam and could well wake up to find that the woman had robbed her blind while she was sleeping. But now she'd extended the invitation and Melanie had accepted, she couldn't find it in her heart to tell the woman that she'd changed her mind and kick her and the child out.

Chapter 10

The sound of footsteps on the stairs woke Isla the next morning. She'd had difficulty getting to sleep and had resorted to drinking a couple of shots of whisky to knock her out. Disorientated now, her heartbeat pounding in her ears, she held her breath and strained to hear which direction the footsteps were heading in. They seemed to be receding rather than coming closer, and she eased herself up in the bed and groped for her phone. About to call the police, she hesitated when the muffled sound of a child crying down below drifted up to her. The events of the previous night came back to her in a rush and she released the breath she'd been holding when she remembered that she had invited Melanie and the boy to stay the night. Still shaking, but massively relieved that she wasn't being burgled, as she'd feared, she quickly got up and pulled on her dressing gown.

Melanie was filling Jacob's bottle with milk when Isla entered the kitchen.

'Sorry,' she apologised, guiltily putting the bottle back into the fridge. 'I was going to ask, but I wasn't sure if you were awake yet.'

'It's fine,' Isla said, noticing that Jacob had stopped crying and was staring up at her from the pushchair. 'Did you sleep OK?'

'Yes, thanks; it's a really comfortable bed,' Melanie said politely as she handed the bottle to her son. 'Thanks again for letting us stay, but we'll be out of your hair in a minute.'

'There's no rush,' Isla said, yawning as she filled the kettle. 'I'm making a coffee if you want one?'

'I'd best not.' Melanie sat down and tucked the blanket around the child's legs. 'It's a long bus ride and I don't want to end up needing the loo before I get home.'

'So you've decided to go back then?'

'Yeah, I think it's for the best. Jacob's going to need his dad when I'm ...'

'When you're what?' Isla frowned when Melanie tailed off. 'Please don't tell me you're planning to dump Jacob there and take off without him, because that's a terrible idea. You're his mum and he needs you.'

'It's not that simple,' Melanie said quietly. 'I didn't tell you yesterday because it's not your problem, but ...' She paused and swallowed loudly. Then, her voice breaking, she said, 'I've got cancer.'

Shocked, because she genuinely hadn't expected to hear that, Isla pulled out a chair and sat heavily down.

'I'm so sorry. Do you mind if I ask what kind?'

'Breast, and it's OK,' Melanie murmured. Then, shaking her head when her chin began to wobble, she said, 'Obviously I don't mean it's OK that I've got it, 'cos it's not. It just feels so unreal. I only found out yesterday and they want me to start chemo in a couple of weeks. I was on my way home from hospital when I saw you and my head was all over the place.'

'I can imagine,' Isla said softly. 'But that makes what Carl did to you even worse. I mean, what kind of man beats up a woman who's got cancer?'

'He doesn't know. I haven't told him yet.'

'Why not?' Isla was confused. 'Surely he's the first person you should have told? If he'd known, it might have stopped him.'

'I honestly don't care what he does to me anymore.' Melanie sniffed. 'I just need to know that Jacob will be safe if anything happens to me.'

'But you *don't* know that,' Isla argued.

Melanie jumped when her phone suddenly started ringing, and she pulled it out of her pocket and stared at the name on the screen. It stopped after a while and, a few seconds later, a voice message notification popped up. She raised the phone to listen to the message, and Isla saw the blood drain from her already-pale face.

'Was that him?' she asked when Melanie lowered the phone. 'What did he say?'

Hands shaking, Melanie played the message on loudspeaker, and Isla's stomach churned when a deep voice growled: '*Where the fuck are ya? You think you're so smart spiking my drink and doing a runner, but let's see what happens when I get my hands on you. And you know I will, 'cos you've got nowhere else to go. Just wait, bitch... If you think last night was bad, you ain't seen nothin' yet!*'

'You need to call the police,' Isla said when it had finished.

'No!' Melanie shook her head. 'I can't! He'll kill me if he gets arrested again.'

'It sounds like he's planning to do that anyway,' said Isla. 'But you're not there, so he won't be able to get at you when they pick him up. We can ring them now. Or I'll drive you to the station so they can see what he did to you.'

'I need to go back before it gets worse,' Melanie said, turning to strap Jacob in before leaping to her feet. 'Thanks so much for everything you've done, and please don't worry about us. We'll be OK.'

'No, you won't,' Isla argued, going after her when she started walking towards the door. 'Please just stop and think about this for a minute. He's already hurt you, and I've just heard him threaten to do it again. You're about to start chemotherapy. Do you really think you'd survive another beating when your body's going through that? Because *I* don't. And what if he kills you and ends up in prison? Then Jacob won't have *either* of you, and you'll have gone through all that for nothing.'

'Why do you care?' Melanie sobbed, swiping at her tears. 'You should be glad to see the back of me.'

'If I thought you were going to be safe, I probably would be,' Isla replied truthfully. 'But you're not, and I can't stand by and watch you put your child at risk. I know you're too scared to do it for yourself, but if you insist on taking Jacob back there, *I'll* call the police.'

'No . . .' Panic flared in Melanie's eyes. 'Please don't. He's never hit me in front of Jacob, and you'll just make everything a million times worse.'

'Then let me help you,' Isla urged. 'There are refuges for women in your situation. You'd be safe there, and they could give you and Jacob the support you need while you're going through your treatment.'

'But what if I die?' Melanie whimpered. 'I can't let them send Jacob to live with strangers. He'll need his dad.'

'If that happens, which I'm sure it won't, you can leave instructions for them to contact Carl,' Isla said. 'But, right now, you need to forget about him and concentrate on getting better and finding somewhere safe for you and Jacob to live. You've already done the hardest part by leaving, so sit down and let me make you that coffee. We'll talk it all over when you've calmed down and see if we can come up with a plan. OK?'

Melanie nodded her agreement, so Isla guided her to a chair.

'I think he might need changing,' she said when she glanced

down into the pushchair and saw a wet patch spreading across the blanket. 'Do you have any nappies?'

'No.' Melanie shook her head and gingerly dabbed at her tears with the back of her hand. 'I only had one and I used it last night.'

'OK, I'll nip into the village after I've made your coffee and pick some up for you,' Isla said. Then, taking a notepad and pen out of a drawer, she passed them to her, saying, 'Write a list of whatever else you both need.'

'But I don't have any money,' Melanie reminded her.

'I didn't ask for any,' Isla said, walking over to switch the kettle on. As she waited for it to boil, she watched Melanie out of the corner of her eye. She wasn't sure why she felt compelled to help her given the trouble she'd caused. No-nonsense Tia would undoubtedly have sent her packing when she had turned up last night, and Isla knew that she should probably have done exactly that. But Melanie was so beaten down, both physically *and* mentally, she couldn't help but feel sorry for her.

Melanie had stopped crying and had written a tiny list when Isla placed her coffee on the table in front of her. Isla slipped the paper into her pocket and told Melanie to help herself to whatever she and Jacob wanted for breakfast. Then, heading upstairs, she took a quick shower and got dressed before setting off.

She didn't feel entirely comfortable about leaving a virtual stranger alone in her house. But now she knew the truth of Melanie's situation, she didn't want to put her at risk of being spotted by somebody who knew Carl. It was highly unlikely, because the village was an hour's bus ride from Manchester. But she'd seen documentaries about violent, controlling men like him, and they often went to extraordinary lengths to track down the women who had dared to leave them. She hoped that she would be able to find an alternative place for Melanie to stay before it got to that. But the woman was safe for now, so she pushed the misgivings out of her mind and drove on into the village.

Chapter 11

It had been a tense morning, but it only got worse as the day wore on. Isla had returned home from her shopping trip to find that Melanie had turned on the TV in the snug and put on a children's channel on YouTube. The same batch of infuriatingly chirpy nursery rhymes had been playing on a loop ever since, which Isla had found irritating. But Melanie said it was the only thing that seemed to settle Jacob, so she'd let that fly. What she couldn't ignore, however, was Melanie's phone. It had been pinging all day, as Carl bombarded her with messages; alternating between begging her to go home, or threatening to hunt her down and kill her and Jacob if she didn't. With no sign of him letting up, Isla reached her breaking point after lunch and ordered Melanie to switch it to silent. But the damage had already been done by then, and Melanie was a nervous wreck for the rest of the day. And, Jacob, obviously picking up on the tension, had bawled his head off for hours.

Worn out and seriously questioning her decision to invite them to stay longer, Isla waited until Melanie took Jacob to bed after dinner and then opened a bottle of wine. She poured an extra-large glassful, carried it out into the garden and flopped onto a patio chair. It was dark and cold, but the sky was clear, and she felt the tension lift off her shoulders as she sipped her drink and gazed up at the stars. She had always enjoyed sitting out here with Jerry in the evening, and she still missed him dearly. But, right then, after the sheer chaos of the day, she had never felt so happy to be alone.

Melanie hadn't come back down after taking Jacob to bed, so Isla had decided to have an early night after she finished her drink. Rested and determined to get things back on track when she woke up the following morning, she was already showered, dressed and in the kitchen making coffee when Melanie brought Jacob down at 8 a.m.

Melanie had only written a couple of essentials on the shopping list Isla had told her to write, so Isla had added a few of her own; including toiletries for Melanie, and a few little outfits and toys for Jacob. The child was dressed in one of those outfits now, and his freshly washed hair looked almost golden in the sunlight coming through the window. Melanie was wearing the blouse and slacks Isla had gifted her from her own wardrobe, and she looked a lot brighter, despite the livid bruises still marring her face.

Isla greeted her with a smile and handed a cup of coffee to her. 'Did you sleep well?'

'Yeah, really good, thanks.' Melanie returned the smile and took a seat at the table. 'I, um, wanted to apologise for yesterday. We must have done your head in with all the noise.'

'Not at all,' Isla lied. 'But you should probably keep your phone off today so we can work in peace. I've already made a start.' She gestured towards her laptop, which was standing open on the table. 'I was looking for numbers of nearby refuges for women, but it seems they don't like people to apply to them directly, so we'll have to go through the domestic abuse helpline.

Apparently, they're connected to every refuge in the country, so they should be able to find one that has space for you both.'

Melanie nodded and gazed down at Jacob, who was sitting on her lap; shyly watching Isla from beneath his lashes.

'Why don't you give him his breakfast and get him settled before we make a start,' Isla suggested.

Melanie put Jacob down on the rug and started preparing a bottle for him, and Isla took a seat and watched him as she drank her coffee. She'd babysat for a couple of her neighbours' children when she was a teenager, but they had always been asleep by the time she'd got there, so she'd never spent any one-on-one time with them. Tia didn't have children, and Jerry's friends' children had already been grown by the time she'd met them, so she had no clue at what age they started to walk and talk. Melanie had told her that Jacob was almost two and a slow starter, but Isla hadn't yet heard him utter a single word. And he wasn't even attempting to crawl away from the spot where he'd been left.

Melanie came back just then and placed the boy in the pushchair. She gave him the bottle and propped it up with the blanket, then took her seat at the table.

'Ready?' Isla asked.

'I guess so,' Melanie murmured, clutching her cup between both hands.

'Hopefully it won't take too long,' Isla said, clicking on the link for the helpline's contact number. 'I'm not sure how these places work, but I imagine they'll want to speak to you in person, so I'll pass the phone to you when they answer.'

Melanie didn't reply and Isla gave her a questioning look.

'Are you OK? Only you've gone very quiet since I mentioned the refuges. Please don't tell me you're still thinking about going back?'

'I honestly don't know what I want to do,' Melanie admitted. 'I know you don't approve, but I think Jacob needs his dad.'

'We talked this over yesterday and you agreed that you need a fresh start,' Isla reminded her. 'What's happened between then and now to make you change your mind? Have you spoken to him? Has he threatened you again?'

'No.' Melanie shook her head. 'This is my decision.'

'Well, something must have happened to make you start rethinking everything,' Isla said, trying not to let her irritation show. She had only invited her to stay an extra night because Melanie had agreed to seek help, and she had been up since the crack of dawn looking into her options, only for Melanie to start flip-flopping again.

Melanie was staring down into her cup and Isla sighed when she saw that her chin was wobbling.

'Look, I don't want to upset you,' she said. 'But will you at least speak to the helpline people to get some advice before you make a decision?'

'There's no point,' Melanie replied quietly. 'I've dealt with them before, and they'll tell me I have to report him to the police and get a case number before they can help me. I can't do that, because then I'll get into trouble as well.'

'No, you won't,' Isla argued. 'You've done nothing wrong. This is all on him.'

'It's not,' Melanie countered. 'You don't know the full story.'

'So tell me.'

Melanie closed her eyes and dropped her head into her hands. Then, sighing, she said, 'When I was pregnant, a neighbour heard Carl hitting me and called the police. I was covered in blood and the flat was wrecked when they got there. They were going to arrest Carl, but I told them a man had followed me home from the club and forced his way in while he was sleeping.'

'Why didn't you just tell the truth and let them take him?' Isla frowned.

'I was too scared,' said Melanie. 'He'd been arrested for it before, but they let him off with a caution and he battered me again as soon as he got home. I couldn't risk that happening again.'

Isla heard the tremble in her voice and saw the tears glistening in her eyes. She was clearly terrified of the man, and it had to be especially terrifying to think that the police couldn't even help her.

'They knew Carl had done it, but I wouldn't change my statement,' Melanie went on. 'So they said I was putting the baby at risk and called social services in. They said they'd get a court order to take the baby away if I was still with Carl when he was born. I didn't want to lose him, so I said I'd ask my mum if I could go and stay with her. But Carl said he'd leave instead, so they let him pack a bag and escorted him out.'

'I thought you said the flat was in his name,' Isla said when she paused to take a sip of her coffee. 'So how would you have been allowed to stay there without him?'

'Oh, er, no.' Melanie shook her head. 'That happened at the flat we were in before the one we've got now. That one was in my name.'

'Oh, I see,' Isla said. 'But if Carl had gone and you knew you'd lose the baby if you got back with him, why did you?'

'He didn't really leave,' Melanie said sheepishly. 'He stayed out that night in case they were watching, then came back the next day. Things settled down for a bit and I thought we were going to be all right. But I was scared they'd come back when I had Jacob, so Carl found us a new place and put it in his name so they wouldn't be able to find me. My job was cash in hand, but when I lost it I couldn't claim benefits in case they traced me through that. If I put myself back on social services' radar now and they find out I've been with Carl the whole time, I'll lose Jacob. And I can't do that. I just can't.'

'You also can't carry on living like this,' Isla replied bluntly. 'It's not fair to you *or* Jacob.'

'I know you think I'm a terrible mother, but what choice do I have?' Melanie asked. 'Now you know why I can't involve the police or social services, what am I supposed to do? I'm not on the housing list, so it'd take years to get a place off the council. I can't even rent somewhere private because they'll want references and a deposit. And there's no way I can ask my family for help. So what's left? Me and Jacob end up on the streets and I lose him anyway?'

Isla couldn't answer that. Melanie's dilemma was partly of her own making, because she'd chosen to stay with Carl despite being warned that she would lose her baby if she did so. As a result of that decision, she'd been trapped in a violent relationship with a man who knew he could treat her as badly as he liked without consequence. She had reached her breaking point and had drugged him in order to escape. But she was now facing the realisation that she had burned all her bridges because of him and had nobody to turn to for help.

After mulling everything over for several minutes, Isla said, 'OK, I can see why you don't want to go to the authorities, so I won't try to persuade you. But I genuinely don't think it's safe for you to go back, so why don't you stay here for a few more days while you think about your options.'

'Thanks, but I can't do that to you,' Melanie protested. 'I know you don't really want me here, so—'

'Stop.' Isla held up her hand. 'If you want the truth, then, *no*, I wouldn't want you here if I thought you had anywhere else to go. I hardly know you and you did a terrible thing by telling me that you'd had an affair with my husband. But I locked you in my car that night and made you get home late, which makes me partly responsible for you getting beaten up. This is my way of trying to put that right.'

'That wasn't your fault,' Melanie insisted. 'I was already late and Carl was already angry, so he'd have done it anyway. Please don't blame yourself.' She reached across the table and touched Isla's hand, then immediately snatched her own hand back. 'Sorry. I didn't mean to do that.'

'Don't worry about it,' Isla said, rising to her feet and gathering up their cups. 'Jacob's asleep and I think we could both do with a break, so why don't you go and take a bath or go for a walk to clear your head. I'll watch him if he wakes up while you're gone.'

'Are you sure?' Melanie asked.

'Positive,' Isla said, carrying the cups to the sink.

Melanie decided to go for a walk, so Isla let her out and closed the gate behind her. Then, locking the front door, she checked that Jacob was still sleeping before going upstairs.

The guest bedroom door was standing slightly ajar and she pushed it open when she picked up on an unpleasant smell coming from inside. The bed had been made, but the clothes Melanie and Jacob had been wearing when they arrived were sitting in an untidy heap at the end of it. They were grubby and there were spots of dried blood on both sets, which made Isla wonder if Melanie had lied about Jacob being in a different room when the beating took place. If so, Carl was even more of a disgusting scumbag than he'd already proved himself to be – and Melanie a bigger fool.

Isla shook that last thought out of her head, reasoning that the blood had probably transferred onto Jacob's clothes when

Melanie had lifted him out of his cot. She looked around for the source of the bad smell and traced it to a bag of soiled nappies wedged between the base of the bed and the bedside cabinet. Nose wrinkled in disgust, she pulled it out with her fingertips and carried it and the clothes downstairs at arm's length.

She deposited the nappies in the outside bin and put the clothes onto a hot wash. Then, gently pushing the pram into the snug so that the washing machine wouldn't wake Jacob when it started spinning, she did a quick tidy round before sitting at the table to check her emails and messages.

Jacob began to stir after a while, so Isla put down her phone and walked over to him. His face crumpled at the sight of her, and she was alarmed when he let out an ear-piercing scream. She rocked the pram in an effort to calm him down, but it seemed to make him worse. So she grabbed his empty bottle and quickly made him a new one before lifting him out of the pram.

Still screaming, Jacob thrashed around in her arms as she carried him over to the armchair in the corner. Unsure what to do, Isla held him close and rocked him until, at last, he began to run out of steam. She was sweating as much as he was by then, and she breathed a huge sigh of relief when he sucked the teat of the bottle into his mouth and started to drink the milk.

His little chest was still heaving and his eyes were glossy with tears, and Isla couldn't help but wonder what terrible things he must have witnessed in his short life. Even if Melanie had been telling the truth and Carl had never hit her in front of him, he must have heard her screams and seen the injuries on her face. He was too young to understand what it meant, but he would undoubtedly have picked up on his mother's fear and his father's rage, and that made Isla both sad and angry on his behalf.

*

Jacob had settled down and was sitting quietly in front of the TV playing with one of his new toys when Melanie came back an hour later. Isla let her in and then went back to stirring the pot of soup she was making for lunch.

'Oh wow, he's not crying,' Melanie remarked as she slipped off her jacket. 'He usually goes nuts if I'm not there when he wakes up. I think that's why Carl has such a hard time with him when I'm out.'

'He wasn't too happy when he saw me,' Isla admitted. 'But he's been good as gold since he had his bottle. Does he like chicken soup, by the way?'

'Yeah, he'll eat anything,' Melanie said, looping the jacket over the back of a chair. 'Can I help?'

'No, I'm almost done,' Isla said. 'Sit down while I share it out.'

Melanie picked Jacob up and sat him on her lap.

'Did you enjoy your walk?' Isla asked, carrying their bowls to the table and sitting down. 'You look a lot brighter than when you went out.'

'It was lovely.' Melanie smiled. 'I found some woods at the end of the road and it was so peaceful in there, I totally lost track of time. It was like all the outside noise disappeared and all I could hear was birds singing and leaves rustling. All you ever hear on the estate is sirens and doors getting booted in.'

'I know, I grew up there,' Isla reminded her. 'It took a while to get used to how quiet it is round here, but I couldn't imagine living in the city again.'

'You're so lucky,' Melanie said, casting a longing glance around the kitchen. 'This is like heaven compared to my flat. And your garden's bigger than our local park. Jacob would love it if he could play out there.'

'You're welcome to take him out there any time you like,' Isla said. 'But please don't leave him alone, because there's a stream at the back, and if he gets out of the gate he'll fall down the slope.'

'Yeah, it looks really dangerous,' Melanie agreed, spooning soup into Jacob's mouth.

Isla was confused by that comment, because Melanie hadn't been out into the garden, and the fence was far too high for her to have seen what lay on the other side from the house. But she supposed it was possible that Melanie might have stumbled across it on her walk.

'It's a lovely area, but I don't think I could live out here by myself,' Melanie went on. 'Don't you ever get scared?'

'Not really.' Isla shrugged. 'Nothing's ever happened in all the time I've been here, so I reckon I'm safe.'

'Yeah, but it gets really dark at night,' Melanie mused. 'If it was me, I'd be paranoid someone was out there prowling around.'

Isla's frown deepened when Melanie gave a visible shudder. She had always felt safe in the house when Jerry was alive, but she hadn't really thought about what she would do if someone were to break in now he was gone. She'd known Peter for years, so she had been annoyed rather than scared when he'd let himself in that day. But now Melanie was here, hiding out from a violent man who was probably desperately trying to track her down, she dreaded to think what might happen if he turned up and forced his way in. It was unlikely since she and Tia were the only ones who knew Melanie was there. But, just in case, she decided she should probably follow Tia's advice and look into getting some cameras fitted when Jerry's money went into her account.

Chapter 12

The next few days passed without incident, and Isla gradually began to get used to having Melanie and Jacob around. Jacob still hadn't spoken, but he seemed more alert than when he'd first arrived and was crying far less. He had even started to try to feed himself at mealtimes, which was messy but fun to watch.

Melanie was also doing well. She wasn't eating very much, but Isla figured that the stress of the cancer diagnosis had probably affected her appetite. That aside, her bruises were fading and there didn't appear to be any signs of permanent scarring. And, since Carl seemed to have given up on her and had stopped bombarding her with nasty messages, she no longer jumped at every little sound.

All in all, things were heading in the right direction, and Isla was happy to see the progress they were both making. It was only a temporary solution, because Melanie really needed her own place. She still seemed resistant to the idea of seeking the professional help she needed in order to achieve that. But now Carl was out of the picture, Isla was convinced that social services would see that she had acted out of fear in the past and was now doing her best to keep her child safe.

But it was still early days, and Isla didn't want to push Melanie too hard in case she ran back to Carl. So she kept her thoughts to herself and did her best to ease Melanie's burdens while she healed from the trauma.

It was Jacob's second birthday at the end of the week. Conscious that he hadn't left the house since they'd arrived, *and* that Melanie's first chemotherapy session was just around the corner, Isla decided to treat them to a day out to celebrate. She had found a farm online which had a petting zoo for children, and it looked like the perfect, stress-free environment for both Melanie and Jacob. She had already bought a car seat so that she could drive Melanie to the hospital on Monday morning. It had been delivered the previous evening, so she quickly unboxed it and fitted it into her car. That done, she made a packed lunch for them all and then woke Melanie and told her to get ready.

It was a long drive and Jacob started to get restless long before they got there, but he quickly settled down when Melanie took him out of the car and strapped him into the pushchair. The farm was nestled in a valley and all they could see for miles around was grassland, hills and more farms in the distance. The air smelled of a combination of sweet hay and manure, and the sun beat down on them as they strolled around the grounds.

It was obvious to Isla that Jacob had never been anywhere near the countryside before as he swivelled his head from side to side, trying to take it all in. He got really excited when they wheeled him through the petting zoo and he saw the lambs, rabbits and meerkats up close. But it was the alpacas that brought the biggest reaction from him, and he squealed with delight when one of the girls who was working in the enclosure led a baby over for him to stroke.

They had walked miles by lunchtime and Isla could see that

Melanie was starting to flag. They found a little clearing next to a stream, far away from the buildings and the other visitors, and settled down to eat. Melanie said she wasn't hungry and lay back to enjoy the sunshine, so Isla gave Jacob a sandwich and ate her own before lifting him out of the pushchair and sitting him on the grass.

Melanie hadn't yet taken him into the garden at the house, and Isla wondered if he'd ever even seen grass before when he tentatively reached out and touched it. He snatched his hand back and then immediately touched it again. Then, seeming to decide that it was safe, he tore out two handfuls and went to stuff them into his mouth. Isla stopped him when she noticed ants crawling on it and turned to get the wet wipes from the bag Melanie had packed. When she turned back, she was shocked to see that Jacob had risen to his feet. It was the first time she had seen him stand up on his own, and she grinned when he wobbled for a moment before taking a couple of tentative steps towards a patch of bluebells he'd spotted.

'Melanie!' She nudged the woman. 'Look!'

Melanie sat up and, shielding her eyes with her hand, turned to see what Isla was pointing at.

'He went there by himself,' Isla told her. 'Is that the first time he's walked?'

'Yeah.' Melanie nodded. 'He tried a few months ago, but he fell and split his head open on the table and it put him off trying again.'

'Well, now he's started, there'll be no stopping him,' Isla said, watching as the boy plucked a tiny flower out of the ground and stared at it as if he'd never seen anything quite like it before.

'God, that's all I need,' Melanie murmured.

'It'll be fine,' Isla reassured her, guessing that she was probably worried that she wouldn't be able to keep up with him if he got too mobile while she was having her treatment. 'You've got this.'

'I hope so,' Melanie smiled. ' And thanks for today. It's been a really nice birthday for him.'

'It's my pleasure,' Isla said, watching as Jacob put the flower into his mouth before immediately spitting it out again.

'You're so good with him,' Melanie said. 'I reckon you'd have been a great mum. How come you never had any of your own? Didn't you want kids?'

Isla's stomach clenched and her smile slipped.

'Sorry,' Melanie apologised when she noticed the change in her expression. 'I shouldn't have asked. It's none of my business.'

'It's OK,' Isla sighed. 'Truth is, I *did* want children, and I was ecstatic when I found out I was pregnant shortly after marrying Jerry. Sadly, I miscarried a few weeks later, and the same happened with my next two pregnancies. Jerry didn't want me to go through the heartache and grief again, so we decided to stop trying.'

'I'm so sorry,' Melanie murmured. 'I had no idea.'

'I've learned to live with it, but I don't really like to talk about it,' Isla said. Then, eager to get off the subject, she nodded at Jacob, saying, 'He's starting to look a bit sleepy. Shall we take him for one last walk around the zoo then head home?'

'Yeah, the fresh air's probably knocking him out,' Melanie said. 'And he's not the only one,' she added, covering a yawn with her hand. 'I'm absolutely knackered.'

'Are you OK?' Isla asked, concerned that they might have overdone it. She had wanted to do something nice for Melanie, to help her to relax, but she hadn't thought about the physical toll the cancer might already be taking on her.

Melanie opened her mouth to answer, but the words froze

on her tongue, and her eyes widened in horror as she gazed at something over Isla's shoulder.

'What's wrong?' Isla asked.

'I think I saw Carl,' Melanie whispered, scrambling to her feet.

'What? *Where*?' Isla snapped her head around to look. 'I don't see anyone.'

'He was over by that barn,' Melanie said, scooping Jacob up off the grass. 'He must have followed us.'

'Does he have a car?' Isla asked, dusting her jeans off as she, too, stood up.

'No.' Melanie shook her head. 'But he could have got a lift off someone, or a taxi.'

'Hey, take it easy,' Isla said when Melanie roughly bundled Jacob into the pram, banging his head in the process.

'Sorry,' Melanie mumbled, leaning down to kiss his head when he started grizzling.

'Calm down,' Isla said, peering into her eyes when she straightened up. 'Look, I've asked you this before, but I'm going to ask again – and I want the truth. Have you been talking to Carl and told him where I live?'

'No!' Melanie cried. 'I wouldn't do that, I swear. I don't want him to know where we are.'

'OK, then it can't have been him,' said Isla. 'I know you're scared, and that's understandable after everything you've been through. But the only way he could have followed us is if he'd been near my house when we left. And that's not possible if you haven't told him where I live. So, whoever you saw over there, it wasn't him.'

Melanie squeezed her eyes shut and inhaled deeply. Then, releasing the breath, she said, 'Yeah, you're right. Sorry. It just really freaked me out. I hope I haven't ruined the day for you?'

'Not at all,' Isla said. 'But I think we've all had enough excitement, so how about we give the zoo a miss and go straight home?'

Melanie nodded her agreement and turned to strap Jacob into the pushchair, and Isla quickly bagged the remnants of their lunch before heading back to the car.

Chapter 13

Jacob had started to cry as soon as they left the farm, and the more Melanie had tried to quieten him down, the louder he'd screamed. Isla felt guilty for taking him out and causing him to get overstimulated, but her head was banging by the time they got back to the house and she was desperate for a break. So, leaving Melanie to it after throwing together a quick dinner for the pair, she escaped to her bedroom and swallowed a couple of painkillers. Then, running a bath, she lit an aromatic candle and plugged in her earbuds to drown out the sound of Jacob's screams.

Soothed by the music and the sweet scent of the candle, she didn't realise she'd fallen asleep until she was woken by Melanie banging on the bathroom door and calling her name through the wood. The water was almost cold by then, and the candle had burned itself out, so she groped for the towel and quickly wrapped it around herself before opening the door.

'What's wrong?' she asked when she saw the panicked look on Melanie's face. 'Is Jacob OK?'

'Someone keeps ringing the bell,' Melanie told her. 'But I daren't look in case it's Carl and he sees me.'

As soon as the words had left her mouth, the doorbell rang

again. And then again, and again, as if someone was jabbing their finger down on the button.

'What are we going to do?' Melanie whimpered.

'Go to your room,' Isla said. 'I'll get dressed and see who it is.'

'If it's Carl, please don't let him in,' Melanie pleaded as she backed out onto the landing. 'He can be really charming, but he's dangerous.'

'Don't worry,' Isla said calmly. 'If it *is* him, I'll have the police here so fast, he won't know what's hit him.'

Melanie retreated to the guest bedroom, and Isla quickly pulled on some clothes before heading downstairs. She looked through the spyhole and saw a shadowy figure on the other side of the gate. But she couldn't see their face, because the headlights of the car parked next to them were beaming too brightly. Melanie had sworn that she hadn't given Carl the address, and she'd also said that he didn't drive, so Isla genuinely didn't think it could be him. But she gripped her phone tightly in her hand as she opened the door, just in case it was and she needed to call the police.

'About bloody time,' a voice called out when she stepped outside. 'I've been out here so long, I was starting to think you'd given me a dummy address.'

'*Benny*?' Isla shielded her eyes with her hand as she walked over to the gate. 'What are you doing here?'

'You invited me for dinner,' he said. 'Don't tell me you forgot?'

'I'm so sorry,' she apologised, recalling that she had issued the invitation as she was leaving his house the previous week. 'Things have been a bit crazy for the last few days and my head's all over the place.'

'So I see.' Benny looked pointedly at her still-wet hair.

'I fell asleep in the bath,' she said, self-consciously running her fingers through her hair to untangle it as she pressed the fob to open the gate.

Benny drove in and parked alongside Isla's car, then climbed out and cast an approving gaze over the house.

'So this is where you've been living while I've been roughing it in the ghetto, eh? Talk about rags to riches. I'm not sure if I should call you Cinders or Your Majesty.'

'It's not that grand,' Isla said, giving him a hug.

'Oh, please.' He gave her a bemused look. 'Don't pull that fake modest crap on me. This place is bigger than our whole block back home.'

'OK, I guess it is pretty impressive the first time you see it,' Isla conceded. 'But I'm used to it, so I forget what it looks like to other people. Come on in.'

Benny followed her inside and looked around as he slipped his jacket off, checking out the furnishings and décor. 'Well, this is … *quaint.* Looks like someone's been single-handedly keeping the local charity shops in business.'

'I'll have you know these are all antique family heirlooms,' Isla informed him.

'Well, they sure as hell ain't from *your* family,' he shot back. 'No offence, but I still have nightmares about that orange plastic sofa your mum had. It was like something out of a seventies porno.'

'It was pleather not plastic,' she laughed. 'And she was really proud of it.'

Benny opened his mouth to deliver another comeback, but snapped it shut again when he glimpsed a pale face peering down at him from the top of the stairs.

'What the hell was *that*?' he asked, turning back to Isla when it immediately disappeared again. 'You told me you lived alone, so please don't tell me you've got a ghost? That stuff scares the crap out of me.'

'It wasn't a ghost,' Isla reassured him, lowering her voice as she waved him towards the kitchen. 'Go through there, I'll be with you in a sec.'

She padded up the stairs and tapped lightly on the guest bedroom door.

'It's OK, it's not Carl,' she whispered when Melanie peeped out. 'It's a friend of mine.'

'Yeah, I saw him,' Melanie replied quietly. 'But thanks for letting me know.'

'No worries.' Isla smiled. 'We're going to have something to eat and drink if you'd like to join us?'

'No, I'm all right,' Melanie said, glancing back at the bed. 'I don't want to leave Jacob in case he wakes up.'

Isla nodded her understanding and then said good night before heading back down to the kitchen.

Already seated at the table, Benny gave her a questioning look when she came in and closed the door. 'Everything OK?'

'Yeah. She was scared you were someone else, so I just needed to let her know she's safe.'

'So who is she?' Benny asked.

'The woman I told you about the other day,' said Isla. 'The one who turned up at Jerry's funeral and then came here the next day.'

'Really?' Benny looked confused. 'So how come she's here? I thought you said she was a weirdo.'

'It's a long story,' Isla said, taking a bottle of wine out of the rack and pouring two glasses. She carried them to the table and handed one to Benny, then sat down and told him about her encounter with Melanie after leaving his house that day – and everything that had transpired since.

'Let me see if I've got this right,' Benny said when she paused to take a sip of wine. 'She claimed she'd had an affair with your husband, then turned up asking for help. And you not only let her in, you tell her she can stay?'

'She didn't come for help; she came to tell me she'd lied about Jerry, because she felt guilty,' Isla corrected him. 'And I only let her stay because she had nowhere else to go.'

'That's her problem, not yours,' Benny said. 'I mean, I get that you feel sorry for her, but what do you even know about her? If she's already admitted she lied about the affair, what's to say she's not lying about everything else?'

'She's definitely not lying about getting beaten up,' Isla said, taking her phone out of her pocket and pulling up the photo she'd secretly taken of Melanie on the first night. Melanie didn't know she had it, but she'd decided to keep it in case the woman ever wanted to report him and needed evidence of the injuries he'd caused.

Benny peered at the photo and shook his head in disgust as he took in the cuts, bruises and swellings on Melanie's battered face. 'OK, that is pretty bad,' he said after a moment. 'But if he can do that to the woman he's supposed to love, what do you think he'd do to *you* if he finds out you've been letting her hide out here? I'm not trying to scare you, but you need to think about that.'

'He doesn't know anything about me,' Isla assured him. 'And this is only temporary, so she'll be gone soon.'

'I hope so,' Benny said. 'But please be careful.'

'I will,' Isla promised. Then, eager to change the subject, because she didn't want to think about what Carl might do if he found out that Melanie was there, she pushed her chair back. 'Right, I'm supposed to be feeding you, so let me see what I've got in the freezer. But it won't be anything fancy, I'm afraid. I haven't had a chance to do a proper shop this week.'

'I don't do fancy,' Benny said. 'Just keep the wine coming and bung me some cheese and crackers. That'll do me. Good stuff, by the way.' He held up his glass. 'Better than the plonk they sell on the Grange.'

'Jerry had contacts and got it by the caseload dirt-cheap,' Isla said, getting up to take the cheese out of the fridge and prepare the crackers.

As she worked, her phone started ringing on the table where she'd left it, and Benny grinned when he glanced at the screen.

'It's Tia,' he said. 'Can I get it? It's been years since I spoke to her and I want to see if she can guess who it is.'

'Yeah, go for it,' Isla said.

Benny answered the call and put it on loudspeaker.

'Hey, babe,' Tia's voice drifted out. 'How's it going?'

'I'm good,' Benny replied in a high-pitched imitation of Isla's voice. 'How the hell are *you*?'

'Who is this?' Tia asked warily.

'It's me… Isla,' Benny said, raising a finger to his lips to shush Isla when she almost started laughing. 'Don't tell me you don't recognise my voice. Some friend you are.'

'Whoever this is, I don't find you funny,' Tia snapped. 'Put Isla on right now or I'll call the police and report you for stealing her phone. It's got a tracker on it, so it'll be easy for them to find you.'

'Damn, you got me,' Benny said, dropping his voice to a sinister growl. 'But don't you be worrying your sweet little head about Isla. I've got her wrapped up nice and tight.'

'If you've touched her, you're a dead man!' Tia yelled. 'I swear to God I'll—'

'Whoa!' Benny jerked his head back when her voice rose in

volume. 'Christ, you haven't changed a bit. Same old savage Tia. Bite first, ask questions later.'

'Who is this?' Tia demanded.

'It's Benny,' Isla called out. 'He wanted to see if you'd guess it was him.'

'You absolute dick!' Tia tutted. 'Have you any idea how close I was to driving over there and knocking you out?'

'Come,' Benny urged. 'It'd be great to see you.'

'I wish I could, but I'm stuck in London for another week.'

'So let's hook up when you get back. You up for that, Isla?'

'Absolutely,' Isla agreed, smiling as she carried the plate of cheese and crackers to the table.

After a brief three-way conversation, Tia said she had to go because she'd been invited to go for drinks with her bride and the bridesmaids. Isla and Benny said their goodbyes and then carried their food and drinks out into the garden.

It was a balmy night, and they spent the next few hours chatting and laughing as they reminisced about the past and filled in the spaces from their previous conversation.

When the night drew to a close, Isla felt happier than she had in ages as she waved Benny off from the doorstep. She had always enjoyed hosting parties for Jerry's friends, but she hadn't realised how much she had missed her own friends. Benny had always been funny, and she still found him hilarious. But she'd seen a deeper side to him tonight that she found quite fascinating, and she admired that he'd done so many things in his life; some of which had been successful, some not so much. But rather than allow the failures to derail him, he'd taken time out to re-centre himself while he healed from the trauma of losing first his partner and then his mum. And, contrary to what she'd thought he had said during their first conversation, he hadn't given up on his career, after all. He had just realised that London wasn't the best base for him and had decided to start over in Manchester.

That news had pleased Isla, and she was still smiling as she made her way upstairs after turning off the lights and locking the doors. On the landing, she hesitated when she saw a sliver of light under the guest bedroom door. Immediately feeling guilty, she tapped on the wood.

'Sorry to disturb you,' she whispered when Melanie opened the door a few seconds later. 'I just wanted to apologise if we kept you awake with our noise. We haven't seen each other for a while, so we had a lot of catching up to do.'

'I didn't hear anything,' Melanie assured her. 'I had a few things on my mind and couldn't sleep, that's all.'

'Carl or hospital?' Isla ventured.

'A bit of both.'

'Want to talk about it?'

'No. Honestly, I'm OK.'

'All right, I'll see you in the morning, then,' Isla said, backing towards her own room. 'Sleep well.'

'You too,' Melanie said, smiling as she closed the door.

Chapter 14

Melanie's first chemotherapy appointment had been scheduled for Monday morning, and Isla could immediately see that she was nervous when she brought Jacob downstairs. She was shaking from head to toe and the bags under her eyes were deeper and darker than usual, so Isla ordered her to sit down and drink her coffee while she gave Jacob his breakfast.

It was rush hour by the time they hit the motorway, and Isla could feel Melanie's anxiety rising as they inched their way along in the gridlocked traffic. They arrived at the hospital with minutes to spare, so Isla pulled in as close to the main doors as possible.

'You don't have much time, so why don't you go and get yourself booked in while I find a parking space,' she suggested. 'I'll follow you in with Jacob. Or I can keep him for the day, if that's easier for you?'

'No, I want him with me,' Melanie said, already unclipping the straps of his car seat. 'I rang the unit last week and the nurse told me they've got a special room for kids next to the chemo ward.'

'Are you sure? I don't mind.'

'No, honestly, I'll feel better knowing he's there. Thanks for offering, though. I really appreciate it.'

'No worries,' Isla said, climbing out of the car to get the pushchair out of the boot while Melanie lifted Jacob out. 'You've got my number, so ring me when you're done and I'll come and pick you up.'

'You don't need to do that,' Melanie said. 'It's a long drive and I don't want you getting stuck in traffic again. I've still got a few days left on my bus pass, so I'll make my own way back.'

'Are you sure you'll be up to that?' Isla asked.

'I don't know.' Melanie shrugged. 'But I can't stay with you forever, so I need to get used to doing this by myself.'

Isla admired her spirit, but she'd heard that chemotherapy left people feeling quite weak, and she didn't want Melanie to have to suffer a long bus ride if it affected her badly. So, reaching back into the car, she took a twenty-pound note out of her purse and handed it to her.

'Take this and get a cab back to mine. If it comes to more than that, I'll pay the rest when you get there.'

Melanie looked down at the note and bit her lip, as if trying to decide whether or not to accept it. Then, slipping it into her pocket, she murmured, 'Thank you.'

'Good luck,' Isla said, giving her an awkward hug.

Melanie nodded and then turned and scuttled in through the hospital doors. Isla watched her go and then climbed back into the car. She had offered to look after Jacob so that Melanie wouldn't have to worry about him, but she was secretly relieved that her offer had been rejected. She had managed to keep him occupied whenever she'd looked after him while Melanie was out walking. But that had only been for an hour or so at a time. And, after his meltdown on Saturday when they visited the farm, she wasn't sure she was ready for a full day of him.

*

The house was silent when Isla got home. But it wasn't the dark, heavy blanket of silence that had settled over her when Tia and Sam had left after Jerry's funeral. That had felt unbearable, and she had struggled to imagine how she was ever going to get out from under it. Now, all she felt was relief that she had the house to herself – even if only for a few hours.

Determined to make the most of it, she walked into the kitchen and switched the kettle on. It was a nice day and she gazed out through the window as she waited for the kettle to boil. A vision of Jerry riding around on his lawnmower flashed into her mind and she swivelled her gaze onto the machine. She hadn't touched it since that awful day when she had found Jerry's body, and she wondered if she ought to turn the engine over to prevent the battery from dying. The grass had already grown quite considerably since it had last been mowed and would soon be out of control. But she couldn't face sitting on that seat, knowing that Jerry had probably died on it before falling to the ground. So, instead, she rooted out the number of the gardener they had used before Jerry had retired and decided they no longer needed him.

Isla made the call and arranged a date for the man to resume his twice-monthly visits. It was a tiny step, but after weeks of drifting around in a fog of grief and inaction, it felt huge. And now she'd dealt with that, she decided to tackle the cleaning that she hadn't felt able to do while Melanie and Jacob were under her feet. She started in the kitchen, and then worked her way around the rest of the rooms; polishing, vacuuming and mopping.

It was late afternoon by the time she finished, and the house looked and smelled fresher than it had in weeks. Tired, but conscious that Melanie could be back at any time, Isla prepared dinner and then relaxed with a glass of wine while she waited for the bell to ring.

*

It was almost 8 p.m. when Melanie arrived back at the house. Already concerned, because she'd expected her to be back a lot earlier, Isla rushed outside to help with the pushchair when she saw how exhausted the woman looked.

'How did it go?' she asked, speaking quietly when she noticed that Jacob was sleeping.

'Horrible,' Melanie said, stopping to take a deep breath before following her inside.

'I'll get him,' Isla said, leaning down to unstrap Jacob before lifting him out of the pram. 'You go and sit down while I take him to bed. Your dinner's in the oven.'

Melanie visibly blanched and shook her head. 'I'm sorry, but I can't face eating. I feel really sick and just need to lie down. Sorry.'

'There's no need to apologise,' Isla said, carrying Jacob up the stairs as Melanie slowly followed.

In the bedroom, Isla laid Jacob on the bed and gently took off his jacket and shoes before covering him with the quilt. Still fully clothed, Melanie took off her own shoes and lay down beside him. Isla asked if she wanted a glass of water, but Melanie didn't answer and her eyes were already closed, so she backed out of the room and quietly shut the door.

Chapter 15

It took Melanie a couple of days to recover after her first chemotherapy session, and she spent most of that time curled up under a duvet on the sofa in the snug while Isla looked after Jacob.

Surprisingly, given how difficult it had been to settle him at the start, that task was turning out to be a lot easier than Isla had anticipated. He had been shy around her when they'd first moved in, but the more time Isla spent with him, the more he seemed to gravitate towards her. Unlike his mother, who she often had to cajole into eating, he ate whatever Isla put in front of him and was becoming quite bonny. He was also getting more active; exploring, instead of just sitting in front of the TV for hours on end. But the first time he reached out to her when he got tired and then fell asleep in her arms, her heart positively melted.

Isla and Melanie settled into a smooth routine over the next few weeks. On the mornings of Melanie's hospital appointments, Isla would drop her and Jacob off at the hospital and then go home and do the shopping and cleaning that she wasn't able to do when they were around. She always offered to keep Jacob for the day, but Melanie refused; insisting that it comforted her to know he was nearby. Isla thought it sad that he was left to spend the day with strangers when he could have been at home with her. But Melanie was his mother, so she had to respect her decision.

On those days, Jacob would always be asleep when they arrived home in the evenings. And Melanie usually felt too weak and nauseous to eat and would go straight to bed. She would then spend the next couple of days on the sofa, after which she would have a couple of good days before the cycle started again.

On the day before Melanie was due to have her fourth session, Isla received a call from Tia; letting her know that she was home and wanting to know if they could have the reunion dinner with Benny that night.

'I know it's short notice, and I'm really sorry for springing it on you like this,' she apologised. 'But I've been booked for another job in Dublin and have to fly out first thing Saturday. Obviously, I want to spend some quality time with Sam, so we've made plans for tomorrow. But he's at a conference today and won't be home till the early hours, so this is the only free time I'll have before I go. It's already been a month since I saw you, and I'm going to be away for another six weeks, so please say yes.'

Isla was torn. On the one hand, she had really missed Tia and didn't want to miss out on the chance to spend some time with her before she left again. But, on the other, she knew that Melanie was nervous about her upcoming session, and she didn't want to make her feel uncomfortable.

'Isla?' Tia's voice cut into her thoughts. 'Are you still there?'

'Yeah, I'm here,' Isla said. 'OK, let's do it. I'll message Benny to see if he's free. If he is, I'll tell him to come over at eight? Is that all right for you?'

'Perfect,' Tia said. 'Unless you want me to come earlier to

help you cook? I've got a bit of washing to do and I need to get changed, but that shouldn't take too long.'

'No, I'll be fine,' Isla assured her. 'You do whatever you need to do. I've got this.'

'You're an angel. See you at eight.'

When Tia had hung up, Isla messaged Benny to ask if he was free. He replied almost immediately that he was, so she let Tia know that they were on and then walked over to the fridge-freezer to check if she had anything to feed them.

As she looked, she heard Melanie coming into the room and turned to look back at her. The woman had taken Jacob upstairs to give him a bath shortly before Tia rang, but Isla sensed that it hadn't gone too well when she saw the tears in the child's eyes and the frazzled look on Melanie's flushed face.

'Are you OK?' she asked.

'Not really,' Melanie muttered, rolling her eyes when the boy suddenly started grinning and reaching out to Isla. 'I can't do right for doing wrong with this one. He was having a proper meltdown up there. But one look at you, and he acts like butter wouldn't melt.'

'He's probably picking up on your tension, so why don't you sit down and relax,' Isla said, taking the boy from her arms. 'I've got a couple of friends coming over and need to nip into the village to pick up a few bits. How about I take him with me to give you some breathing space?'

'No, I don't want to put you out,' Melanie said.

'I honestly don't mind,' Isla assured her. 'Oh, and you're more than welcome to join us for dinner, if you're up to it?'

'Thanks, but I was just going to give Jacob a quick snack, then put him down,' Melanie said. 'And I'm not really hungry, so I think I'll get an early night, as well.'

Isla nodded her understanding, but she was secretly relieved that Melanie had turned down her invitation to join them for dinner. She'd offered out of politeness, because she hadn't wanted the woman to feel excluded. But it would be a lot less awkward if Melanie wasn't around when Tia arrived.

Tia and Benny arrived within minutes of each other that evening. It was a warm night, so Isla led the pair out onto the patio before serving up the lasagne she had baked. After they had finished eating, Isla cleared the plates away and opened another bottle of wine as Tia and Benny brought each other up to date on what they had been doing since they last saw each other. Isla already knew both accounts, so she listened in silence as Benny regaled Tia with the same stories he'd already told her about his crazy time in London. He was a fantastically visual and hilarious storyteller, and he had them both in stitches when he described some of the zany characters he'd met. But the atmosphere became markedly more sombre when he reached the part about losing his partner and moving back to Manchester, and Tia scooted around the table to give him a hug.

'I'm so sorry we weren't there for you at that time,' she said. 'We might not have known Victor, but you loved him, so I'm sure we would have, too.'

'Sorry, *what*?' Benny drew his head back and stared at her in confusion. 'Where did you get Victor from? Her name was Victoria. And she was a she, not a he.'

'Oops!' Tia grimaced. 'When you told Isla his – sorry, *her* – name was Vic, we just assumed it was Victor. I really hope I didn't offend you. I'm totally rubbish with the whole pronoun thing.'

'What on earth are you talking about?' Benny asked bemusedly. 'Don't tell me you actually think I'm gay?'

'Well, yeah…' Now it was Tia's turn to be confused, and she flicked a glance at Isla, as if to say *help me out here*.

'It was pretty obvious,' Isla chipped in. 'But you never outright told us, so we figured you didn't want anyone to know.'

'Well, I appreciate your loyalty,' Benny chuckled. 'But you were way off track.'

'Oh, come off it, you were camp as hell,' Tia scoffed. 'We haven't forgotten the hours we spent in your dad's shed listening to you sing along to those show-tune CDs. And don't even get me started on all the old musicals you used to make us watch. No straight man I've ever known is into that kind of shit.'

'Well, I am, and I've made a pretty good career out of it so far,' Benny countered. 'As for being camp, that was just me being theatrical. Honing my craft, so to speak. Theatre isn't like TV and film, you see. On screen it's all got to be drawn right back, but on stage you have to project and exaggerate.'

'Thanks for the acting class, but that doesn't explain why you never had a girlfriend,' Tia pounced.

'Ah, but that's where you're wrong.' Benny winked. 'My drama group didn't call me the Italian Stallion for nothing.'

'Bullshit!' Tia laughed. 'You were always with me and Isla, so we'd have known if you had any girls on the go.'

'I didn't tell you everything,' Benny shot back with a grin. 'But you know what the hilarious thing is about all this? All the time you two thought you were keeping my little secret, I thought I was keeping yours.'

'What do you mean?' Tia pulled a face. Then, eyes widening, she said, 'Are you saying you thought me and Isla were lesbians?'

'Well, you were rather close.' Benny shrugged. 'Always hugging and whispering to each other; having sleepovers and swapping clothes. It was like you couldn't bear to be apart.'

'*All* girls are like that with their best mates,' Isla said. 'But surely you remember us falling out after I kissed Kyle that time? She didn't speak to me for weeks over that.'

'Oh Christ, did you have to remind me?' Tia groaned. 'I had the biggest crush on him. What an idiot.'

'I thought she was mad at you for cheating on her,' Benny laughed. 'Makes you wonder how we got on so well back then when we clearly didn't know each other at all.'

'Well, that's my head blown,' Tia said, reaching for the bottle to pour herself another glass of wine. 'Mind you, it's probably a good thing that we did think you were gay, or things could have got very messy.'

'How so?' Benny asked.

'She means she fancied you,' said Isla. 'And if she'd known you were straight, she might have gone for it.'

'You fancied him, as well,' Tia shot back.

'Oh wow, this is all news to me,' Benny chuckled.

'Bullshit!' Tia gave him a knowing look. 'You knew damn well that all the girls round our way thought you were gorgeous. You just chose to ignore it with me and Isla, because you weren't interested in us. The way you treated us, we might as well have been lads.' She paused at that and pursed her lips thoughtfully. 'Then again, if you *had* been gay, then you treating us like lads would have meant that you *were* interested. Wouldn't it?'

'That makes zero sense,' Benny said.

'No, it makes *perfect* sense,' Tia insisted. 'Tell him, Isla.'

'I haven't got a clue what you're talking about,' Isla said, pushing her chair back when she heard the slur in Tia's voice. 'But it's getting late, so I'm going to make coffee. I don't want Sam blaming me for letting you get too drunk to drive home.'

'He'll be fine.' Tia flapped her hand dismissively. 'I'll ring him and tell him to come over.' Then, drawing her head back as if she'd just had a revelation, she said, 'Oh, but I can't do that, because you've given our room to Little Miss *I-Fucked-Your-Dead-Husband*.'

'Hey, there's no need for that,' Isla berated her. 'I've got other bedrooms you can sleep in.'

'But not *my* room,' Tia argued. 'You know that's the only one I like.'

Unsure if she was joking, Isla said, 'Oh, come on; it's the same as the others.'

'That's not the point,' Tia muttered, reaching for her glass and swigging the rest of her wine before reaching for the bottle to refill it again.

'Do we have to do this now?' Isla sighed. 'You know why she's here.'

'Yeah, because you're a soft touch and she spotted you from a mile off,' Tia replied bluntly. 'I'm sorry, babe…' She held up her hands. 'You know I love you and I'll always have your back, but she shouldn't be here. Should she, Benny?'

'I didn't know she *was* still here.' Benny gave Isla a questioning look. 'I thought you said it was temporary?'

'It is,' Isla replied defensively. 'But she's got nowhere else to go right now.'

'There's probably a very good reason for that,' said Tia. 'Most people are smart enough to cut her type loose once they realise what they're dealing with. But not you, baby. You invited her in, and now she's bleeding you for all she's worth.'

'None of this is her fault,' Isla argued, irritated that her friend couldn't see the parallels between Melanie's situation and her own. 'She lost her family for the same reason I lost mine: because she fell in love with a man they didn't approve of. The only difference is Jerry was a good man, whereas *her* man is a violent pig who's made her life hell.'

'I get that she's had a hard time, and I wouldn't wish that on anyone,' Tia replied. 'But this whole set-up has been ringing massive alarm bells from the start. First she gate-crashes Jerry's funeral, and then turns up here at the house like some sort of stalker. Then you just happen to bump into her on the Grange, where she tells you she had an affair with your husband, only to turn up here again later and retract it. I don't know what her game is, but it stinks to high heaven.'

'I know how it looks, but she's honestly not as bad as you think,' said Isla. 'You haven't spoken to her, so you don't what she's been through. I do, and I feel really sorry for her.'

'And that's exactly what she wanted,' Tia shot back. 'She fed you a sob story and reeled you in. And now she's got her feet under your table and made herself your new best friend, you're never going to get rid of her.'

'She's not my friend, she's my guest,' Isla countered. 'And she's only staying until she finds her own place.'

'And what if her psycho ex finds out she's here before that happens?'

'That's not going to happen. But she'll be gone soon, so even if he *does* turn up, there'll be nothing here for him to find.'

'I hope so, for your sake,' Tia said ominously. 'You're vulnerable out here on your own, and I don't want the police knocking on my door in the middle of the night asking me to come and identify your body.'

'Come on, now,' Benny interjected, placing his hand on Tia's arm. 'This is getting a bit dark, and you're going to scare her to death talking like that.'

'Good,' said Tia. 'She needs to know the danger she's putting herself in.'

'All right, that's enough,' Isla said firmly. 'I'm going to make that coffee, and when I come back, I don't want to hear another word about this. OK?'

Tia pursed her lips, as if contemplating whether or not to continue. But after looking from Isla to Benny and back again, she shrugged, and said, 'Fine. If that's what you want, I won't say another word.'

In the guest bedroom, directly above the patio, Melanie was lying on top of the bed with her phone clutched to her chest. Unlike her flat, which was always freezing, Isla's house was always cosy. Tonight, however, it was too hot, so she had opened the window to let in some cooler air. The windows were triple-glazed, which blocked out all external noise, so she hadn't realised that Isla and her friends were sitting below until their voices drifted up to her. She'd only caught a snatch of their conversation before Isla had shut it down and gone to make coffee, but it had been enough to tell her that Isla's friend, Tia, didn't like her being there and wanted Isla to kick her out.

Isla had said that Melanie was a guest, not a friend. That had come as a bit of a blow to Melanie, because she'd thought they had been getting along quite well. But now she'd heard how strongly Tia felt about it, she supposed it was understandable that Isla might have decided to downplay it in order to avoid dragging the argument out.

When Isla left them, Tia and the man had talked some more, but their voices had been too low for Melanie to hear what they were saying. Things seemed to settle down when Isla rejoined them a few minutes later, and the women were now laughing as their male friend cracked jokes.

The issue had obviously been resolved for them, but it had left Melanie feeling unsettled to the point that she was tempted to call Carl to ask if she could go home. It was past midnight, however, which meant that the buses would already have stopped running. She could walk, but it would take hours, and she didn't really want to put herself or Jacob through that. Also, Carl would undoubtedly have been drinking for the last few hours. And he was a nasty drunk, so even if he agreed to let her go home, there was no guarantee that he'd let her in when she got there.

Too tired to think about it any longer, Melanie decided against ringing Carl and placed the phone on the bedside table before rolling onto her side. Still able to hear Isla and her friends chatting and laughing outside, she gazed at Jacob's sleeping face. He'd recently started to put on weight, and his complexion and general mood were far brighter than when they had arrived. He had never been a particularly happy child, but he was smiling a lot more than usual of late. Particularly, she'd noticed, when Isla was around. He really seemed to have taken a liking to her. And Isla, in turn, seemed to be growing quite fond of him.

Isla had been kind to them both, which was more than Melanie deserved given the circumstances of how they'd met. But she was the one who had invited them in, and she had just defended that decision, so she obviously wasn't in any hurry for them to leave. That cemented it for Melanie, and she decided that she and Jacob would stay for as long as Isla was happy for them to do so. And to hell with what that interfering bitch, Tia, had to say about it.

Chapter 16

Isla was woken by her phone ringing on the bedside table the following morning. It was Tia, and she rubbed the sleep out of her eyes as she answered it.

'Morning. You got home OK, then?'

'I know you thought I was too pissed to drive, but I honestly wasn't,' Tia replied. Then, sheepishly, she said, 'I might have had one too many earlier on, though, and said some stuff that I shouldn't have.'

'Yeah, you did,' Isla agreed.

'I'm sorry,' Tia apologised. 'I've been feeling really guilty about it and needed to make sure we were OK before I go to Dublin. I know we ended the night on a better note, but I hope you know that I only spoke out because I love you.'

'I know, and I love you too,' Isla sighed. 'Contrary to what you obviously think, I'm not stupid, and I totally get why you're concerned about me letting Melanie stay. I'd feel exactly the same if this was happening to you. But I had to do what felt right in the moment.'

'I know, and I'm not knocking you for that,' Tia said. 'I'm just scared you'll get caught in the crossfire if he finds out she's there.'

'Let's not start it up again,' Isla said wearily. 'I've already told you there's no way he can find out unless she tells him. And she's not going to do that, because she's absolutely terrified of him.'

'I hope you're right,' Tia said. 'But if you're determined to keep her there, will you please think about getting CCTV cameras fitted, like I told you to a while back? At least then you'll be able to see him coming and call the police before he does any damage.'

'OK, fine. If it makes you feel better, I'll get some,' Isla agreed. 'But I can't do anything until Marcus transfers the money into my account. I've only got what I found in the tin, so I'm trying to be careful and eke it out while I'm waiting.'

'What's taking him so long?'

'No idea.' Isla shrugged. 'I haven't heard from him since I went to his office that day. I've tried to call him, but his secretary always tells me he's unavailable, so I'll just have to wait till he gets back to me.'

'That doesn't sound right to me,' Tia said. 'Is he getting paid for being the executor?'

'I don't remember any mention of it at the reading,' said Isla. 'But he was Jerry's solicitor, so I'm assuming they'll have sorted that out between them when he wrote the will.'

'Do you know how much money is involved overall?'

'No. I tried to check, but Jerry's online banking app is set to facial recognition, so I couldn't get into it. And his bank said they're only allowed to discuss it with Marcus.'

'Why? You're his wife, and the sole beneficiary.'

'I know. But my name wasn't on Jerry's accounts, so they're not allowed to give me access to them.'

'Well, I think you've got a right to know how much is at stake. I know Marcus was Jerry's friend, but after seeing the way his other friends treated you at the wake, I wouldn't trust any of them.'

'I doubt Marcus would do anything dodgy.'

'But he *might*,' Tia countered. 'If he's the only one with access, he could swipe half the money before he hands the rest over to you and closes the accounts. And you'd never know, because the history will have been deleted. I know you said you can't check the app, but what about paper statements?'

'I didn't even think of that,' Isla said thoughtfully. 'Jerry kept all his important paperwork in his study, so I'll take a look in there.'

'Do it now,' Tia insisted.

'I need to get ready to take Melanie to hospital, so it'll have to wait till I get back.'

'Well, make sure you don't forget,' said Tia. 'Hopefully Marcus is a straight shooter and it'll all be fine. But if there's one thing I've learned in business, it's that you can't take anyone at face value. And don't forget Sam's an accountant, so if anything looks iffy, get him to take a look.'

'Thanks,' Isla said. 'And let me know when you get back from Dublin. I'm going to miss you.'

'No, you're not,' Tia shot back. 'You've got your new bestie to keep you company.'

'Oi! Don't start that again,' Isla chided.

'Only joking,' Tia laughed. 'Love you.'

'Love you, too,' Isla said, smiling when Tia blew her a loud kiss before hanging up.

Isla was showered, dressed and making coffee when Melanie brought Jacob downstairs a short time later. She seemed a little more subdued than usual, but Isla didn't read too much into it, because she knew from previous experience that the woman was always a nervous wreck before her chemotherapy sessions.

Tia's warning about Marcus was still playing on Isla's mind, so she drove straight back home instead of stopping off at the supermarket as she usually did after dropping Melanie and Jacob off at the hospital.

She hadn't stepped foot in Jerry's study since Melanie's arrival. The sight of his chair had almost brought her to tears on that occasion, and it still made her sad to see it sitting there empty. Her grief had been all-consuming then, but it was far less intense now, and she realised that was partly due to Melanie and Jacob, whose presence in the house had filled the huge void Jerry had left behind. So, as much as Tia thought that Melanie was using her, the mere fact of them being there had helped Isla as much as she was helping them. And, more, she'd had the pleasure of watching Jacob blossom into the lovely, happy little boy he might never have become under the terrifying watch of his father. That alone convinced Isla that she had done the right thing by inviting them to stay.

Refocusing on her reasons for being in the study, Isla walked over to the filing cabinet. Dust rose into the air as she crossed the floor and she wafted her hand in front of her face to prevent it from going up her nose. The cabinet was packed with files, but after flicking through them, she found that they were all related to Jerry's former clients. They were of no use to Isla, but they contained sensitive information and financial details, so it didn't feel right to throw them away. Guessing that a lot of the clients might still be connected to the company, she wondered if she ought to contact Peter to ask if he wanted them. It would be the first time she'd spoken to the man since he'd tried it on with her the morning after Jerry's funeral. But she was over the shock of that now, and didn't feel anything other than slight revulsion and pity for him.

Deciding that she would contact Peter later, she turned her attention to the piles of papers that were stacked on the shelving unit behind the desk. There were several of them, all coated with dust, and she grimaced when she lifted the first pile down and saw a dead spider lying on top of it. As she turned to dump the pile on the desk, she heard a tiny clunk and glanced back over her shoulder. A small object was wedged in the shadows at the back of the shelf and she was shocked, when she reached in for it, to find that it was the mobile phone Jerry had lost a few months earlier. He'd sworn that he had searched that room, but he obviously hadn't looked hard enough if it had been sitting right there all along.

As Isla had expected, nothing happened when she tried to turn the phone on. She had no idea if the battery would still be viable after being dead for that long, but the phone was the same model as the one Jerry had replaced it with, so she carried it into the bedroom and dug his charger out of the drawer. The tiny charging symbol appeared on the screen when she plugged it in. She perched on the edge of the bed and waited to see if the phone would power on.

It took quite a while and Isla was about to give it up as a lost cause when the phone suddenly lit up in her hand. There were several missed call notifications on the screen, but it was a message preview that caused her heart to momentarily freeze in her chest, and she blinked in confusion as she read the words.

I know you love me and I still love you – and always will. But this isn't fair. You say you want to start a new life with us, but how can we when you're still with...

It was only an extract, but it was more than enough for Isla to know that the sender was referring to her at the end of it.

Hands trembling wildly, she tapped in Jerry's old password. It didn't work, so she tried it again. Again, it didn't work, and she guessed that Jerry must have changed it at some point before he lost the phone. No doubt to prevent her from seeing the damning evidence of his affair.

She tried a few variations of significant dates that Jerry might have used instead. His birthday, her birthday, their anniversary… the date she had miscarried their first child, which was indelibly etched on her heart. None worked. So, as a last resort, she tapped in the old default numbers: 1, 2, 3, 4, 5, 6. Surprised when that opened the phone, she took a deep breath to calm her nerves before clicking into Jerry's messages.

The message she'd seen on the lock screen was at the top of the list, and she felt her heart pounding when she read it in full.

> *I know you love me and I still love you – and always will. But this isn't fair. You say you want to start a new life with us, but how can you when you're still with her? You've promised to divorce her loads of times, and I've waited like an idiot. It's obvious you're too scared to leave her in case she takes your money. That's all you really care about, but it never meant anything to me. You were enough. But we weren't enough for you and never will be, so please stop messaging and let me get on with my life. He doesn't know Jacob isn't his and I'll never tell him, so don't worry about that. I've already sent you all the photos you asked for, so now please forget about us and get on with your own life. You must have loved her once, so I'm sure you'll be able to make it work again if you try. Love and best wishes, M xxx*

Jerry had listed the sender as *Nee*, which was obviously a shortened version of Mela*nie*, and Isla hissed, 'You fucking bastard,' between her teeth.

That message, clearly a response to one that Jerry must have sent to Melanie, was the only one on there. Isla guessed that he must have deleted any they had exchanged prior to that. The fact that this one was still there and hadn't been opened told her that it must have come through after Jerry had lost his phone. Tears of pain and fury coursed down her cheeks at the thought of him conducting an affair and sneakily covering his tracks right under her nose, while continuing to play the dutiful husband.

Isla rarely drank alcohol during the day, but she needed a stiff drink by then, so she dug her powerbank out of the drawer and plugged the phone into it. Then, heading downstairs, she poured herself a glass of neat whisky and took a seat at the kitchen table. Hands shaking, she clicked into Jerry's photos to find the ones Melanie had mentioned in her message. The images that came up were mostly selfies that Jerry had taken at various events. There were also ones he had taken of Isla, along with shots of buildings that had obviously caught his eye. But not one single picture of Melanie or Jacob. That confused her, because Melanie had specifically mentioned that she had sent all the photos he'd asked for.

Remembering that iPhones had a hidden file feature, she scrolled down and clicked on it. It asked for a passcode, so she tapped in the same one she'd used to open the phone. It worked and her jaw clenched painfully when her gaze landed on the first photo in the album. It was a shot of Jerry and Melanie gazing into each other's eyes across a small, candlelit table; each with a glass of champagne in one hand, while the fingers of their free hands were entwined on the tabletop. It had been taken inside a dimly lit restaurant, but daylight was showing through one of the windows in the background, which confirmed what Melanie had initially said about them meeting up in the daytime when Isla had thought Jerry was working.

In the following photos, Melanie's hair was different lengths and shades, indicating that they had been taken over a period of months. It was a visual timeline of the double life Jerry had been living behind Isla's back, from that first cosy dinner, to photos of them dancing at what appeared to be some kind of club – probably, Isla guessed, the strip joint where the woman had initially claimed they had met and started their affair.

The most hurtful shots, by far, were those of Jerry and Melanie at various stages of her pregnancy, followed by several of Jerry proudly holding new-born Jacob as a sweaty-faced Melanie smiled wearily up at them from a hospital bed. Those could only have been taken if Jerry had been present at the birth, and her heart started pounding again when she saw the loving way Jerry was looking at the child.

Devastated to think that her husband had not only impregnated another woman, but had been with her all the way through the pregnancy and had also attended the birth, Isla swallowed the rest of her drink in one before pouring another glassful. Jerry had been supportive when she had suffered her miscarriages, but nowhere near as present as he appeared to have been with Melanie. In fact, he had continued working throughout; leaving Tia to comfort her and soak up her tears during the agonising days following each loss.

In light of his detachment regarding her own losses, the tenderness in Jerry's eyes as he'd gazed at his son in those photos was devastating for Isla. And it cut her to the bone that he had apparently begged Melanie to let him be the father Jacob deserved. Jerry had known how desperately she had wanted to be a mother, but he had insisted that they should stop trying after her third miscarriage. He'd told her that she was enough for him and he didn't need a child to make his life complete. But that had obviously been a lie, because he had clearly been excited about Melanie's pregnancy given the gentle way he'd cradled her swollen stomach in some of the earlier photos. And the pride and love in his eyes when he'd held the child was undeniable.

Tears streaming, Isla swigged her drink and scrolled through the rest of the photos. In the last few, Jacob appeared to be almost as big as he was now, which told her that it must have been taken shortly before Jerry had died. But he'd barely left the house in the last two months, so how had he managed to sneak away to meet up with Melanie and the boy?

As she stared at that last photo, trying to figure out when it had been taken, her own phone pinged and a WhatsApp message from Benny appeared on the screen. It was a photograph, and she almost dismissed it, presuming it to be another of the funny memes he'd taken to sending her since they had reconnected. But when a second message popped up seconds later, she swiped away the tears that were blurring her vision and opened it.

Hey gorgeous, it read. *Just checking if this woman is the one who's staying at your place? xx*

Confused, Isla clicked onto the photo he'd sent and enlarged it. It was a grainy shot of several people outside a shop, but it seemed to be focused on a man and a woman who were at the centre of it. The man's head was turned so she couldn't see his face, but the woman, when she zoomed in, did look like Melanie.

Jumping when her phone suddenly started ringing, she took another sip of her drink before answering it.

'Hey, how's it going?' Benny asked chirpily. 'I wasn't going to ring in case you were busy, but I thought I'd chance it when I saw you were online. Not disturbing you, am I?'

'No, it's fine,' Isla sniffed.

'You sound like you're coming down with a cold,' Benny said. 'Or are we in hangover hell?' he added with a chuckle.

'Hay fever,' Isla lied, unwilling to admit that she'd been crying, because then he'd want to know what was wrong, and she wasn't ready to talk about the devastating discovery she'd made. How could she, when she hadn't fully processed it herself yet?

'Ah, the curse of summer,' said Benny. 'So, is it her in the picture? Your ghostly house guest.'

Isla stared at the photo again. 'It looks like her, yeah. But where did you get it? Did you find it online on one of those street-view things?'

'No, I took it,' Benny said. 'I nipped out to get some milk earlier and saw her outside the newsagents.'

'Today?'

'Yeah, about half an hour ago.'

'Oh, well, it can't be her, then. I dropped her off at the hospital an hour ago. She's having chemo today.'

'Are you sure?' Benny asked. 'I could have sworn it was her. And the pushchair looks exactly like the one I saw in your hallway.'

Confused, because she hadn't noticed a pushchair, Isla zoomed in on the photo again. It took a few seconds, because it was partially concealed behind the people; but then she spotted its reflection in the shop window.

'Do you see it?' Benny asked.

'Yeah, and it does look similar,' Isla agreed. 'But Melanie's definitely in hospital. I dropped her off and watched her go in, so it must just be someone who looks like her.'

'With the same disgusting yellow pram?' Benny didn't sound convinced. 'Maybe her appointment got cancelled and she came back out after you left,' he ventured. 'Then again, it'd be a bit weird for her to come back to the estate when she's supposed to be terrified of her ex, so maybe you're right.'

Isla stared at the photo again, this time focusing on the man. His face wasn't visible, but he had the same lanky build and dark, curly hair as Carl.

'It is her,' she spat, anger building inside her again at the thought of Melanie meeting up with Carl behind her back when she'd spent the last few weeks trying to protect her from him. 'You and Tia were right, and I'm an absolute fucking mug. She's obviously been lying to me this entire time. Like you said, she's supposed to be terrified of him, but she doesn't fucking look it there.'

'Hey, I didn't send you that picture to turn you against her,' Benny said. 'I know Tia's got really strong opinions about it, but you had your reasons for taking her in, and I respect that. There could be a really simple explanation for why she was here today. I'm presuming that bloke's the kid's dad, so maybe she needed to talk to him about child support, or visitation, or whatever.'

'He's not the dad,' Isla said through gritted teeth. '*Jerry* was.'

'Jerry?' Benny repeated. 'As in *your* Jerry? No way.'

'I've seen the evidence with my own eyes,' Isla said, unable to hold it in any longer. 'I found his old phone and it's full of photos of them together. My saintly husband, who supposedly worshipped me and wanted to take care of me, played me for a fool and I never suspected a thing. I'm such a fucking idiot!'

'No, you're not,' Benny countered. 'You trusted him and he betrayed you, so *he* was the idiot, not you. You're a beautiful woman and he was lucky to have you.'

'But I couldn't give him the child he clearly wanted,' Isla replied bitterly. 'He always said it didn't matter; that I was more than enough. But now I've seen how ecstatic he looked when *she* had *hers*, it's obvious he was lying. The worst thing is, when I lost mine and he made me stop trying, he refused to even consider adopting instead. He said it would never feel like our child, but *I* would have loved it.'

'I'm so sorry,' Benny murmured. 'That must have been hard for you.'

'It nearly killed me,' Isla spat. 'But he was my husband and I thought he was trying to protect me from having my heart broken again, so I learned to live with it. And then he goes and has a baby with *her*.'

'Obviously, I never met him, so I've no idea why he did what he did,' said Benny. 'But I don't believe for one minute that he didn't love you, or he would never have stayed with you so long. If you ask me, it was probably a midlife crisis type of thing.'

'He would have been fifty-seven or eight when he met her, so that's hardly midlife,' Isla argued. 'And what's to say there weren't others before and after her? For all I know, he could have been at it the whole time we were together.'

'I honestly doubt that,' Benny said sincerely. 'As stupid and selfish as most men are, I can assure you that, deep down, we all want a woman who's as beautiful, kind and intelligent as you.'

'According to her message asking him to leave her alone, he only stayed with me to stop me from getting my hands on his money,' said Isla. 'It must have hit him really hard when she ended it, and he probably decided it was worth losing the money if it meant he could be with her and his precious son.'

'He left everything to you in his will,' Benny reminded her. 'Why no mention of her if they were so in love and he desperately wanted to be the kid's father?'

'Who knows?' Isla sniffed. 'He probably got mad at her for turning him down and did it to punish her.'

'Or maybe he loved *you* and wanted to make amends before he died,' said Benny. 'Whichever way you look at it, he chose you in the end, so don't let this ruin the memory of all the good times you shared with him.'

'It's way too late for that,' Isla replied coldly. 'He had a child with his bit on the side, and there's no getting past that. Of everything he could ever have done to hurt me, that's the absolute worst. I just don't understand how I didn't see any signs. If I'd cheated on him, I would have felt so guilty I wouldn't have been able to look him in the eye. But he acted exactly the same as always. And now he's gone, I can't even confront him and find out why he did it.'

'Maybe you should speak to her,' Benny suggested. 'See if she can fill in any of the gaps for you.'

'She's already proved she's a liar, so what's the point?' Isla shot back. 'I just want her out of here.'

'Personally, I'd need to have it out with her,' Benny said. 'But you have to do what's right for you. Whatever happens, you know me and Tia are here for you.'

'I know, and I love you both for that,' Isla said gratefully. 'But please don't tell Tia about this. She saw through Melanie from the start and I'm so ashamed of myself for letting the bitch come between us. I need to be the one to tell her, but not while she's working, 'cos she'll only get worried and try to come home early. She already pulled out of one job to be with me after Jerry died, and I don't want her losing out on more money because of me.'

'I won't say anything,' Benny promised. 'But you shouldn't have to deal with this by yourself, so why don't I come over later? I've got a meeting with a producer this evening, but I'll be free for the rest of the night.'

'No, it's fine; I'll be OK,' Isla assured him. 'Thanks for letting me vent, though. I feel a bit calmer now.'

'Any time,' Benny said.

Isla thanked him again and promised that she would call

him later to let him know what happened. When the call was ended, she reached for her glass and raised it to her lips. She immediately changed her mind and threw the liquid down the drain before tearing two bin bags off the roll she kept in the drawer under the sink. She still intended to kick Melanie out, but Benny was right: she did need to talk to her first. The photos and Melanie's text painted a pretty definitive picture, but they didn't explain the whys and wherefores of the affair. And, as painful as it would undoubtedly be, she needed to know exactly what had happened so she could try to gain an understanding of why Jerry had betrayed her. Had he made a mistake and got dragged deeper into it when Melanie told him she was pregnant; or had he started the affair because Isla hadn't satisfied him sexually? Or, worse, had he deliberately chosen to sleep with another woman in the hope that she would provide him with the child that Isla couldn't give him?

In the guest bedroom a few minutes later, Isla opened the wardrobe doors. There were several outfits hanging in there, all of which Isla had either bought for, or gifted to, Melanie. Annoyed with herself for being so generous, Isla yanked the items off their hangers and stuffed them into a bin bag. She piled Melanie's underwear on top of them, and then gathered the woman's toothbrush and toiletries – again, all bought by her – from the bathroom and threw them in.

She knotted that first bag and dumped it by the door before turning to the chest of drawers. Jacob's clothes were kept in there and an unexpected wave of emotion washed over her at the sight of the tiny vests and jumpers in the first drawer. Tears welled in her eyes as she lifted the first pile out, and she swallowed hard to clear the lump that was forming in her throat as she inhaled the sweet scent of the washing powder on them. She had held the boy in her arms so many times that the scent was now indelibly connected to him in her mind. Now that she knew he was Jerry's child, she wanted to hate him as much as she hated his mother. But none of what had happened was his fault. He was as innocent as she was, and it killed her to think that she would never again see his beautiful little smile or rock him to sleep in her arms after that night.

Chapter 17

Isla had managed to get her emotions under control by the time Melanie arrived back at the house that evening, and she watched from the doorstep as the weary-looking woman pushed the pram across the gravel. She usually rushed out to help her, but she stayed put on the doorstep this time; only stepping aside at the last minute to allow Melanie to wheel Jacob into the hallway.

'How did it go today?' she asked after closing the door.

'Horrible,' Melanie said, sighing as she leaned down to unstrap Jacob. 'They keep telling me it'll get better, but it still wipes me out. I threw up before I left today, so they made me sit down and have a cup of tea and some biscuits. But that just made me feel even more sick.'

Isla had hoped that the woman might confess that she hadn't attended her session that day, so hearing her lie so easily *and* add embellishments made her want to punch her. Instead, she forced a sympathetic smile, and said, 'I need a quick word, so why don't you leave him there for a minute.'

'Is everything OK?' Melanie asked, giving her a wary look.

Isla walked into the kitchen without answering and took a seat at the table. Hands clasped on the tabletop in front of her, she waited until Melanie joined her and sat down, before saying, 'So how did it *really* go today? And please tell me the truth this time.'

'I-I'm not sure what you mean,' Melanie stammered, shifting in her seat as a flush crawled up her throat and spread out across her cheeks. 'I've already told you.'

'Really?' Isla slid her phone out of her pocket and pulled up the photo Benny had sent her that morning. 'Care to explain why you were on the Grange an hour after I dropped you off at the hospital this morning?' She turned the screen towards Melanie. 'And, more importantly, why you were with Carl?'

Melanie's mouth flapped open and she blinked rapidly as she stared at the image. Then, shoulders slumping, she said, 'It's not what it looks like. I didn't go to see him. Well, obviously, I *did*,' she corrected herself. 'But not for the reasons you're probably thinking. He … he started messaging me again yesterday. He said he knew where I was staying and was going to break in and smash the place up if I didn't meet up with him. I didn't want you to get hurt, so I skipped my appointment and went to see him.'

'We've had this conversation before, and there's no way he could have randomly found out you were here unless you told him,' Isla said accusingly. 'The only other people who know are me and two of my closest friends, and we definitely didn't tell him.'

'I don't know how he found out, but I swear it didn't come from me,' Melanie insisted. 'To be honest, after talking to him, I'm not even sure he *does* know. I think he was just bluffing to get me to stop ignoring him.'

'Why did he want to see you?' Isla asked. 'You said he'd given up trying to contact you weeks ago, so why start it all up again now?'

'He says he still loves me,' Melanie murmured. 'And he's been missing Jacob, so he wants us to go home and be a family again.'

'Missing his boy, is he?' Isla said sarcastically. 'I take it he still thinks he *is* the father? Unless he knows the truth and doesn't care?'

Melanie's blush deepened at that, and she gave Isla a cautious look. 'I don't know what you mean.'

'Yes you do, so quit playing games,' Isla said sharply as she yanked Jerry's old phone out of her other pocket. 'I found this today.' She slammed it down between them on the table. 'It was Jerry's and it went missing a while back. Imagine my surprise when I managed to turn it on and saw the message you sent my husband. And all the photos of the pair of you; and the ones of you, him and Jacob playing happy families.'

'Oh God,' Melanie murmured guiltily. 'I'm so sorry.'

'Sorry for what?' Isla glared at her. 'For having an affair with my husband? Or for worming your way into my house with his bastard child and laughing at me behind my back while I was doing my damnedest to keep you both safe?'

'It wasn't like that,' Melanie whimpered. 'I … I tried to tell you the truth in the car that night. I didn't know you when it was happening, so I didn't really care if I hurt you. But when I met you and you were so nice to me, I felt terrible about it. When Carl battered me, I knew I had to get away. But I couldn't leave without trying to put things right with you.'

'By lying and telling me you'd made it all up so I'd feel sorry for you and let you stay?' snapped Isla. 'Do you hear how fucking twisted that sounds?'

Melanie had never heard Isla swear before, and she shrank back in her seat when she saw the fire in her eyes. 'I'm sorry,' she whimpered, using her sleeve to soak up the tears that were sliding down her cheeks. 'I was in a mess and my head was all over the place, but I promise I didn't do it for sympathy. I just wanted to make you feel better.'

'More like you were trying to make yourself feel better,' spat Isla. 'You took full advantage of the fact that I was grieving, and I'm disgusted with myself for falling for it. All I want now is for you to tell me exactly what happened with you and Jerry, from the start. And then you can get out.'

Melanie nodded and sniffed back the tears. Then, quietly, she repeated the story she'd originally told Isla about meeting Jerry at the club and him paying for private dances before asking her on a date.

'Like I told you before, things weren't good with me and Carl at that time, so I enjoyed having someone like Jerry chasing after me,' she said. 'He was a proper gentleman and treated me like a lady; always buying me flowers and gifts and taking me out for dinner. No man had ever been that nice to me before and I started to fall in love with him. Then I got pregnant, and I knew it couldn't be Carl's, 'cos we hadn't slept together in weeks.'

'Hang on a minute,' Isla held up her hand. 'You said Carl thinks he's the father, but how could he if you hadn't had sex in that long? And why wasn't he at the birth if he thought the baby was his?'

'He, um, wasn't around when I went into labour,' Melanie explained. 'We'd had a fight and he took off for a few days. He gets drunk most nights and has blackouts, so he never remembers anything he's done the night before,' she went on. 'He doesn't even know what day it is half the time, so he never clicked about the dates.'

'So you told Jerry the baby was his. And he just accepted it, even though you were still living with Carl?' Isla asked.

'I wouldn't have told him if I hadn't been positive it was his,'

Melanie said. 'The dates added up, but it was more than that. I just knew in my heart that he was the dad.'

'So you told him, and then what?'

'He was really happy; said he'd always wanted to be a dad, but…' She paused and flashed Isla a guilty look, before murmuring, 'He said you didn't want kids, so he'd resigned himself to never having any.'

'Well, you know that was a fucking lie, because I've already told you how much I wanted to be a mother,' Isla spat. 'It was *him* who made me stop trying after my last miscarriage. Bastard!'

'I'm sorry,' Melanie murmured. 'Obviously I know the truth now, but I believed Jerry at the time. If I'm honest, I don't think I would have cared that he was lying at that point. I loved him and he said he loved me, so that was all that mattered.'

'If you loved him so much, why did you stay with Carl the whole time you were seeing him?' Isla asked. 'I could never be with two men at the same time.'

'I had nowhere else to go,' Melanie said. 'Jerry kept saying he was going to rent a flat for me, but it never happened.' She paused and released a heavy sigh before continuing. 'Like I told you when we talked in your car, I honestly thought he'd come to surprise me when I saw him pulling into the restaurant car park as I was leaving work that night. So when *you* got out and I saw the way he was looking at you, I realised he had no intention of leaving you. That broke my heart. But Carl already thought he was the dad, so I finished with Jerry and tried to make the best of it.'

'Well, that went well, didn't it?' Isla muttered sarcastically. 'But when exactly did you finish with Jerry? Only there's recent photos of him with Jacob, so it couldn't have been that long ago.'

'I actually finished it twice,' said Melanie. 'The first time was after I saw you together, but I missed him, so I started seeing him again a few days later. Then Carl started getting suspicious and I was worried he'd find out, so I ended it for good a few months ago. It really threw me when Jerry messaged to say he was ready to leave you, but I was scared he'd change his mind again and I'd be left homeless, so I told him it was over. Then I saw his obituary in the paper, and the rest you already know.'

'Yeah, I do,' Isla agreed, tiring of the conversation when she realised that she wasn't going to learn anything new. 'You saw me as a soft touch and latched onto me, and I was stupid enough to take you in. But I'm done now, so you can go. Your stuff's in the hall.'

'I know you won't believe me, but I really am sorry,' Melanie said quietly as she rose to her feet. 'Now I've had a chance to get to know you and see how lovely you are, I totally get why Jerry wouldn't leave you. I honestly thought I was doing the right thing when I told you I'd lied about the affair, and I really wish you hadn't found his phone and seen all that.'

'Well, I'm glad I did,' Isla countered as she, too, stood up. 'Now I know the truth, at last, I don't have to waste any more time grieving for him. And I'm not blaming all this on you, by the way, because Jerry was the one who betrayed me. But I *do* blame you for the lies you've told since I met you. You knew I would never have let you step foot in my home if I'd known, and you should be ashamed of yourself for accepting my hospitality.'

'I am,' Melanie said, guiltily dipping her gaze. 'I didn't deserve your kindness and I hate myself for putting you through this. But I'll always be grateful for the way you treated Jacob. He's a different child since he met you, so thank you for that.'

Isla acknowledged Melanie's thanks with a curt nod and waved her out into the hallway. She had left the packed bin bags in the corner by the door, and she watched as the woman stuffed them into the tray beneath the pushchair before opening the front door and pulling the pushchair backwards over the step. Jacob had been sleeping until then, but the movement woke him, and Isla's heart almost broke when he saw her and gave her a sleepy smile. Then, as if sensing that something was wrong, his face suddenly fell and he reached out his arms to her.

Unable to bear the sound of his cries when his mother turned the pram around and pushed him towards the gate, Isla closed the door and leaned her back against the wood; hugging herself tightly as the tears she'd been holding in began to fall. She knew she shouldn't care; that the child was nothing to do with her and needed to be with his mother. But what kind of life was he ever going to have with Melanie and Carl? Melanie had insisted that the man had never taken his anger out on Jacob, but Isla had not forgotten the anger on his face when she'd seen him screaming at the child outside the shop that day. She dreaded to think what Carl would do if he ever found out that he wasn't Jacob's father. And Jacob would be completely at his mercy if the chemotherapy failed and Melanie died.

As the awful thoughts swirled inside her mind, Isla knew she had to do something. She yanked the door open and ran across the driveway and out through the gate onto the pavement. It was already dark and the spaced-out street lamps were dim, so it was difficult to see too far ahead. Melanie and Jacob had already been swallowed by the shadows, but there was only one way they could have gone if Melanie was planning to catch the bus back to Manchester.

Determined to catch up with them before it was too late, Isla rushed back inside and grabbed her keys off the hall table. Then, running upstairs, she reached into her bedside cabinet and grabbed the money box she had found in Jerry's desk drawer. She had used quite a bit of it feeding and clothing Melanie and

Jacob, but there was still a fair amount left, so she grabbed two bundles and stuffed them into her pocket, then ran back down the stairs.

The village centre was deserted and pitch-dark when Melanie reached the bus shelter. Back home on the Grange estate, she would have been on high alert for muggers and rapists lurking in the shadowy shop doorways. But she didn't feel scared tonight; she just felt sad to be leaving this quiet, peaceful place. In the short time she had spent there, she had relished the freedom of being able to walk around without fear of being attacked. She would miss that. And she would also miss the comfort of staying in Isla's beautiful, clean, warm home. And, surprisingly, she realised that she was going to miss Isla, too. But it was over, so she would just have to put it behind her and return to her own shitty corner of the world.

Jacob had started crying as soon as they had left the house, and his wails bounced off the walls of the nearby buildings. She sat down on the bench and rocked the pram in an effort to get him back to sleep, but he seemed determined to fight it, and her nerves jangled at the thought of the screaming fit that would undoubtedly follow the tears if the bus didn't get there soon.

Hope flaring when she heard a vehicle approaching a short time later, Melanie pulled her bus pass out of her pocket. But it wasn't the bus that pulled up alongside her, it was Isla.

'Are you OK?' she asked when Isla leapt out of the car and rushed towards her. 'Has something happened?'

'I'm fine,' Isla said. 'I just need to know if you're going back to *him*?'

Melanie gave a tiny shrug and stuffed her hands into her jacket pockets. 'It's where we belong, and I honestly think we'll be all right this time. When I saw Carl earlier, I could tell he really meant it when he said he loved me and wanted me to come home.'

'Words are cheap,' Isla shot back. 'And you really need to think about how this is going to affect Jacob. I know you think you can protect him, but we both know you won't be able to do a damn thing if Carl kicks off again.'

'I won't let anything happen to him,' Melanie insisted. 'It'll be different this time.'

'You don't know that,' Isla argued. 'Carl might behave for a while if he's been missing you as much as you say. But what happens when the novelty of having you back wears off?'

'I'm not sure what you want me to say,' Melanie sighed. 'You know I've got nowhere else to go, so I either take him back or we'll end up on the streets.'

'Let him stay with me,' Isla blurted out.

'*What*?' Melanie stared at her in confusion. 'You just kicked us out.'

'I don't mean you, I mean *him*.' Isla pointed at the pushchair, in which Jacob was now only softly sniffling and had his tired eyes fixed on her. 'He doesn't deserve to live in fear, so let him stay with me until you find a place of your own and get back on your feet.'

'How's that ever going to happen?' Melanie gave her a pained look. 'You already know I can't go to the council or sign on.'

'I'll help you,' Isla said, yanking the money out of her pocket and holding it out to her. 'There's two thousand here. Take it and book yourself into a hotel to give yourself some breathing space while you decide what you want to do. Or book a ticket to Devon and try to mend bridges with your family. I'm sure they'll help you when they hear what you're going through.'

'I can't just leave Jacob,' Melanie protested, pulling the pushchair closer. 'I'm his mum. He needs me.'

'Nobody's saying he doesn't, but please think about it,' Isla persisted, taking a seat on the bench beside her. 'I'm not trying to be insensitive, but you've got cancer and you need to think about what will happen to him if your treatment stops working. I know you think Carl will do right by him, but do you honestly believe that? You've already told me that he hardly paid him any attention when you were still living there; that you were the one who had to do everything for him. At least with me you'll know he's being fed and bathed and played with, like every child deserves to be.'

Melanie looked shell-shocked by the time Isla had finished, and she stared down at Jacob in silence for several long moments. Still clutching the money, Isla held her breath as she waited for a response to her suggestion. She wouldn't blame Melanie for turning her down, because any mother would baulk at the idea of giving up their child – even temporarily. But most mothers would never put their own children into such a situation in the first place. Isla had lost her own babies, but if she had been blessed to go full-term with any of them, she would have protected them with her life.

'If I let you take him,' Melanie said quietly, breaking into Isla's thoughts. 'Will you promise to give him back when I'm ready?'

'Absolutely,' Isla agreed.

'Swear on your life.' Melanie looked her in the eye.

'On my life.' Isla placed a hand on her chest.

Melanie chewed on her lip for a moment. Then, shaking her head, she said, 'It's too risky. What if someone who knows me sees me without him and starts asking questions? Or Carl finds me and wants to know where he is. I can't just give my child away to a stranger. And I don't mean that badly, because you've been amazing with him. But if anything happens to me, he needs to be with his family.'

'I was his father's wife, so, technically, I *am* family,' Isla pointed out. 'You're his mother, so it would have been your right to let him live with Jerry if you'd thought it would be a better life for him. He's already lived with me for the last few months, so it's no one else's business if you decide to let him stay.'

'This is starting to sound complicated,' Melanie said cautiously. 'You said you'd give him back to me, but now it sounds like you want custody of him.'

'That's not what I'm saying at all,' Isla reassured her. 'Chances are, Carl will give up looking for you if you take the money and disappear. As soon as you get settled somewhere you'll both be safe, ring me and I'll bring Jacob to you. You have my absolute word on that.'

Melanie stared down into the pram again and Isla could see that she was torn between allowing Jacob to stay with her and taking him back to Carl. The latter was a terrible option, in her opinion, so when she heard the distinctive rumble of a bus engine in the near distance, she decided to up the pressure.

'Look, I know you're scared you're going to lose him, but I only want to keep him safe,' she said. 'I don't want to threaten you, but if you insist on taking him back, I'll have no choice but to report you. I don't want to do that, because I think that you're a great mum and you'll make a better life for Jacob if you start over on your own. I can't stop you if *you* want to go back, but I won't let you drag that innocent child down with you. So it's your choice.'

Melanie didn't reply and Isla's stomach lurched when the woman stood up and gripped the pushchair's handles as the bus came into view.

'Please, Melanie, I'm begging you,' she said, placing her hand on Melanie's arm when the vehicle squealed to a stop beside them. 'Do the right thing.'

Again, Melanie stayed silent, and Isla's hopes faded when the bus door swished open. Convinced that Melanie was going to take the boy and go home, she was confused when the woman suddenly released the handles, then leaned down and kissed Jacob before snatching the money out of her hand and jumping aboard the bus. Half expecting her to change her mind and jump straight back off again, she watched as Melanie stumbled along the aisle in tears. Seconds later, the door swished shut again and the bus pulled away, plunging Isla and Jacob back into darkness as its rear lights faded into the distance.

Chapter 18

After the second hour-long bus ride of the night, Melanie was exhausted, and her legs felt like blocks of concrete as she trudged the rest of the way home. Her flat was on the second floor of the block, but the lift was broken so she had to drag herself up the stairs. Halfway up, she picked up the muted sound of screaming coming from above. It wasn't unusual to hear people fighting or arguing round there, but this sounded like someone was literally being murdered.

The screams got louder when she reached her floor, and her heart lurched when she walked up to her front door and realised the horrendous noise was coming from inside. Hands shaking, she pulled out her keys and quickly let herself in. The screaming appeared to be coming from the living room and she hesitated outside the door, torn between rushing in or running back outside to call the police. Muttering, 'Holy shit!' when sinister music suddenly blared out and she realised it was coming from the TV, she pushed down the handle and walked into the room.

Carl was sprawled on the sofa watching a slasher movie with the volume turned right up. It was unbearable and Melanie covered her ears with her hands and yelled at Carl to turn it down. He didn't hear her, so she walked further into the room and leaned down to shake his shoulder. He leapt to his feet as if she'd electrocuted him, and she raised her arms to protect her head when he yanked a metal bar out from under the cushion and swung it at her. 'Carl, stop!' she cried. 'It's me!'

'What the *fuck*?' he squawked, breathing heavily as he lowered the bar and stared at her. 'I nearly caved your head in, you stupid cow! What the hell are you doing sneaking in like that?'

'She's kicked me out,' Melanie yelled. 'For God's sake, turn that down! I can't hear myself think.'

Carl shoved the bar back under the cushion and then used the remote to mute the TV before slumping down onto the sofa again. 'What d'you mean she's kicked you out? You said everything was cool this morning?'

'It was,' Melanie said, flopping down beside him. 'But one of her mates saw us together at the shops and sent her a photo.'

'I thought you said you'd never met them, so how did they know it was you?' Carl asked.

'I haven't spoken to either of them. But the woman's seen me a couple of times, and the man spotted me once not long after I moved in, so they both know what I look like. I told you we needed to be more careful.'

'Don't be blaming me. You're the one who insisted on stopping off at the shop to get Jacob some fucking sweets.'

'It doesn't matter whose fault it is; she was going to kick me out anyway,' Melanie sighed. 'She found her hubby's old phone while I was out and saw the message and the photos. She had a right go at me for lying to her, then told me to do one. But what I *didn't* expect was for her to come after me and ask me to leave Jacob with her.'

'You what?' Carl pulled a face. 'Why the fuck would she do that?'

'She was worried you might hurt him if I brought him back here,' Melanie said, reaching into her pocket for the money Isla had given her. 'So worried, she gave me this and told me to move away and start a new life without you.'

Carl's eyes widened and he snatched the notes out of her hand. 'How much is it?'

'Two grand.'

'Wow. I take it her money's come through, then?'

'No idea.' Melanie shrugged. 'She doesn't talk to me about that stuff. Like she told her mate, we're not friends, so why would she?'

'You ain't friends, but she wants your kid so bad she's willing to pay for him,' Carl snorted. 'Sounds like a right weirdo.'

'She's actually really good with him,' Melanie said quietly. 'I told you about her not being able to have kids, but I didn't realise how desperate she'd been to be a mum. I think that's why she bonded with Jacob so fast.'

'I don't see why,' Carl sneered, stuffing the money into his own pocket. 'All he ever does is cry.'

'He's not like that with her,' Melanie said. 'You won't have noticed, 'cos you always make me put him in his room when we come over and that sets him off again. But he hardly ever cries at her place. And he eats whatever she cooks without trying to chuck it back at her. I think he really likes her and feels like that's his home now, so it's going to be murder when I take him away from her again.'

'When's that going to be?'

'Whenever I want.' Melanie shrugged. 'She said to call her when I get settled and she'll bring him to me.'

'Cool.' Carl looped an arm around her shoulder and pulled her closer. 'That'll give us time to have some fun without him squawking and making me lose my boner.'

Squirming when he started kissing her neck and tried to slide his hand up under her T-shirt to grope her breasts, Melanie pushed him away.

'Not now. That bus ride's exhausting, and I've had to do it twice tonight. I need a wee and a brew, then I'm going to bed.'

'Nah, we can't let this free time go to waste,' Carl said, jumping up and grabbing his jacket off the back of the sofa. 'I'll go get something to wake you up.'

'Don't go crazy with that money,' Melanie cautioned. 'You need to pay Wozza the rest of what you owe him before he sends his boys round again. I can't take another kicking. They nearly killed me last time.'

'I know, and I promise that won't happen again,' Carl assured her. 'But you've got to admit it was perfect timing, 'cos there's no way she'd have let you in that night if you hadn't turned up in that state.'

'I suppose so,' Melanie agreed. 'But now we can afford it, please pay him off. There won't be any more money after that.'

'Yeah, there will,' Carl said slyly as he pulled on his jacket. 'Now she's shown she's willing to pay for what she wants, she's gonna find out there's a price for stealing things that don't belong to you.'

Melanie forced a smile when Carl leaned down and kissed her before heading out, but her shoulders slumped as soon as the front door closed behind him. Whenever she came home after Isla dropped her off at the hospital on chemo days, he always dragged her straight to bed, to make up for not seeing her all week. And they stayed there till it was time for her to leave and take the bus back to Isla's, so she hadn't noticed the mess he'd made in her absence. There were heaps of clothes, empty takeaway cartons and crushed beer cans all over the floor and the chairs, and the air stank of stale smoke and damp. She'd never really noticed how scruffy everything was before, but after experiencing the luxury of Isla's lovely, clean home, it looked like an absolute shithole.

Too tired to be bothered dealing with it right then, Melanie got up and went to the toilet. About to head to the kitchen to put the kettle on when she'd finished, she stopped outside Jacob's open bedroom door and felt the sting of tears in her eyes at the sight of his empty cot. He had always slept in his own room at the flat, and she wondered now if being alone in there was the reason he'd always cried so much. He'd been sleeping with her at Isla's house, and he had obviously enjoyed it, because she often woke to find him snuggled up to her. That, in turn, had made her feel closer to him, and she'd grown used to falling asleep to the sound of his soft breathing, and waking to his sleepy little smiles. Now Isla would be the one to get him up in the mornings, and a bitter taste flooded her mouth at the thought that her son might not even notice that she was gone. Why would he, when Isla had already made such an impact on him? It was her he had reached out for and cried over tonight as they were leaving the house, but he had barely reacted when Melanie had kissed him before getting on the bus. It was almost as if he thought Isla was his mother now, and that hurt. But she was the one who had taken him there and allowed him to bond with the woman, so she only had herself to blame.

The sound of the front door opening snapped Melanie out of her reverie, and she quickly pulled Jacob's bedroom door shut as Carl walked in.

'You were fast.'

'I'm on a promise, so I ran,' Carl grinned. 'Here, I got you these.' He held out a wilted bunch of flowers.

Touched, because she couldn't remember the last time he'd bought her flowers, Melanie said, 'That's so sweet. Thank you.'

'Don't get too used to it,' he laughed. 'You looked like you needed cheering up, so I got these, an' all.' He pulled a bottle of vodka and a small plastic bag of coke out of his pockets.

'Did you see Wozza?' Melanie asked.

'Yep. All sorted,' Carl said, slinging his jacket onto the already heaving coat-hooks behind the front door. 'Now let's go get this party started,' he said, grabbing her hand and pulling her into their bedroom.

Chapter 19

Isla was exhausted after two full weeks alone with Jacob. The first week had been particularly hard, because he'd cried non-stop; obviously missing his mum. That had made Isla feel really guilty, and she had been tempted to call Melanie to tell her she'd changed her mind and needed to give him back. But the thought of him being taken back to a life of misery and potential physical harm with Carl had stopped her. And that was what would happen, she was sure, because Melanie had already proved that she wasn't capable of looking after him on her own. Hopefully that would change if she'd used the money as Isla had intended and was trying to sort herself out away from him. But the fact that she hadn't rung or messaged to ask how Jacob was doing since she left made Isla suspect that she had probably gone straight back to him that night. She had messaged her a couple of times to let her know that Jacob was OK, but Melanie hadn't replied. So, as hard as it was to listen to the boy cry himself to sleep, she put her doubts aside and continued to comfort him as best she could.

Jacob gradually began to settle down and Isla felt that she had made the right decision when she saw the progress he was starting to make in her care. Melanie had told her that their GP had classed him as a slow starter, but Isla had always thought he was a bright child. And now she was free to give him her undivided attention, he was picking things up really quickly. She had bought him a cot and had placed it in her own bedroom so he didn't have to sleep alone, which seemed to have helped. And she had also bought a potty to train him how to use the toilet. It had taken a while, but something seemed to have clicked into place after a few days, and he now let her know when he needed to go. The third milestone she'd attempted to get him over was to teach him to speak actual words instead of grunting and pointing at the things he wanted. She'd started with their names; saying her own while pointing at herself, then his while pointing at him. He had quickly started to repeat the words, but Jacob came out as Bake-up and Isla as Yaya. Both names stuck, despite her efforts to get him to say them properly. But it sounded so cute, she stopped trying after a while; concentrating on teaching him other basic words instead.

All in all, things were going well, and Jacob seemed to be enjoying their time together as much as she was. She was relieved about that, because it signalled that he felt safe with her. That made her happy, but also a little sad that she had never had the opportunity to give love to a child of her own. She had long ago accepted that she was never going to be a mother, but having Jerry's child in the house had shown her what it would have been like to be a complete family. And, strangely, considering that Jacob was the product of her husband's betrayal, she believed that if Jerry were still alive, she would eventually have found the strength to accept the boy into their lives.

At the end of her second week with Jacob, Isla decided to take him out for the day. Summer would be coming to an end soon and it wasn't quite as sunny or warm as it had been a few weeks earlier. She would usually have taken him out into the garden to play for a while after breakfast. He loved it out there, but there wasn't much for him to do, other than run around tearing up the flowers the gardener had nursed back to life. Afraid that he might get bored with doing the same thing every day, and in desperate need of a change of scenery herself, she decided to head to the seaside to take advantage of the last of the mild weather.

She made a packed lunch for them both and loaded it and Jacob's pushchair into the boot of the car. As she was strapping him into his seat, a car pulled up at the gate and Benny leaned out through the driver's side window and called her name.

'Hey, what are you doing here?' she asked, pressing the fob to open the gate. 'You never said you were coming over?'

'I wasn't aware I needed to book an appointment,' he teased. 'Or is that what us commoners have to do now you're a lady?'

'Don't be cheeky,' she chided, slapping his arm when he climbed out after parking up. 'You're lucky you caught me. We're on our way to Rhyl.'

'*We*?' Benny looked around. 'Is Tia back?'

'No, she's not back till next week. I was talking about me and Jacob.' Isla nodded towards the child who was staring up at him from the back seat. 'We've been stuck inside all week, so I thought he deserved a bit of fun.'

'You picked a good day for it,' Benny said, leaning down to waggle his fingers at the boy. 'You all right there, little man?'

Jacob gave him a shy grin and then covered his eyes with his hands to play peek-a-boo.

'Looks like you've made a friend,' Isla said, smiling when Benny started playing the game. 'Hey, why don't you come with us,' she suggested. 'Unless this was only going to be a short visit?'

'You think I'd drive all the way over here for a quickie?' Benny asked.

'Well, if you're coming, we need to get a move on,' Isla said. 'He'll start getting bored if we leave it too long.'

'Let's do it,' Benny grinned. 'I haven't been to the seaside in years.'

'Neither have I,' Isla said, handing Jacob one of the bottles of juice she'd prepared before closing his door. 'Jerry was a workaholic, so our honeymoon was the first and last holiday we ever took together. When he retired, I booked us into the same place as a surprise for our anniversary and his sixtieth. But he died that day, so Tia had to cancel it for me. I couldn't half do with it right now, but Rhyl will have to do.'

'Wow, that's a coincidence,' Benny said. 'Me and Vic had booked tickets to Portugal the week before she died.'

'We were going to Portugal,' Isla exclaimed.

'No way! Which hotel?'

'Vila Joya. Please don't tell me you were booked into that one?'

'I wish.' Benny grinned. 'I saw it online, but it was way out of my pay grade. Hey, maybe *we* should go together when your guests have gone and you're free,' he suggested, casting a hooded glance towards the front door. 'Is she any closer to finding a place yet?'

Remembering that she hadn't updated him on the events of the night when she'd found Jerry's phone and he'd sent her the shot of Melanie and Carl, Isla said, 'She's already gone.'

'Really?' Benny frowned. 'How come the kid's still here, then?'

'Long story.' Isla rolled her eyes as she climbed into the driver's seat.

Jacob quickly fell asleep after they set off, and Isla quietly filled Benny in on everything that had happened since they had last spoken.

'I asked her how her session had gone, and she lied to my face, saying she'd been so sick they made her stay longer to have biscuits and tea. She admitted it after I showed her the photo you sent me, but she claimed she only went to see him because he'd told her he knew my address and was going to come and kill us all.'

'If you're in danger, you need to report him,' Benny said concernedly.

'She reckons he only said that to force her hand and get her to meet up with him,' Isla assured him. 'He told her he'd missed her and wanted her to go home, but she didn't believe he knew where she'd been staying.'

'Did she go back to him after you kicked her out?'

'No idea. I haven't heard from her since she left, and she hasn't answered any of my messages.'

'Mother of the year, right there,' Benny remarked sarcastically. 'I hope she was telling the truth about him not knowing where you are, but if you think there's any chance she was lying, I'm happy to come and stay for a bit.'

'Thanks, but I honestly don't think he knows where I am or he probably would have come already,' Isla replied. 'This is the second week I've had Jacob and I haven't heard a peep from either of them.'

'Well, the offer's there,' Benny said, glancing back at Jacob to check he was still sleeping. 'How long do you reckon you'll have him?'

'No idea.' Isla shrugged. 'But he's no problem, so I'm not in any rush for him to go. He's been making great progress with his walking and talking, so I'm kind of glad she's gone off the radar. I know she's had a rough time of it, but she doesn't give him the attention he needs. She hardly ever talked to him; she just used to plonk him in front of the TV when they got up and leave him there. It was me who played with him and fed him.'

'He's lucky to have you,' Benny said, smiling as he reached out and squeezed her bare shoulder.

A shiver rippled down Isla's spine, and she prayed that Benny couldn't see the flush that was heating her cheeks. She'd had a bit of a crush on him when they had first met as teens, but she hadn't thought about him in any sort of romantic way in years, so she didn't understand why her body had reacted so strongly to his touch. She also felt guilty, as if she had somehow betrayed Jerry. But *he* was the one who had betrayed *her*, so she determinedly pushed that last thought out of her mind and drove on.

It was quite breezy and there weren't many people on the beach when they arrived, so they found themselves a good spot and settled down to enjoy the weak sunshine. Jacob was so excited by the sight of the sea, he immediately started toddling towards it. Benny grabbed him and took off his shoes, then held his hand and walked him across the sand. Jacob's little legs went up and down like pistons in an attempt to get there faster, and Isla smiled when she heard him squeal with delight when they reached the water and he felt it lap around his ankles. She had never seen this gentle side of Benny before, and she loved how at ease Jacob was with him, despite it being the first time they had ever met.

The pair paddled for a while longer, and then Benny scooped Jacob up into his arms and carried him back to Isla. After eating the sandwiches she had made, Benny taught the boy how to dig in the sand for shells and build little sandcastles with his hands.

Later in the day, when Jacob started to get tired, they put him in his pushchair and took a stroll around the town, checking out the shops and the arcades before stopping to buy ice creams from a kiosk on the pier. They sat on a bench to eat them and gazed out over the sea as the tide came closer to the shoreline. Glancing down at Jacob after a while and seeing that he was asleep, Benny nudged Isla.

'I think the sea air's done him in.'

'Yeah, he'll sleep well tonight,' Isla said.

'So will I,' Benny yawned. 'It's been a lovely day, though, hasn't it?'

'It has,' Isla agreed. 'Thanks for being so great with him. I doubt he's ever had a positive male influence in his life before. He really took to you.'

'He's a great kid,' Benny smiled. 'And the way he says our names is super cute. Bebby and Yaya. I think that's what I'll call you from now on.'

'Don't you dare,' Isla laughed.

'You love it,' Benny teased, winking at her.

Their eyes met, but Isla quickly looked away when she felt a tingling sensation in the pit of her stomach. Relieved when her phone suddenly started to ring, she pulled it out of her bag and leapt to her feet when she saw that it was the solicitor, Marcus.

'Sorry, I just need to get this. Won't be a minute.'

'No worries,' Benny said. 'I'll watch little man.'

Isla was gone for quite some time, and Benny gave her a questioning look when she came back with a stunned look on her face.

'Are you OK?' he asked.

'No.' She shook her head. 'That was Jerry's solicitor who's been executing his will. He called to let me know that everything's completed and he's transferred the money into my account.'

'Bad news?' Benny peered at her.

'Shocking,' Isla said. Then, glancing around to make sure that nobody was within hearing distance, she whispered, 'Almost two million.'

'Whoa.' Benny's eyebrows shot up. 'That's a lot. I take it you weren't expecting that much?'

'Nowhere near,' Isla murmured. 'I figured it'd be a fair amount, because he co-owned his business and had only recently sold his shares when he died. But that's just crazy.'

'Well, I'd keep it to yourself for now,' Benny advised. 'You'll have people crawling out of the woodwork begging for handouts if that gets around.'

'That's what Marcus said,' Isla replied. 'And he reckons I'll be inundated with requests for donations from charities, if word gets out.'

'It's no one's business, so don't let anyone pressurise you into doing anything you don't want to do,' Benny said, squeezing her hand.

Isla nodded her agreement and blew out a tense breath. In the aftermath of finding Jerry's old phone, she had forgotten to go back into his study to look for bank statements, so she'd had no idea he'd had that much in his accounts. He hadn't been the kind of man to splash out on luxuries and had often queried her own spending habits when her credit card bills came in; asking if she couldn't find a cheaper hairdresser, or tut-tutting over the price of her shoes and handbags. So to hear that he had been sitting on a fortune all along was staggering, and she couldn't quite believe that it was real.

'Shall we get him home?' Benny asked, breaking into her thoughts and nodding towards Jacob. 'You look like you're in shock, so I reckon you could do with a drink or ten.'

'You're not wrong there,' Isla said. 'My legs feel like jelly.'

'If you're angling for a piggyback, you can jog on,' Benny grinned. 'You might be rich now, but this boy's not for sale.'

Laughing, but still in shock, Isla firmly grasped the handles of the pushchair to keep her legs from giving way as they walked to the car park at the other end of the promenade.

Jacob was still asleep when they arrived back at the house that evening, so Benny gently lifted him out of the car seat and carried him up to the bedroom. Isla quickly changed his nappy and slipped him into his pyjamas, then laid him in the cot, covered him with the blanket and turned off the lamp before quietly backing out of the room.

In the kitchen, sure that Benny must be as hungry as she was considering they had only eaten sandwiches and ice cream that day, Isla handed him a bottle of wine to open and then quickly reheated some leftover lasagne she'd had in the fridge. They carried their plates and glasses out onto the patio and sat side by side on the padded bench. The sky was clear, and they relaxed under the glow of the heater as they ate.

Pouring more wine when they had finished eating, they chatted about the events of the day and talked over their plans for a foreign holiday when they were both free. The atmosphere was so relaxed, neither of them was aware of how long they had been sitting out there. So when Benny caught Isla yawning for the fourth time in a row and glanced at his watch, he was shocked to see that it was almost midnight.

'It's getting late, so I'm going to head off and let you get some sleep,' he said. 'Thanks again for letting me tag along today.'

'Thank *you* for agreeing to come,' Isla said, smiling as she rose to her feet. 'I don't think Jacob would have had half as much fun with me on my own.'

'Don't underestimate the effect you're having on him,' Benny replied as he, too, stood up. 'I saw the way he kept looking back whenever I took him off to do anything without you. And it's obvious you're really fond of him, too. I just hope he doesn't suffer too much when his mum takes him back, 'cos the longer she's gone, the more he's going to feel like this is his home.'

Isla's smile slipped at that, and Benny, thinking that he'd upset her, said, 'Hey, I'm sorry. I didn't mean to put you on a downer.'

'You haven't,' she assured him. 'But I've been thinking about that, too. Obviously, I've enjoyed having him with me, but it does make me wonder if I'm doing the right thing by keeping him here. If it's going to unsettle him when she takes him back, maybe I should have just let her take him when I kicked her out. The last thing I want to do is hurt him.'

'You did this to protect him, and that's a good thing,' Benny said. 'His mother's the one who decided to go no contact and ignore your messages, so all you can do now is wait for her to get her act together and reach out. If she's got any sense, she'll do that soon to avoid him getting hurt. But that's on her, not you.'

'Yeah, you're right,' Isla agreed. 'There's nothing I can do if I can't get hold of her, so I'm going to carry on looking after him and deal with whatever comes *when* it comes.'

'Chin up,' Benny said, pulling her into a hug. 'You've got this.'

Isla squeezed her eyes shut when she got the shivers again, and then quickly pulled herself free and walked into the kitchen. Benny followed and picked up his jacket, keys and phone. At the front door, he leaned down and kissed her cheek before walking to his car.

'I'll pop over again in a couple of days,' he called out through the window. 'But if you need me before that, call me. And make sure you lock the house up tight.'

'I will,' Isla promised. 'Drive safely.'

'Always do,' Benny said, waving as he reversed out through the gate.

Chapter 20

Benny had said he would pop over in a couple of days, so Isla was surprised when he pulled up outside her gate and honked his horn the following morning.

'What are you doing here again so soon?' she asked as she let him in.

'I was passing and thought I might as well drop in and say hello,' he answered. Then, giving a sheepish smile when she raised a disbelieving eyebrow, he said, 'OK, so maybe I wanted to see my little mate again. And *you*, of course. But mainly him.'

Amused, Isla shook her head and waved him towards the kitchen. 'He's having his breakfast.'

Benny kissed her cheek before heading in to see the boy, and Isla's stomach fluttered when she picked up the musky scent of his aftershave as she followed him into the kitchen. Annoyed that her body was going rogue and creating sensations that she had no business feeling given that Jerry had only been gone a few months, she shook it off and walked over to the kettle to make Benny a coffee.

Jacob had stopped eating his cereal and was excitedly bouncing in his high chair while reaching out to Benny to lift him up.

'Let's finish this first,' Benny said, perching on a chair beside him. 'Don't worry, I won't be staying long,' he added to Isla when she walked past him to get the milk out of the fridge.

'It's always nice to see you, so you can stay as long as you like,' Isla said, smiling as she watched him feed Jacob. 'It'll give me a chance to get a few things done, if you're happy to watch him for a bit?'

'Of course,' Benny agreed. 'But if you're heading out, I've got a couple of things in the car I need to get before you go.'

'No, I'm staying in. I just need to strip the beds and put a wash on, but I can never get anything done when he's awake. And I'm always too tired by the time he goes to bed.'

'I've got something that'll keep him occupied,' Benny said, jumping to his feet after feeding Jacob the last spoonful of cereal. 'Won't be a sec.'

He walked out to his car, and Isla's eyes widened when he came back carrying a big red fire engine.

'Wow, that's huge. He's going to love that.'

'Nah, that's for you,' Benny said. '*This* is for him.' He whipped a bottle of champagne out from under his jacket. 'Only joking,' he laughed, handing the bottle to her. 'It's yours. To celebrate the end of your troubles and the start of your brand new life.'

'Thank you,' Isla murmured, touched by his thoughtfulness. 'I hope you're going to stick around long enough to share it with me?'

'I guess it's my duty,' he said, rolling his eyes as if it was the last thing he wanted to do. 'Now go get on with your chores and leave me and the boy to have fun.'

'Knock yourself out.' Isla placed the champagne in the fridge as Benny lifted Jacob out of the high chair and got down on the floor with him. 'Your brew's on the ledge,' she said, leaning into the utility room to get the washing basket. 'Won't be long.'

The deafening wail of the fire engine's siren eclipsed her

words, and she smiled when Jacob started laughing and clapping his hands together as the lights began swirling. She left them to it and headed upstairs to strip the beds.

The boys were still playing when she came back down with the bedding, so she put it in the wash and then sat at the table to drink her coffee and do some shopping on her laptop. Now that she was over the shock of how much money Jerry had left her, she had made a list of things that she'd been too scared to buy while she was still waiting for it. Jacob was already growing out of the outfits she'd bought him when he first arrived, so she ordered some lovely new clothes for him and a couple of things for herself. That done, she ordered groceries for the week ahead. Then, switching sites, she ordered the swing and slide set and the small trampoline she'd been planning to get for Jacob. The garden was his favourite place and she couldn't wait to see his little face when they arrived. He'd loved the swings when she'd taken him to the park a few days earlier, and she wanted him to enjoy his time outside while the weather was still warm. Plus, it would distract him from digging up any more of her flowers, so it was a win-win.

She knew she had more than enough money to pay for it all, but she hadn't quite shaken off the fear of being left with nothing and had set herself a budget. Pleased with herself now for not straying too far outside of it, she closed the laptop and logged into her email account. The first few were confirmations of the orders she'd just made, along with the delivery dates. But the fourth one was totally unexpected, and she frowned when she saw that it was from Peter's wife, Felicity. It was an e-invite to their fortieth wedding anniversary party and had been sent just after midnight.

'What the hell…' she murmured.

'S'up?' Benny asked, standing up and dusting the knees of his jeans as Jacob amused himself with the fire engine.

'This.' Isla pointed at the screen.

Benny came up behind her, rested his hands on her shoulders and leaned forward to read the email. Barely able to breathe, Isla sat stock-still until he'd finished and stepped back.

'Remember I told you about Tia having an argument with the wife of Jerry's old business partner at the wake, after she caught her calling me a gold-digger?' she asked. 'Well, that's from *her*. I haven't heard from her since, so God knows why she's contacting me now.'

'Maybe she wants to put things right?' Benny mused, reaching down for Jacob, who had got up and was tugging on the leg of his jeans for attention. 'Are you going to go?'

'After what she said about me? Absolutely not.' Isla pulled a face. 'She probably forgot I was in her contacts and sent it to me by mistake, knowing her.'

'I'd go to get a rise out of her and make her feel awkward,' Benny chuckled. 'And I'd take Tia as my plus-one.'

'God, that would be hilarious,' Isla laughed. 'But I've got Jacob, so I couldn't go even if I wanted to.'

'I'd be happy to look after him,' Benny offered.

'Thanks, but that's one chapter of my life I've got no intention of revisiting,' Isla said, closing the laptop when she noticed that Jacob had laid his head on Benny's shoulder and was starting to look tired. 'I'll get him a bottle and make us some lunch. What do you fancy?'

'Do you really want me to answer that?' Benny asked, his dark eyes twinkling mischievously as he gave her a piercing look. Laughing when he saw the shock on her face, he said, 'Relax. I was joking.'

'I knew that,' Isla said, smiling to disguise how flustered she felt. 'Right, bottle,' she muttered, quickly turning away from him.

Bottle made, she put Jacob down for his nap and then prepared sandwiches for herself and Benny. As they sat at the table to eat, the doorbell rang, so she excused herself and went out into the hall to see who it was. Surprised to see Peter standing beside his car on the other side of the gate, she walked over.

'Hello, Isla.' He gave her a tentative smile. 'I hope I'm not disturbing you?'

'I am kind of busy,' she lied.

'I shan't keep you long,' he assured her. Then, glancing past her towards the house, he said, 'I don't suppose I could come inside for a moment?'

'I have guests, so it's not really a good time,' Isla said, folding her arms. 'And, to be honest, I'm surprised you'd even ask, given what happened last time you were here.'

'That was regrettable,' he murmured, awkwardly shifting his weight onto his other foot. 'I've been meaning to reach out to you for some time, but it's taken me a while to summon the courage. I know I apologised at the time, but I am deeply, deeply ashamed of myself and I truly hope you can forgive me. I also want to thank you for not telling Felicity.'

'I told you I wouldn't, so let's just forget it,' Isla said, giving him a tight smile. 'But while we're on the subject of Felicity, I think she might have accidentally sent me an invite to your anniversary party. Can you please assure her that I won't be coming, as I'm sure she'd rather not have me there.'

'On the contrary,' said Peter. 'That's why I came, actually: because we guessed that you might think it was a mistake. We'd both love to see you there, and she's really keen to have you back in the fold. She talks about you often. And the other ladies have missed you, too.'

'I kind of doubt that,' countered Isla. 'But it doesn't matter. We've all moved on.'

'So I see,' Peter murmured.

Confused when she saw that his narrow-eyed gaze was locked onto something behind her, Isla turned her head and saw Benny on the step.

'Sorry, didn't mean to interrupt, but someone's calling you,' he said, holding up her ringing phone. 'And I think you might want to take it,' he added pointedly.

Isla told him that she wouldn't be a second and then turned back to Peter. The sneer on his lips told her that he thought she and Benny were together, and she opened her mouth to assure him that they were only friends. Immediately changing her mind, she smiled and said goodbye instead. He could think whatever he liked; it was none of his business and she owed him no explanations. If he'd had his way, *he* would be the new man in her life, so he could stick his sanctimonious display of disapproval up his fat old arse!

That last thought tickled her and she was still smiling when she reached Benny, but it slid off her lips when she took her phone from him and saw the name on the screen.

'Melanie?' she answered it warily as she stepped inside.

'Yeah, it's me,' Melanie replied. 'Sorry I didn't get in touch sooner, but I've been trying to find a place.'

'And have you found one?' Isla asked, feeling a little sick at the thought that she might be about to ask to take Jacob back.

'No, not yet,' Melanie sighed. 'Everyone wants references and I can't get any, so I'm kind of stuck.'

'What about your family?' Isla took a seat at the kitchen table and nodded to Benny when he gestured to the kettle, asking if she wanted a brew. 'Have you spoken to them yet?'

'I thought I'd best try to get a place up here first,' Melanie said. 'I'd have to change hospitals if I move to Devon, and I was scared that would interrupt my treatments.'

'I get that,' Isla said. 'But if you're still in Manchester, where have you been staying?'

'I'm in a B and B in Levenshulme,' Melanie told her. 'It was the cheapest one I could find, but it's sixty quid a night, so it's eating through that money you gave me. I've had to buy food and pay to get to hospital and round all the estate agents looking at flats, so it'll run out soon and I'll have to leave.'

'And where will you go?' Isla asked. 'If you can't stay there and you don't want to go to Devon because of your chemo, you're pretty much back at square one. And we both know where that'll lead, don't we?'

Melanie didn't reply to that and Isla guessed that the woman had probably already decided to go back to her ex – if she hadn't already done so. Whether she had or not, it was her business, but it pissed Isla off that she was so consumed with herself she hadn't even asked about her son yet.

'Jacob's fine, in case you're wondering,' she remarked coolly. 'I take it that's why you're calling, since you haven't seen him in weeks?'

'Yeah, I was about to ask,' Melanie replied guiltily. 'You must be sick of him by now, so I can come and get him if you want?'

Isla's jaw clenched with disgust that Melanie was speaking about Jacob as if he was a burden. If she allowed her to take him back, she had no doubt that Melanie would go back to plonking him in front of the TV for hours on end, with little to no attention or interaction. And God only knew how long it would be before he was subjected to hearing his so-called father beating the shit out of her again. It was unacceptable, and she couldn't allow it to happen.

'Jacob's no problem,' she said when she'd decided what she

would do. 'You're obviously under a lot of stress and I think you need to concentrate on getting yourself better, so I'm going to send you some more money to tide you over until you get your chemo out of the way without worrying about looking for a place to live. Did they tell you how long that would be?'

'I think they said I've got four more sessions,' Melanie told her. 'But they're going to start staggering them, so it might be every fortnight instead of every week.'

'OK, well stay there and get that out of the way, then go and see your parents and try to get your life back on track. When you're settled and know you can properly take care of Jacob, I'll bring him to you.'

'That's really kind, but I can't take more money off you,' Melanie protested. 'You've given me more than enough already.'

'I'm not offering, I'm *telling* you this is what's going to happen,' Isla said firmly. 'Jacob's happy here and he's doing really well. If you care about him, let me take care of this. OK?'

Melanie stayed silent for several moments. Then, sighing, she murmured, 'OK.'

'Good,' Isla said. 'Now how do you want to do this? I don't want you coming here and upsetting Jacob if he sees you and you leave again. So, I can either transfer the money to you, or you can give me the address of the B and B and I'll see if my friend can drop it off for you.'

'I haven't got a bank account, so it'll have to be cash. But the woman who runs this place doesn't allow visitors, so it's probably best if I meet your friend somewhere.'

'OK, leave it with me. I'll have to go to the bank to draw the money out, so it might take a while. But it'll definitely be today.'

'Are you sure you can afford it?' Melanie asked. 'Only I saw how careful you were being with your money when I was there, so I don't want to put you to any trouble.'

Reluctant to reveal that her inheritance had come through, Isla said, 'I've got a little put by, so I'll manage. I'll call you later – and please don't ignore it this time.'

'I won't,' Melanie promised. 'And thank you so much. I'll pay you back as soon as I can.'

'Don't worry about it,' Isla muttered.

She cut the call and released a weary breath as she slumped back in her seat.

'Are you OK?' Benny asked, placing one of the cups of tea he'd made on the table in front of her. 'You look wiped.'

'I feel it,' Isla said, massaging her temples. 'The thought of her taking Jacob back to that shithead did me in.'

'Is that what she said she was going to do?'

'Not outright, but I knew that's where she would have gone,' Isla said, realising that he'd only heard her side of the conversation. 'She asked if I wanted her to pick Jacob up, because she reckons I must be sick of him by now. Can you believe that?'

Benny raised his eyebrows and took a seat. 'Is that why you offered her more money?'

'Yep.' Isla sighed. 'But it's a small price to pay to keep Jacob safe, so I'm not bothered about that. It's not like I can't afford it.'

She relayed what Melanie had told her about staying in a B and B and how she was struggling to find a place to live, and Benny listened with an expression of increasing incredulity.

'I'm sorry,' he said when she'd finished. 'But how the hell has she gone through two grand in two weeks? And sixty quid a night for a B and B in *Levenshulme*? Pull the other one.'

'I don't really care what she's done with the money, *or* where she is,' Isla replied flatly. 'I know she went through hell with her ex, and I wouldn't wish cancer on anyone. But she didn't even ask about Jacob and she hasn't seen him in weeks, so how can I be sure she'll look after him properly if I let her take him back?'

'Well, you're keeping him for a while longer, so at least he's safe for now,' Benny said. 'And I'm happy to drop the money off, by the way.'

'Thanks.' Isla gave him a grateful smile. 'I was going to ask, but I didn't want you to think I was being cheeky.'

'I figured as much,' Benny grinned. 'Tia's away, so that only left me. Unless you've got some secret mates stashed away that I don't know about?'

'Nope. You and Tia are pretty much it,' Isla sighed. 'I gave up everything for Jerry and wasted fifteen years trying to be the perfect wife, and this is what I'm left with. Great achievement, huh?'

'It wasn't wasted,' Benny said softly. 'You loved and trusted him, and there's no shame in that. You're a beautiful, kind and intelligent woman, and a real man would know your worth.'

Isla blushed and dipped her gaze, and Benny tipped his head to one side and gave her a bemused smile.

'Why do you keep doing that?'

'Doing what?' She forced herself to look at him.

'Every time I give you a compliment, you look away,' he explained. 'It's almost like you don't believe that anyone could possibly think good things about you. I know he hurt you, but I guarantee he regretted it or he would have left you.'

'He was planning to,' Isla reminded him. 'He was begging Melanie to give him another chance in his last text, but she said no and asked him to leave her alone. If she'd agreed, he would have gone.'

'Then he was the prick who didn't deserve you in the first place,' Benny said bluntly. 'And it's time you stopped putting yourself down and started moving on.'

'I'm trying,' Isla sighed. 'It's not easy, but I'll get there, so don't worry about me.'

'I'm not worried,' Benny smiled, taking a sip of tea before sitting back. 'So what was with the old dude at the gate earlier?' he asked. 'He's lucky I didn't deck him, the look he gave me when I brought your phone out.'

'That was Peter.' Isla rolled her eyes. 'Jerry's ex-business partner. He came to check if I'd got the invitation to their party, and he apologised for what he did after the wake, as well. When he saw you, I think he thought you were my new boyfriend. And I didn't correct him, 'cos it's none of his business.'

'Too right,' Benny chuckled. 'Hey, maybe you should get Tia to babysit and take *me* to that party as your plus-one. If he already thinks we're a thing, we can really go to town with it.'

'God, can you imagine?' Isla laughed. 'They already think I'm a gold-digging tramp, so that would give them even more to gossip about. To be honest, I don't even know why they'd want me there. They were Jerry's friends, not mine. And Marcus reckons he and Peter weren't even talking when he died, so why try to pull me back into their group?'

'Maybe they've heard about the inheritance coming through,' Benny mused.

'I don't think it's that,' Isla said. 'Peter's loaded, so they'd have nothing to gain from me. I don't even know how they would have found out about it. Unless Marcus told them. I don't know if he's Peter's solicitor too, but he did used to represent the company whenever they had legal issues, so they definitely know each other.'

'Is that legal?' Benny asked.

'Probably not.' Isla shrugged. 'But rich people don't follow the same rules as the rest of us.'

'Says the woman who's a millionaire twice over,' Benny chuckled.

'You know what I meant,' Isla chided. 'Jerry's the one who

earned it, so I still think of it as being his. I'm just a council estate girl who got lucky. That's why Felicity and the others have always looked down on me: because I don't come from their world. But they forget I've seen them with their knickers down. Figuratively speaking, obviously.'

'Now that sounds like a story I need to hear.' Benny leaned forward and rested his elbows on the table.

Without naming names, Isla recounted the events she'd witnessed at some of the parties she and Jerry had attended over the years, where inhibitions had dropped as fast as the booze flowed. From the wives, who acted like the best of friends during the lunch dates, flirting outrageously with each other's husbands; to the pair – from different couples – who she'd walked in on having sex in Peter's downstairs toilet.

'They didn't see me, so I was able to back out without them realising they'd been caught,' she said. 'But me and Jerry had a right laugh about it when we got home that night. In hindsight, it's no wonder Peter thought I'd be up for it when he tried it on with me. They've probably all had each other over the years. It wouldn't surprise me if he was the one who groped Melanie in the strip club the day she met Jerry. She said he was with a group of men, and Peter and the others were the only ones he hung out with socially.'

'Wow. And I thought actors were a wild bunch,' Benny laughed. 'This lot sound like a right bunch of degenerates.'

'You'd never guess it to look at them, though,' Isla grinned. 'When Jerry first introduced me to them, I thought the women were all Stepford Wives.'

'Thank God you didn't turn into one of them,' Benny said.

'No chance.' Isla rolled her eyes. Then, glancing at her watch, she said, 'Right, I'd best wake Jacob up so I can get to the bank.'

'If you want to let him sleep, I can stay here and listen out for him while you're gone,' Benny offered.

'Thanks, that'll be really helpful,' Isla said, smiling as she stood up. 'It's not far, but the bank shuts at noon today and it's murder getting him in and out of the car and pram.'

'No worries,' Benny said. 'You can pay me back with dinner, and then we'll crack open that bottle.'

'Absolutely,' Isla agreed, picking up her handbag. 'See you in a bit.'

Chapter 21

Sinister shadows were rapidly forming as the sun dipped behind the empty warehouses that loomed over each side of the narrow backroad. Huddled in a doorway on the corner, Melanie's eyes darted every which way as she listened out for the sound of approaching vehicles. It had been Carl's idea to meet Isla's friend there, but she wished he'd chosen somewhere less isolated, because this wasn't a particularly safe area. In fact, it was a notorious hotspot for working girls to ply their trade. Which made her vulnerable not only to their pimps and men looking for a quick, cheap shag, but also the police, who might think she was a sex worker.

A glance at the clock on her phone told her that Isla's friend was already fifteen minutes late, and she bit her lip as she shoved the phone back into her pocket. She had no clue which friend to expect, but if it was one of the two she'd overhead on that patio that night, she already knew they both vehemently disapproved of her. The female more so, but both had voiced their concerns about her, so Melanie was already nervous about the digs they might take at her when they handed over the money.

Ten more minutes crawled by, and Melanie began to wonder if Isla had changed her mind. She hoped not, because she knew exactly how Carl would react if she went home empty-handed.

He'd been ecstatic when she'd returned with the two grand Isla had given her. They had never been in possession of that much money before and she'd done her best to persuade him that, if they were careful, they could clear their debts, fill their freezer and put a sizeable amount of credit on their electric card. He'd agreed in the moment, but as soon as he took control of the cash, she'd had no say in how it was going to be spent. In less than three short weeks the money was gone. He had splashed out on daily bottles of booze and bags of coke; new trainers and clothes for himself, and a second-hand PS5 console.

Melanie had watched with a sinking heart as he burned through the money during the first week. But when, for some inexplicable reason, he'd suddenly switched from coke to smack in week two, she'd known that it would a downward spiral from there. And she'd been right. That drug had been his downfall before, and she didn't understand why he'd tempted fate by playing with it again after going through hell to get off it the previous year. He had insisted that he was stronger now and wouldn't get hooked again, but it had taken mere days for him to fall firmly into its grasp.

After spending the last of the money on a bag the previous night, he'd woken up rattling, and Melanie had been helpless to do anything but watch in horror as he tore the flat apart in search of loose change. His search hadn't yielded anywhere near enough for a bag, and she'd been genuinely afraid that he was going to take his anger out on her when he'd lunged and snatched her phone off the arm of her chair. Instead, he'd shoved the phone into her face and ordered her to call Isla to demand more money.

She really hadn't wanted to ask Isla for more when she'd already been so generous, and she'd had to think on her feet to come up with a feasible explanation for why she'd gone through the two grand so fast. But Carl had been in such a volatile mood, she'd had no choice but to make the call.

To her surprise and relief, she hadn't even needed to ask for the money; Isla had volunteered it. Melanie knew she'd only done that to safeguard Jacob for longer, and that had made her feel bad all over again. But if it kept Carl off her back for a while, she was happy to accept whatever Isla was prepared to give her.

Another ten minutes passed, and Melanie was contemplating whether she ought to text Isla to ask if there was a problem, when the glow of headlights suddenly illuminated the white-washed building at the other end of the road. Seconds later, a car turned onto the road and drove slowly along. Unsure if it was Isla's friend or a kerb-crawler, Melanie stuck close to the wall and watched as it approached. It pulled up alongside her and the driver's side window slid down.

'Melanie?' the man in the driver's seat asked.

Relieved to see that it was the man she'd glimpsed from the top of the stairs, Melanie nodded and stepped forward.

'This is from Isla,' the man said, holding out an envelope.

Melanie murmured a thank you and reached out to take the envelope, but the man suddenly pulled it back again.

'Before I give it to you, I want to know what you did with the last lot,' he said, staring at her intently.

It was the one question Melanie had dreaded Isla asking her when she'd rung her earlier that morning, and she'd had to wing it and come up with the story of staying at a B and B. Isla had seemed to buy it, but Melanie could tell that this man wasn't going to be so easy to convince.

'I already told Isla,' she said, trying to sound as sincere as possible as she went on to reiterate the same story she'd told Isla. 'I know it sounds like a lot, but it was honestly the cheapest place I could find. And with bus fares and food, it all adds up fast.'

'Funny that,' the man said. 'Because I did a quick Google search before heading out, and I found tons that were cheaper. And in better areas, too.'

'I must have missed them,' Melanie muttered, dipping her head to let her hair fall forward to conceal her flaming cheeks. 'But I've been under a lot of stress, so maybe I didn't look hard enough.'

'Or maybe you're just lying to extort money out of a good woman?' the man replied smoothly.

Sure by then that he wasn't going to give her the money, Melanie blinked rapidly when tears welled in her eyes. 'I know it probably looks like that,' she said shakily. 'But I wouldn't do that to Isla. She's been really good to me and I owe her a lot.'

'Yeah, you do,' the man agreed, once again holding out the envelope. 'If you do anything to hurt her, you'll have me to deal with,' he warned. 'And that's not a threat of violence, because, unlike *your* so-called man, I'm not a woman-beater. But I know who you are and what you're hiding, and I can make life very difficult for you if you mess Isla around. Got that?'

Melanie nodded and cautiously reached for the envelope again. This time, the man let her take it and she felt her legs turn to jelly when he stared at her one last time before driving away.

Isla had opened the gate and was waiting on the doorstep when Benny arrived at her house after dropping the money off. She already knew that he had completed the handover, because he'd sent her a text as she was putting Jacob to bed, to let her know he was on his way back. Now she wanted to know how Melanie had looked.

'To be brutally honest, like a junkie,' he said, following her inside. 'I've never seen her up close before, so I don't know if that's how she always looks. But she's really skinny, her hair's greasy, and her face looks grey and sunken in.'

'You think she's been doing drugs?' Isla asked, frowning as they took seats at the kitchen table.

'Who knows?' Benny shrugged. 'She sounded pretty coherent when we spoke, to be fair. But she looks rough as hell. Not just rough; ground down.'

'I hope her chemo hasn't stopped working,' Isla murmured, feeling a stab of sympathy for the woman. 'She was always really weak and sick when she got home after a session, and it must feel ten times worse now she's stuck in a B and B on her own.'

'*If* that's where she is,' Benny countered, still not convinced that Melanie hadn't been lying about that, given her guilty reaction when he'd mentioned finding cheaper places.

Isla's expression was gloomy, so he reached across the table and took her hand in his.

'Whatever you're thinking, *stop*,' he ordered. 'You've already helped her far more than anyone else in her life seems to be doing. And you're the one who owes her the least.'

'I know,' Isla replied quietly. 'But—'

'But nothing,' said Benny. 'Like you, I wouldn't wish cancer on anyone after watching it destroy my mum. But she didn't contact you for weeks after you gave her that last lot of money, which tells me that she got on just fine without you until she needed more. Now she's got it, you probably won't hear from her again until *that* runs out. Whatever choices she makes during that time, be it drugs, going back to her ex, whatever; that's up to her. You've done your bit, now leave her to it and stop worrying.'

'Yeah, you're right,' Isla agreed, smiling when he gently squeezed her hand.

'OK, then.' Benny sat back and rubbed his hands together. 'I don't know about you, but I'm ready for my drink.'

Still smiling, Isla got up and took the bottle out of the fridge.

Glasses filled after Benny had popped the cork, he raised his and said, 'To new beginnings.'

'And old mates,' Isla added, clinking her glass against his.

Benny gave her one of his piercing looks, and Isla felt the little flutter in her stomach that was becoming more and more frequent in his presence. He held her gaze for several seconds, as if he was about to say something else. Then, seeming to think better of it, he nodded towards the patio door, and said, 'Shall we?'

Isla felt a little deflated. Benny had given her that same intense look on several occasions now, and her instincts had made her wonder if he might be seeing her as a woman rather than just a friend. But, then, she had absolutely believed that Jerry was a good, faithful husband, which had turned out to be false, so her instincts obviously couldn't be trusted.

Pushing the foolish thoughts out of her mind, she took a swig of her drink and followed him outside.

Chapter 22

Tia was home from Dublin and bursting to fill Isla in on all the things she'd been unable to tell her over the phone during her time away. The last-minute booking she'd taken at the end of her London job had turned out to be a secretive affair, and she'd been made to sign an NDA as part of her contract. She'd worked with wealthy clients before, and even some celebrities. But never an actual billionaire.

It had been a fascinating experience to see how the people who lived at the top end of the money tree behaved behind the scenes. In her experience, wealthy clients could either be really polite and gracious, or totally arrogant and shitty to their staff. She had hit the jackpot with these clients and had been staying in a luxurious suite within the castle they had hired for their wedding. It had been a real eye-opener, and she had been blown away when the couple gave her a cheque for ten thousand pounds before she left, as a mark of their appreciation.

Sam had picked her up from the airport that morning and they had spent the rest of the day in bed. He had a conference in Scotland the following morning, so she had repaid the favour and dropped him off at the airport to catch his flight before driving over to Isla's that evening.

She hadn't told her friend that she was coming, because she'd wanted to surprise her. But she was the one who had been surprised when Isla answered the door holding the child who'd been staying with her. Isla hadn't mentioned him or his mother during their late-night phone calls while she was away. And Tia hadn't asked, afraid to get into another argument like the one they'd had before she left. It had been six weeks since then, and that was plenty of time for the woman to have found a place of her own, in Tia's opinion. But they were obviously still there; sucking her friend dry.

Seated at the kitchen table now, sipping the glass of wine she'd poured for herself, Tia frowned as she listened to Isla's sing-song voice floating out from a baby monitor that was sitting on the countertop. And that wasn't the only new gadget that had appeared since she had last been there. A child's push-along tricycle was propped against the wall behind the back door, and a large box filled with toys was standing in the corner of the snug behind her. And, in the garden, when she looked out through the window, she could see the silhouettes of what appeared to be a slide, a swing-set and a trampoline standing on the lawn.

If someone who didn't know Isla were to walk in right then and hear the way she was crooning the boy to sleep, they would automatically assume that she was his mother. And that disturbed Tia, because she feared that her friend was becoming far too involved with these people.

Tia was on her second glass of wine when Isla joined her after a while, and she raised an eyebrow when her friend flopped into a seat and sighed as if it was the first chance she'd had all day to sit down.

'Sorry I was so long,' Isla apologised. 'He usually goes straight to sleep, but I took him swimming this morning and he's still a bit hyper. I think it was the first time he's ever been and he was so excited, bless him.'

'Why didn't his mum take him?' Tia asked.

'She's, um, not here anymore,' Isla replied cagily as she reached for the glass of wine Tia had poured for her. 'Is this for me? Thanks, babe. Just what I needed.'

'So where is she and why are you taking care of the boy?' Tia asked. Then, frowning, she said, 'She's not…'

Guessing that Tia was asking if Melanie's condition had worsened, Isla shook her head. 'No, she's fine.' Then, sighing, she sat back, and said, 'A lot's changed while you've been gone, but I didn't want to tell you over the phone, because I knew you'd react badly and I didn't want it to affect your job.'

'So tell me now,' Tia ordered, sensing that she wasn't going to like what she heard.

'It started after I'd spoken to you the morning before you went,' Isla said. 'You'd told me to look for bank statements, so I went into Jerry's study to look through his paperwork when I got home after dropping Melanie and Jacob off at the hospital.'

'And?' Tia prompted when Isla paused to take a drink.

Aware that Isla now had her money, Tia was sure that her friend was about to tell her that she'd been right and there was a discrepancy between what she'd received and what the statements showed, so she was confused when Isla got up and took a mobile phone out of a drawer.

'And I found that.' Isla dropped the phone on the table and pushed it away as if it was contaminated.

'A phone?' Tia gave her a questioning look.

'Not just any phone; *Jerry's* phone,' said Isla. 'The one he told me he'd lost, but I now think he'd just hidden it so I wouldn't discover what was on it.'

'And what *was* on it?' Tia pressed when Isla took another swig of wine.

'Look for yourself.' Isla snatched up the phone and tapped in the code before bringing up the photos she'd found.

Tia's frown deepened as she scrolled through them. 'What the hell am I looking at?' she asked after a while.

'You're looking at the proof that Jerry did have an affair with Melanie,' Isla said bitterly. 'And that he's Jacob's father.'

'Sorry?' Tia shook her head. 'No way. She admitted that she'd lied about the affair.'

'Only to make me feel better,' said Isla. 'What she said in the car before that was the truth. They had an affair and he promised to leave me for her. He didn't leave because he was scared I'd get his money, so she ended it and let her ex think Jacob was his.'

'No, I don't believe it,' Tia murmured as she looked at the photos again. 'These photos are pretty blurry. Are you even sure it's Jerry?'

'I've looked at them a thousand times and it's definitely him,' Isla sighed. 'Even if there had been any doubt about them, the message couldn't be clearer. He begged her to take him back and let him be the father Jacob deserved. She refused and asked him to leave her alone. But if she'd agreed, he'd have gone.'

'Bastard!' Tia hissed. 'How the fuck could he do that to you. And with someone like *her*?'

'It doesn't matter what we think of her,' Isla said resignedly. 'He obviously loved her.'

'Well, thank fuck she didn't change her mind and take him back before he died, or he could have left everything to her instead,' Tia said. 'He's just lucky he *is* dead, because I'd be kicking his arse all the way to hell right now.'

She shoved the phone away in disgust and swallowed the rest of her drink before reaching for the bottle to refill both their glasses. She had always liked and respected Jerry, and it had never even crossed her mind that he might be capable of betraying Isla. He'd been a charmer, but not a player, and his love for Isla had shone through whenever they had all been together. At least, she'd *thought* it had. But if he'd managed to fool her so completely, she obviously wasn't as good a judge of character as she'd thought.

'Benny sent me this that same morning,' Isla said, pulling out her own phone to show Tia the photograph.

Tia squinted at the screen and shrugged. 'What am I supposed to be looking at?'

'That's Melanie and her ex,' Isla explained. 'Benny saw them on the Grange an hour after I'd dropped her off for her chemo session. He wasn't sure if it was her, so he took that and sent it to me. It was Jacob's pram that caught his eye. It's not very clear on there, but you can see it in the window behind them.'

'So this was taken when she was supposed to be having chemo?' Tia asked. 'Which means she was lying about having cancer. I fucking knew it! Didn't I tell you?'

'No, she's definitely got it,' Isla said. 'I confronted her when she came back that night and she admitted that she'd skipped the session to protect me. Carl had messaged and told her that he knew my address, and he threatened to come and kill us all if she didn't meet up with him.'

'What?' Tia's eyes widened.

'Don't panic,' Isla said. 'She reckons he was lying and only said it to force her to meet him. If he knew, he's had ample opportunity to do something. But nothing's happened since I kicked her out.'

'If you kicked her out, how come the kid's still here?' Tia asked.

Remembering that this was the first Tia had heard about any of this, Isla told her what had happened after she asked Melanie to leave. When she reached the part about giving Melanie the two grand, Tia held up her hand.

'Whoa! Hang on a minute ... Are you telling me you *paid* her to leave the child behind?'

'No, of course not,' said Isla. 'I gave her the money so she could book herself into a hotel or buy a ticket to see her family in Devon.'

'Without her son?'

'I didn't force her to leave him. I just couldn't let her take him back to Carl.'

'But she's his *mother*,' said Tia. 'It's none of your business what she does with him.'

'It is my business,' Isla argued. 'He's Jerry's son, so that makes me his stepmum. And I did everything for him when she was here, so what difference does it make?'

'Come on, Isla, you must see how bad that looks. If *I* think it looks dodgy, what do you think the police will make of it if she changes her mind and reports you?'

'She's not going to do that,' Isla insisted. 'She used the money to book herself into a B and B, and I gave her some more last week to help her get through her chemo without having to worry about anything. She's happy with the arrangement, and so am I, so I don't see why you've got a problem with it.'

Tia sat forward and rested her elbows on the table when she saw that Isla was getting agitated. 'Babe, I'm not having a go at you, but you could get into serious trouble if this goes wrong. I'm no fan of Melanie's, as well you know; but she came to you in a vulnerable state and you invited her in. Now you've kicked that same vulnerable woman out and given her money to let you keep her child. Legally, that could be seen as coercion.'

'I didn't coerce her into anything. She *chose* to leave him.'

'Under threat of being reported to social services if she didn't.

Knowing full well that she's terrified of them getting involved, because they'd already told her they would take him away if she went back to Carl after she'd had him.'

'Everything I've done is for Jacob,' Isla replied tersely. 'And I'd do it all over again, because he's safe here.'

'And what are you going to do when Melanie asks you to give him back?' Tia asked. 'Are you going to put more conditions on her?'

Isla didn't answer and Tia released a weary breath when she saw the anger flashing in her eyes.

'I know you think you're doing the right thing, but let's be honest here. You don't even know for sure that the kid is Jerry's.'

'Yes I do. The photos and message prove it.'

'No, they prove that Melanie had a baby, but not who the father was. She was still living with Carl all the way through the affair, so it could just as easily be his.'

'He's Jerry's.' Isla was adamant. 'I can feel it.'

'Is there any legal proof of that?' Tia asked. 'Is he named on the birth certificate?'

'I don't think so.' Isla shook her head. 'Melanie said she'd already realised that Jerry wasn't going to leave me by the time she had to register him, and she had to think about Jacob moving forward. Carl already thought he was his dad, so she decided not to tell him any different.'

'More lies.' Tia rolled her eyes.

'I don't blame her for lying to him,' Isla said defensively. 'She's absolutely terrified of the man. With good reason, considering how badly he treated her.'

'You sound like you feel sorry for the bitch. Are you forgetting that she started all this by fucking your husband?'

'Of course I haven't forgotten,' Isla scowled. 'And I'm not saying I've forgiven her, because I absolutely haven't. But she didn't know me back then, so she had no loyalty to me. It was *him* who betrayed me.'

'I'm not disputing that, but it wasn't your responsibility to save her,' said Tia. '*Or* her child,' she added pointedly. 'And he *is* hers, so she will want him back at some point.'

'I've already said I'll take him to her when she's found somewhere safe to live.'

'And how's she going to do that if she can't apply to the council or get benefits?' Tia asked. 'Or is that what you're hoping for?' She gave Isla a piercing look. 'I know it broke your heart when you had to give up on having children of your own, but please don't tell me you're hoping she'll leave him with you forever?'

'Are you being serious?' Isla gasped. 'I'm not doing this for *my* benefit; I'm trying to help a sick woman and keep an innocent child safe.'

'I know you *think* that's what you're doing, but you need to understand how this looks from the outside,' Tia argued. 'You gave her money to leave him with you. And now you're trying to justify it by claiming some sort of special interest because you were married to his father. But, the truth is, you don't even know that Jerry *is* his father.'

'I've had enough of this,' Isla said, abruptly standing up. 'It's probably best if you leave.'

'So now you're kicking *me* out?' Tia raised an eyebrow. Isla didn't answer, so she reached for her handbag. 'Fine. If that's what you want, I'll go. But we both know there's only one way this is going to end. The longer that boy's here, the more attached you're going to get. And when Melanie takes him back, which she will, because she and Carl are his *legal* parents, you'll be left with nothing. And you'll be lucky if they don't get you arrested for kidnapping him, as well.'

'Are you done?' Isla glared at her.

'Yep.' Tia stood up. 'I won't bother you again while you're determined to keep playing happy families. But you know where I am when you're ready to talk honestly.'

Isla walked out into the hallway without replying and yanked the front door open. Tia stepped outside and turned to say goodbye, but Isla closed the door in her face. Shaking her head, Tia climbed into her car and waited for the gate to open before driving out onto the road. She could see Isla heading for a huge fall. But she'd said her piece and Isla hadn't wanted to hear it, so there wasn't much more she could do.

Isla watched through the spyhole until Tia had gone and then pressed the fob to close the gate before going back to the kitchen. She poured herself a glass of whisky and swigged on it as she paced the floor. She'd never really liked the taste, but it calmed her nerves more effectively than wine, so she'd taken to drinking a glass or two whenever she felt stressed out. And, right then, she needed it more than ever.

She couldn't believe that Tia had gone for her like that. They had always been more like sisters than friends, and she had respected her opinions even when she hadn't always agreed with them. But Tia had crossed a huge red line tonight, and she wasn't sure there was any way back from that.

As she paced, the doorbell suddenly rang. Guessing that Tia had come back, either to apologise or to hurl more insults her way, Isla ignored it. The bell rang again, and then a message popped up on her phone. It was from Benny, telling her that he was outside and asking her to please hurry up and let him in, because he desperately needed the toilet. Unable to bring herself to ignore him when he had gone out of his way to support her while Tia had been away, Isla walked to the front door and opened the gate.

'Thanks,' Benny gasped, leaping out of the car after parking up. 'I nearly had to take a leak in your hedge.'

He kissed her on the cheek, then brushed past her and rushed to the downstairs toilet at the other end of the hallway. Isla went back to the kitchen, poured them both a drink and flopped back into her seat at the table.

'I really need to start reminding myself to go to the loo before I drive over here,' Benny said when he joined her a few moments later. 'It's murder at rush hour, and my bladder's not as strong as it used to be. And to think I used to laugh at my old man for planning our holidays around the number of motorway services we'd pass on—'

'Did Tia tell you to come?' Isla interrupted, sliding his glass across the table to him.

'Tia?' Benny gave her a questioning look. 'No, why? I promised to help my neighbour with some DIY and needed to pick up the screwdrivers I left when I put the garden stuff together for you.'

'She's just been here giving me the riot act about Melanie and Jacob,' Isla muttered. 'I kicked her out, so I thought she might have rung you and asked you to come over and check on me.'

'I didn't even know she was back. But even if she had rung me, there's no way I'd have got here that fast if she's only just left,' Benny said, gazing at her with concern when he saw how dejected she looked. 'What happened?'

'She said some of the worst things she ever could have said to me,' Isla replied, blinking furiously when tears flooded her eyes.

'Hey, come on, I'm sure it can't be that bad.' Benny walked around the table and perched on the chair next to hers. 'Tell me what she said.'

'She basically accused me of forcing Melanie to give Jacob to me,' Isla sobbed, resting her head on his chest when he pulled her into his arms. 'And she as good as said I *bought* him to replace the babies I lost. But that's not why I gave Melanie that money. I was genuinely trying to help her, and I only asked her to leave Jacob with me to give her the space to do that.'

'I know, and I'm sure Tia didn't mean it the way you took it,' Benny said. 'She's your best friend, so she's probably just worried about you.'

'You didn't hear her,' Isla cried. 'She wasn't even trying to see it from my point of view. She just thinks I'm doing this for myself.'

She went on to relay everything Tia had said, and Benny listened in silence until she'd finished.

'OK, I can see why you're upset, because I know you're doing your best,' he soothed. 'But I do kind of get why she's concerned.'

'Oh, my God!' Isla jerked back from him. 'You've spent loads of time with us and you haven't once said you thought I was doing anything wrong, so how can you suddenly start siding with *her*.'

'I'm not siding with her,' Benny replied carefully. 'And I'm not knocking you for what you're doing, because I've already told you Jacob's lucky to have you. But do you think she might have a point about how attached you're getting to him? I can tell you're really fond of him, and he obviously loves you, so this could get messy when Melanie asks you to give him back.'

'So why haven't you said any of this while you've been here playing with him and telling me what a great job I'm doing?' Isla demanded. 'And why did you help me put all that stuff together in the garden if you thought it was such a bad idea?'

'You have done a great job,' Benny replied. 'I just don't want to see you getting hurt. And I'm sure that's all Tia's concerned about, as well.'

'I'm not going to get hurt,' Isla sniffed. 'I know this is only temporary, and I'm good with that. But I'm not going to stop showing him love while he's here and make him think he's done something wrong.'

'Nobody's telling you to change the way you act around him. Just don't get *too* attached.'

Isla reached for her glass and took a swig of her drink. She had loved taking care of Jacob, and it was clear that he'd thoroughly enjoyed his time with her, too. He'd been as good as gold since Melanie had left and barely seemed to have noticed that she was gone. That was hardly surprising because Melanie hadn't done much for him when she'd been there, so he was already used to Isla feeding him, playing with him and rocking him to sleep. But that didn't mean she was trying to replace Melanie, and Tia was dead wrong about giving the money to her as payment for keeping him forever.

Benny finished his drink and gestured towards Isla's almost-empty glass. 'Are you done with that?'

Isla swallowed the last of her drink and held the glass out to him, thinking that he was going to refill it. Instead, he carried them to the sink and rinsed them both out.

'Hey, I need that,' she protested.

'No, you don't,' he said, switching the kettle on and dropping teabags into two cups before walking up behind her. 'You're tense as hell, so let's get rid of some of these knots you've got yourself tied up in,' he went on, moving her hair aside and massaging her shoulders. 'As soon as you're relaxed, we'll have a nice strong cup of tea and set the world to rights – as my old mum used to say.'

'Never mind quoting her, you sound like you're turning into her,' Isla snorted.

'And she's back,' Benny grinned, leaning down to kiss her neck before giving her shoulders one last gentle squeeze.

Isla sucked in a sharp breath at the feel of his lips on her flesh. Thankfully, Benny had already turned away from her to make the brews so he didn't notice how flustered she was.

'OK, let's get down to it,' Benny said when he carried their cups to the table a minute later. 'How are we going to sort this out with you and Tia? I know she upset you, but I think this is fixable. So how about we get her over here tomorrow and I'll mediate while you two thrash it out.'

'Have you met Tia?' Isla said drily. 'She's stubborn as hell, so she's not going to change her opinion on this. In her mind, she's right and I'm wrong, end of.'

'Well, I can see it from both sides, so I'll be able to give her my perspective without it turning into an argument.'

'Good luck with that.'

'Will you at least give me the chance to try?' Benny asked. 'I've only just reconnected with you both, and I don't want this to split us apart again. We're the Three Musketeers, don't forget. All for one, and one for all – and all that shizz.'

'That was a lifetime ago. We were just stupid kids.'

'Maybe so, but we were mates and we stuck together,' said Benny. 'I still think it's hilarious that I thought you and Tia were into each other, while you two thought I was gay. But that's kind of my point. No matter what, we all had each other's backs and protected each other's secrets. And I'm sure Tia's only trying to protect you now.'

Isla fell quiet and sipped her tea as she mulled over what Benny had said. Now he had taken the heat out of her anger and revealed that he, too, had been worrying about her, she had to admit that it possibly did look as if she was growing too attached to Jacob. The affection she now felt for him had grown gradually and naturally, but it didn't mean she was trying to replace his real mother. She just wanted to keep him safe and allow him to flourish.

'Right, I've messaged Tia and she's agreed to come over for a chat,' Benny said, snapping Isla out of her thoughts. 'But she's asking if we can do it the day after tomorrow, when Sam gets home from Scotland, so I can meet him. Is that OK with you?'

'Yeah, whatever,' Isla murmured.

'Chin up,' Benny said, reaching across to squeeze her hand. 'We'll get this sorted.'

Isla nodded and gave him a weary smile.

'You look wiped, so I'll grab my tools and get going,' Benny said, standing up to take his cup to the sink. 'Is there anything you need me to do before I go?'

'No thanks, I'm good,' Isla said. 'I'll probably head to bed. Jacob's been getting up around six in the morning since you put up the swing and slide for him, so I need all the sleep I can get. I know he's excited to get out there, but, my God, it's exhausting.'

'I can stay over, if you want?' Benny offered. 'I'm an early riser, so I don't mind taking care of him in the morning while you have a lie-in.'

'That would be bliss,' Isla sighed. 'I can't remember the last time I got to do that.'

'Cool. I'll take the sofa in the snug.'

'Don't be daft. I've got plenty of spare rooms.'

'Oh yeah,' Benny grinned. 'I keep forgetting we're in a mansion.'

'It's far from a mansion,' Isla protested.

'It's a damn sight bigger than my two-up two-down,' Benny laughed as he followed her out into the hall and up the stairs.

'I do remember where I came from,' Isla said, aware that he was only teasing as she walked him past her bedroom and opened the door of the next room along. 'This one OK for you?' she asked, turning on the light.

'Perfect,' Benny said, looking around as he tossed his jacket onto the king-size bed. 'You've made a lovely home for yourself.'

'It was all here long before I moved in, so I can't take any credit,' Isla replied modestly. 'I'm just next door,' she went on as she backed out onto the landing. 'Let me know if you need anything.'

'Will do,' Benny said. 'See you in the morning. And make sure you have that lie-in.'

'Trust me, I'm going to,' Isla assured him, smiling as she pulled the door to.

Chapter 23

Benny's presence in the house had made Isla feel safe, and she'd slept soundly for the first time since Jerry had died. It was gone 9 a.m. when she woke up, and she smiled when she saw a note from Benny propped up against her bedside lamp; letting her know that he'd taken Jacob downstairs so she could have a lie-in. After taking a quick shower, she made her way down to the kitchen, where she was greeted by the sound of Jacob laughing in the garden as Benny gently pushed him on the swing.

The high chair was standing beside the table and she saw that Benny had already wiped it down. He had also washed out Jacob's bottle and the bowls they had used for their cereal. Jerry had never washed anything, declaring housework to be her domain while he took care of the finances. It hadn't bothered her at the time, because she'd loved taking care of their home. But Benny's small act of consideration had touched her, and she was smiling as she switched the kettle on to make coffee for them both.

She had been on autopilot for so long, she hadn't realised how physically and mentally drained she was. She imagined it was exactly how new mothers felt in the first weeks and months after giving birth; when their time was no longer their own and they had to make compromises and fit everything in around their children. As exhausting as it was, she had enjoyed every moment she'd spent with Jacob and had no regrets about asking Melanie to leave him with her. But she was hugely grateful that Benny had offered to stay the night to give her a break. She felt refreshed after her sleep, and it had been lovely to take a shower without having to worry about Jacob waking up and hurting himself while the water was running. He was getting more active and daring by the day, and she'd already caught him trying to climb out of his cot a couple of times. It had been stupid to buy it, because he had clearly outgrown it and needed an actual bed instead.

She decided that she would ask Benny if he fancied going shopping with her. If he was with her to help with Jacob, she would treat him to lunch at the pub overlooking the canal. When she'd gone there with Tia, she'd noticed a small play area for the customers' children, and she was sure that Jacob would have a great time.

Coffees made, Isla carried them out onto the patio and watched from the bench as Benny played with Jacob. It was a beautiful sight, and she felt a momentary twinge of sadness that she had never had the opportunity to see Jerry playing with a child of theirs. It had been one of her heartfelt wishes to fill their home with the sound of children laughing and playing. It hadn't been meant to be, but at least *his* child was able to experience the kind of life she would have loved to have given hers. And, strangely, she was OK with that. Most likely, she realised, because she had already formed quite a strong bond with the boy before she had found out the truth. Whatever the reason, this house had belonged to his father, which made it his rightful home.

'Hey, when did you come down?' Benny asked when he suddenly noticed her.

'About ten minutes ago,' she told him. 'But you looked like you were having fun, so I didn't want to interrupt.'

'She could never interrupt us, could she, little man?' Benny grinned, scooping Jacob out of the swing and carrying him over to her.

Taking the boy from him when Jacob held out his arms to her, Isla sat him on her lap, cooing, 'Morning, sweetie. Have you been having a nice time?'

'We both have,' Benny said, lifting his cup off the table and taking a swig. 'Did you get a good sleep?'

'Yes, it was lovely,' she said gratefully, putting Jacob down when he started wriggling. 'Thanks again. I didn't realise how much I needed it.'

'Any time.' Benny winked at her and reached down to ruffle Jacob's hair.

'You big softie,' Isla teased.

'Don't say that,' Benny hissed as he sat beside her. 'You'll ruin my tough guy image. Kiddo there thinks I'm the Hulk.'

'I wonder why,' Isla laughed, plucking several strands of grass out of his hair. 'You look like you've been rolling around on the lawn.'

'I was trying to teach him to roly-poly, but he was more interested in trying to get out of your back gate,' Benny said, nodding towards it. 'Did you know you'd left it open? Looks like a pretty steep slope back there, so you might want to keep an eye on that while he's here.'

'I'm sure it was shut,' Isla said, frowning as she gazed at the gate. Then, sighing when she remembered that the last time she'd gone near the gate was on the day she'd found Jerry's body, she said, 'I must have forgotten to lock it last time I closed it. The wind probably blew it open.'

'Well, it's bolted now,' Benny assured her, settling back in his seat. He sipped on his coffee and gazed around. 'This is the first time I've seen this garden in daylight, and it's way bigger than it looks in the dark. Really private, too, with the trees blocking out the neighbours' view. My yard's so small, every bugger off the estate can see right through my kitchen window.'

'You keep talking as if I don't know what the Grange is like,' Isla laughed. 'I *was* born and raised there.'

'Bet you wouldn't come back though, would you?' Benny asked.

'Not by choice,' Isla replied truthfully. 'And that's not because I think I'm too grand,' she added, in case she'd given him that wrong impression. 'But now my mum and all my old friends and neighbours have moved on, there's nothing there for me anymore.'

'Oh, so I don't count?' Benny gave her a mock-offended look.

'You're the one and only reason I would go back,' Isla said. 'But I'm sure you're not going to stay there forever, are you?'

'Nah, doubt it.' Benny pulled a face. 'I mean, there's nothing wrong with it. But like you said, most of our old mates have gone now, and I'm surrounded by Karens and Darrens. Why d'you think I offered to stay here last night?' he added with a twinkle in his eye. 'You don't think that was to give *you* a break, do you?'

Aware that he was joking, Isla smiled, and said, 'You can stay any time you like. You don't need an excuse.'

'Careful, I might just take you up on that,' Benny replied.

'You can stay again tonight, if you like?' Isla said. 'I was going to ask you to come and help me pick out a bed for this one, so you'd be doing me a massive favour if you stick around to help me put it up. I'll treat you to dinner.'

'Hmmm … that might be a bit tricky, so let me just check my diary,' Benny replied, reaching into the back pocket of his jeans.

He tugged on something and then pulled his empty hand out and mimed the action of opening a book and flicking through the pages. Then, closing the invisible book, he shrugged, and said, 'Looks like you're in luck. I've got nothing on today.'

'Idiot,' Isla laughed, slapping his arm.

None of the village shops had what she needed, so Isla drove to a small market town a few miles away. She found the perfect child-size bed with guard rails in the first shop they visited and arranged for it to be delivered later that afternoon, then she and Benny, who insisted on pushing Jacob in the new pushchair she'd bought to replace the grotty yellow one, went for a stroll around the town. They came across an ancient arcade of quaint little shops selling antiques, vintage clothes and old vinyl records. Isla was drawn straight in to one that sold crystals, tarot cards and other witchy stuff, and she immediately zoomed in on a large raw amethyst rock that she thought would look great on her hall table. She then picked out a bronze statue of a curvaceous witch holding a broomstick, with a cat at her feet, and carried it and the rock to the till.

'What on earth is that?' Benny asked, pulling his face when he saw the statue up close.

'It's for Tia,' Isla said. 'A witch for a witch.'

'I know you've fallen out, but that's a bit harsh, isn't it?'

'She *is* a witch, so, trust me, she'll love it,' Isla said. 'I thought I'd best get a peace offering, seeing as you're forcing me to talk to her.'

'I'm not forcing you; you agreed,' Benny countered. 'But, just so you know, if she starts any spooky nonsense around me, I'm gone.'

'Oh yeah, I forgot you're scared of ghosts,' Isla teased. 'Don't worry; she doesn't *do* anything,' she added when Benny frowned.

'She just senses stuff about people and situations. And she's usually right, so I can't knock her.'

Benny looked at her as if she was insane. Then, giving an exaggerated shudder, he pushed the pram towards the door, saying, 'Come on, kiddo; let's get you away from the crazy lady.'

Laughing, Isla followed him out of the shop.

Chapter 24

Tia was relieved to see Benny's car already parked on the driveway when she and Sam arrived at Isla's house the following evening. This meeting had been his idea, but she had no clue if Isla actually wanted to see her or had been cajoled into it. Either way, it was going to be awkward, because Tia was still pissed off with Isla for kicking her out. And Isla was just as stubborn as she was, so it could easily have turned into a battle of wills if Benny hadn't intervened. She knew that Isla had convinced herself that she was doing this out of the goodness of her heart, but the fact that money had exchanged hands had set off massive alarm bells for her.

Isla opened the front door as Tia and Sam were getting out of the car, and Sam immediately walked over to hug her.

'How are you doing?' he asked. 'You're looking well.'

'Thanks,' Isla said, nervously eyeing Tia over his shoulder. 'So are you.'

Benny came out behind Isla and extended his hand when Sam released her.

'You must be the amazing Sam I've been hearing about,' he quipped, pulling Sam in for a man-hug as they shook hands. 'Lovely to meet you at last.'

'You too, mate,' Sam replied gruffly. 'But just so we're clear, I'm straight.'

'Oh no.' Benny pulled back and covered his mouth with both hands in mock horror. 'Please don't break my heart when we've only just met.'

'Sam's messing with you, 'cos I told him me and Isla thought you were gay,' Tia said, rolling her eyes in despair. 'And he's messing with you,' she added to Sam. 'Now, if you've both finished acting like children, go and get a beer.'

'Yes, dear,' Sam replied meekly. Then, both grinning, he and Benny walked inside and headed to the kitchen.

Still on the doorstep, Isla and Tia looked at one another, each waiting for the other to speak. Breaking first, Isla said, 'OK, I'm sorry.'

'For what?' Tia arched an eyebrow.

'Don't play games,' Isla sighed. 'I shouldn't have kicked you out, and I apologise for that. You hurt me, and I guess I overreacted. But it shouldn't have gone that far.'

'No, it shouldn't,' Tia agreed. 'And I apologise if I hurt you, because that wasn't my intention. You threw me for a loop, because you hadn't told me anything, so I just gave you my honest opinion as someone looking at the situation from the outside. And I *was* on the outside, because you deliberately kept this from me.'

'Only because you were working and I didn't want to stress you out,' Isla said. 'Look how you reacted when I *did* tell you. That's what I was trying to avoid. But you know everything now, so where do we go from here?'

'That's up to you,' Tia said. 'I love you to bits, but I really don't like this situation you've got yourself involved in. I don't trust that bitch and it stinks to high heaven that she took money for her child.'

'I know how it looks, but it was my idea, not hers,' Isla said. 'I just didn't want her taking him back to her ex.'

'I get why you did it, but that's another thing that worries me,' Tia said. 'I know you said she thought he was lying when he claimed to know your address, but what if he *does* know? You've already seen what he did to her, and I'm scared for you, babe. You're out here on your own, and all your neighbours are old, so they won't be any use if you need help. Look how long it took for one of them to hear you when you were screaming for help after finding Jerry. And that was in the daytime. If anything happens at night, you'll have no chance.'

'Don't say that,' Isla shivered.

'I'm sorry, but you really need to think about your security,' said Tia. 'I've told you numerous times to get cameras.'

'I know.' Isla held up her hands to indicate that she didn't want to go over that ground again. 'And now I've got the money, I'll do it. But please stop worrying about me, because I'm fine right now. Benny's been coming over a lot while you were away, and he's stayed over for the last couple of nights to give me a break with Jacob. I've been able to catch up on sleep, which has helped massively. And Benny and Jacob have really bonded. You should see them together; it's so sweet.'

Tia narrowed her eyes with suspicion when she noticed that Isla's face had lit up as soon as she started talking about Benny.

'What's going on?' she asked. 'Are you and him a thing now?'

'No!'

'So why are you blushing like a teenage girl?' Tia teased. 'You always used to get flustered around him, and you're doing it again, so something's obviously happened.'

'*Sshhh*!' Isla hissed, casting a glance back over her shoulder. 'Nothing's happened. It was just a bit of a crush, but I've got it under control now.'

'Wow,' Tia grinned. 'Does *he* know?'

'No. And I don't want him to, so please don't say anything,' Isla whispered. 'Please, I'm begging you, don't even joke about it.'

'I won't say anything,' Tia assured her. 'But if you ask me, you could do worse.'

'We're friends,' Isla insisted. 'And he treats you exactly the same way he treats me, so he obviously doesn't see me as anything special. Let's leave it at that. OK?'

'We'll see.' Tia gave a sly smile. Then, more seriously, she said, 'Anyway, thanks for apologising, but I need to apologise as well. I should never have said that about you taking the boy as a replacement for your own babies. It was below the belt, and I'm really sorry if I hurt you.'

'It's OK; I know you didn't mean it the way I took it,' Isla sighed. 'And I'm glad Benny made me see sense, because I've really missed you.'

'Friends?' Tia held out her pinkie finger.

'And you accuse *me* of acting like a teenager,' Isla laughed.

'Just do it, or it's not a pact,' Tia ordered.

Still laughing at the absurdity of it, Isla hooked her own pinkie around Tia's and they did the old shake they used to do when they were kids.

Tia hugged her, and said, 'Now I've got you back, we need to spend more time together. Benny told me how exhausted you've been, so I want to support you while I've got the next few weeks free.'

'You don't have to do that,' Isla insisted. 'I know you don't really want to be around Jacob. And Benny's already given me a break, so I'll be fine.'

'It's his mother I've got a problem with, not him,' Tia countered. 'But she's not here anymore, so I'm going to forget about her and concentrate on helping you and getting to know him. Where is he?'

'In his new bed,' Isla said. 'It's his first night in it and he was so excited when he saw it after Benny put it together. I usually have to stay with him until he falls asleep, but he went out like a light as soon as his head hit the pillow tonight.'

'Ah, well, I'll meet him next time.'

'You're going to love him. And thanks for offering to help. But be warned; he's growing up fast and you need eyes in the back of your head to keep up with him.'

'Benny's already told me he's a little firecracker, so I know what I'm letting myself in for,' Tia said. 'I'm just sorry you never got this chance to bring up your own kids, 'cos it sounds like you'd have been a brilliant mother.'

'Thank you.' Isla smiled. 'That means a lot.'

'OK, that's enough of the sloppy stuff,' Tia said, linking her arm through Isla's when she saw tears in her eyes. 'Let's go see what our men are up to.'

'*Your* man, our *friend*,' Isla corrected her.

'Whatever,' Tia chuckled, squeezing her arm as they walked inside.

'Oh, before we go out, I've got something for you,' Isla said, rushing over to the hall table to retrieve the gift bag she'd put there earlier. 'It's just a little something to say sorry for kicking off at you. Hope you like it.'

Tia opened the bag and lifted out the witch figurine. 'Oh, wow,' she murmured, turning it around to look it over properly. 'It's amazing. Thank you, darling. But you didn't need to.'

'Yes I did,' Isla insisted. 'And there's a pack of angel cards in there, as well. But you're not allowed to take them out while Benny's here,' she added with a chuckle. 'He was with me when I bought them and they really freaked him out.'

'He's such a wuss.' Isla laughed. 'But I'll leave them in here if they bother him that much. Wouldn't want to scare him away and deprive you of his company now you've admitted you've got the hots for him.'

'Seriously?' Isla gave her a warning look. 'I swear to God, if you say anything, I'll never speak to you again.'

'Relax,' Tia purred linking arms with her again. 'My lips are sealed.'

Benny and Sam were sitting out on the patio, bonding over their beers, so Isla and Tia grabbed a bottle of wine and a couple of glasses and went out to join them.

Ice firmly broken, they spent the next few hours chatting and drinking. It was a lovely, relaxed atmosphere, and Isla couldn't help but notice what a contrast it was to the parties she had hosted for Jerry's friends over the years. At those parties, the wives and husbands had always split into separate groups after dinner. Isla had never really felt that she belonged, and she now suspected that the wives had deliberately kept her at a distance so she didn't forget her place. It hadn't mattered that she had loved Jerry and had tried really hard to be a good wife. In their eyes, she had never been worthy of him – or them. To a degree, Isla had believed that, too. But now she knew that Jerry had lied and cheated his way through their marriage, she felt like she had wasted fifteen years of her life on people who didn't deserve her. Now, with her real friends around her, she was beginning to feel like the old Isla again, and that made her happier than she had felt in a very long time.

Chapter 25

Six weeks had passed since Isla had heard from Melanie after sending Benny to give her the money. The silence worried her, because she had no idea if something bad had happened – or if Melanie was even still alive. But at the same time, she dreaded receiving the call to say that Melanie was ready to take Jacob back. He'd been with her for so long, she could hardly remember what it was like to not have him around. She loved taking care of him and watching him thrive, and the sound of his laughter filled her heart with joy. She knew that the day would eventually come when she would have to hand him over, but until then, she was determined to enjoy every moment she had with him.

Tia was also concerned, but for different reasons. She had been vehemently opposed to Isla's involvement with Melanie at the start, but after seeing how well Jacob was doing and how happy he was, she had changed her mind and now fully supported her friend. In her opinion, Melanie's silence showed that she didn't give a crap about her son. So, over a drink one evening after Isla had put the boy to bed, she advised her to get something put in place to safeguard her and Jacob.

'Like what?' Isla asked.

'The way I see it, she's only interested in the money,' Tia said. 'She took the first lot and you didn't hear from her again until it ran out. It's been weeks since you gave her the second lot, so I reckon you're due for a call soon asking for more. If I'm right, what are you going to do? Pay her off for another few weeks, then another, and another? Is this going to be it from now on, or is there a finish line?'

'I haven't thought that far ahead,' Isla admitted. 'For now, I'm happy to support her through her treatment. But, after that, I honestly don't know.'

'What if she's using that money to pay a solicitor to challenge Jerry's will?' Tia mused. 'As Jacob's mother, she'd be able to do that on his behalf.'

'I doubt she could do that,' Isla said. 'And I don't think it would even be possible now. It was all settled weeks ago.'

'I wouldn't put it past her to try,' said Tia. 'If I was you, I'd get legal advice, just in case. She hasn't seen Jacob for months, so what if she leaves him here for another ten years, then suddenly turns up and demands him back? You wouldn't have a leg to stand on.'

'I know,' Isla sighed. 'But I can't risk going legal with this, because it'll probably be me who ends up in trouble.'

'No you wouldn't,' Tia argued. 'His loser parents clearly don't give a toss, but it's obvious you really care about him.'

'I think Melanie does care,' Isla said quietly. 'But she knows he's better off here for now, so she's trying to do the right thing by him. That can't be easy for her, given what she's going through.'

'Don't do that,' Tia said sternly. 'You've already given her far more help than she deserved, and you're still supporting her, so don't start feeling guilty. She chose her path when she went back to Carl after she'd been warned she would lose her baby because of him. Jacob's the only one who doesn't have a choice in any of this, so stop thinking about her as the victim.'

'You're right,' Isla agreed. Then, sighing, she said, 'And I know what you mean about trying to safeguard him legally, but I can't risk it. Look how you reacted when you heard I'd paid her to leave Jacob with me. I know I got mad, but you were right, it does look really bad. I kicked her out, knowing that she's got cancer and had nowhere to go after escaping a violent relationship. If the police heard that, they'd think exactly what *you* thought: that I blackmailed a vulnerable woman into giving me her child. No one in their right mind would let me keep him if they found out about that. So, for now, I think it's better if I stay quiet and carry on doing what I'm doing.'

'So you're going to pay her if she calls asking for more money?'

'If that's what it takes to keep him safe.' Isla shrugged. 'Whatever happens after that, I'll deal with it as and when it comes.'

'Personally, I'd tell her to sling her hook,' Tia said. 'But I get why you're doing it, so I'll support you whatever.'

'Thanks.' Isla smiled. 'I'm not sure how I'd have managed to get this far if I hadn't had you and Benny to help me. You've both been amazing.'

'That's what friends are for,' Tia said, raising her glass. 'What are you doing?' she asked when Isla clinked her glass against it. 'I'm asking for a refill, not raising a toast to you. Christ, I always knew you had a big ego, but that's off the scale.'

'Shut up,' Isla laughed, aware that she was joking. 'I do not have a big ego.'

'Oh, really,' Tia gave a bemused smile.

'*Really*,' Isla said, reaching for the wine bottle.

As soon as she began to pour, her phone started ringing and Tia leaned forward to look at the screen when it rattled across the tabletop.

'Talk of the flaming devil,' she snorted when she saw Melanie's name on the screen. 'How mad is that? Bang on cue.'

Isla's stomach turned over and she quickly put the bottle down.

'Don't answer it,' Tia ordered when she went to pick up the phone. 'We know what she wants, but you've been drinking, so you can't go to her.'

'What if something's wrong?' Isla murmured. 'I can't just ignore her.'

'Yes, you can,' Tia said firmly. 'She needs to learn that she can't go silent for six whole weeks, then ring you out of the blue whenever she feels like it. She can damn well wait till morning.'

Isla withdrew her hand, but Tia could see the worry lines creasing her brow as she stared at the still ringing phone. Determined not to let it spoil the lovely night they'd been having, she snatched up the phone, dismissed the call and then switched it off.

'There. Dealt with,' she said, handing Isla's glass to her. 'I know you've decided to carry on helping her, but there's nothing she could need so urgently that can't wait a few hours. So top that up, have a drink and relax. OK?'

Isla nodded and released a tense breath, then filled their glasses and sat back.

Over in Manchester, Melanie's heart was pounding as Carl paced the floor in front of her. 'She's not answering,' she said, eyeing him nervously after her fourth attempt to call Isla.

'Try again,' he ordered.

'It's going straight to voicemail,' she said. 'It is quite late and she goes to bed early, so she's probably asleep.'

'Piss-taking bitch,' Carl hissed, booting an empty beer can

across the room. 'If she thinks she can mess me around, she's in for a fucking shock.'

'She doesn't know I'm with you, so she's not messing you around,' Melanie said quietly.

'Don't you fucking *dare* defend that whore,' Carl yelled, towering over her and slamming his fists down on the arms of her chair. 'She owes me, and I'm this fucking close to sacking the whole thing off and doing things my way.'

'She'll give me the money,' Melanie croaked, bracing herself in case he started lashing out. 'But she had to go to the bank last time, and no banks are open now, so we'll have to wait.'

'I *can't* fucking wait,' Carl bellowed. 'Don't you get it, you stupid bitch? He's coming round for it tomorrow, and if it's not here, it's game over. Is that what you want? You want him to fucking off me? 'Cos that's what's going to happen if I don't get the money.'

Temper flaring when his spittle dotted her face, Melanie yelled back at him: 'Stop fucking spitting on me, and stop blaming me for this shit that *you* caused. You're the one who ran up another debt with him after paying off the first one. So this is on you, not me.'

Carl seized her by the throat and forced her head back. Then, pressing his forehead hard against hers, he hissed, 'Keep mouthing off and watch what happens, bitch.'

'Stop it!' she gasped, desperately trying to prise his hand off. 'I can't breathe.'

'Good, 'cos you're a waste of fucking oxygen and you don't deserve to breathe,' he spat, squeezing even harder. 'If that two grand ain't in my hand by morning, I'm gonna kill you, and then I'll kill her and the brat. You got that?'

Eyes bulging, Melanie nodded weakly.

'You'd better,' he warned.

Sucking in a sharp breath when he abruptly released her, Melanie watched as he grabbed his jacket and stormed out. His mood swings were becoming more frequent and more violent, and she was constantly walking on eggshells; terrified that he was going to flip out and seriously hurt her – or worse. Heart hammering in her chest now, she leapt up when she heard the front door open and then slam shut behind him. Covering her mouth with her hand when her stomach churned, she rushed to the bathroom, reaching the toilet just in time to throw up.

She hadn't eaten that day, because the last of their food had run out and Carl had refused to hand over any of the money he had left to buy more. *He* had eaten, though, because she'd smelled the onion on his breath when he had pressed his head up against hers. With nothing left in her stomach now but bile, she rested her head on the rim of the stinking bowl and waited for the nausea to subside. A sudden cramping in her stomach doubled her over, and she hugged herself and rocked backwards and forwards until it passed.

It felt like period pains, so she pulled herself up to her feet and looked in the cabinet for a Tampax. There were none in there, so she wadded some tissue and stuffed it inside her knickers before going over to the sink to rinse the bitter taste out of her mouth. The reflection in the mirror caught her off guard, and she stared at herself in disgust; taking in the lank, greasy hair, her pallid complexion and the dark hollows under her eyes. Her throat was red and she blinked back tears when she saw the outlines of finger-shaped bruises that were beginning to form.

After rinsing her mouth and splashing water on her face, she went into the bedroom and dug out a polo-necked sweater to hide the bruising. Then, grabbing her jacket and her keys, she let herself out and pulled the door shut behind her.

In the communal hallway, she bit her lip as she scanned

her neighbours' doors. None of the other residents bothered with her, because they had all had run-ins with Carl at some time or other. But there was one she hadn't yet met: the man who'd moved in next door while she was away. She'd heard him banging on the wall whenever Carl had the TV or stereo on too loud, and she knew he had confronted Carl in person a few times. But she had never had any interactions with him, so she hoped he wouldn't hold Carl's actions against her now.

Ashamed that she even needed to do this, she gingerly tapped on the man's door. She heard footsteps approaching it a few seconds later, and then the sound of two bolts being drawn back before it creaked open an inch.

'What do you want?' the man asked, staring out at her through the crack with unfriendly eyes.

'Hi, sorry to bother you,' she said politely. 'I'm Mel, from next door. I'm really sorry to disturb you, but I need to ask you a favour.'

The man drew his head back and gave her an incredulous look. 'Are you kidding me? After all the shit you two have put me through, you've got the cheek to ask a favour? Get to fuck.'

'Please,' Melanie pleaded, putting out her hand to stop him slamming the door in her face. 'I'm really sorry for everything that's happened, but I wasn't even living here through most of that. And I wouldn't be asking anything of you now if I wasn't desperate.'

The man narrowed his eyes and peered at her for several moments. Then, sighing, he said, 'I reckon I'm not the only one he's a prick to, eh? I've heard the way he yells at you. He's a sack of shit, if you ask me. Why d'you put up with it?'

'I've got nowhere else to go,' Melanie murmured, dipping her gaze in shame.

'And where is he now?' the man asked, popping his head out to check if Carl was in the hall.

'I don't know,' Melanie shrugged. 'He went out and I probably won't see him again tonight.'

'So this favour… Is it for you or *him*?'

'Me,' Melanie lied. 'My, um, son's staying with a friend and she just rang to tell me he's not well, so I need to go over there. But I don't have any money for the bus, so I was going to ask if you could lend me ten pounds? I know you probably think I'm really cheeky, but I promise I'll pay you back.'

The man pursed his lips thoughtfully and Melanie was sure he was going to say no, so she was shocked when he shoved his hand into his pocket and pulled out a handful of notes. He took a tenner from them and handed it to her.

'Thank you so much,' she said gratefully. 'I'll get it back to you as soon as I can.'

'Don't worry about it,' he said, giving her a sympathetic smile. 'Go see your son. Then do *yourself* a favour and get rid of that clown. You seem like a decent girl and you deserve better than the shit I hear going on behind that wall.'

Embarrassed, Melanie nodded her agreement, then thanked him again before quickly scuttling away.

Chapter 26

It was almost 10 p.m. when the bus dropped Melanie off in the village. It was always deserted at night, and there was an eerie quiet that she had never experienced anywhere else. That silence and the almost pitch darkness between lampposts unnerved her as she set off on the walk to Isla's house. But it wasn't nearly as scary as the thought of what would happen tomorrow if she didn't get some money, so she continued on her way.

There were no lights on in Isla's house, and the gate was closed and locked. Melanie had tried to call her several times on the way over, and had also sent a couple of messages, both of which were still marked as unread. She knew that Isla was home, because her car was parked on the driveway alongside the vintage Jag that had belonged to Jerry. The master bedroom was directly above the living room that Isla never seemed to use. Melanie gazed up at the window for a minute, trying to decide what to do. The fear of going home empty-handed overcame her and she pressed her thumb firmly down on the intercom pad attached to the gatepost.

The intercom usually beeped every few seconds until it was either answered or it timed out. No noise came out of it tonight, so Melanie tried it a few more times before stepping back and looking at the fence. She could immediately see that it was too high to climb, and it had also been constructed in such a way that the spaces between the diagonal bars at the front were too narrow for feet to get through to the horizontal bars at the back. She turned her attention to the hedges on either side of it instead, but quickly realised they were too dense to push through. That only left the back of the house as a means to get close enough to wake Isla. She had once walked along the bank at the top of the stream behind the garden, and it had been murder trying to fight her way through the wild brambles. Partway through, she had nearly slipped over the edge and had been forced to turn back. And that had been in daylight, so she dreaded to think how hard it would be in darkness.

The intercom suddenly crackled, and Melanie's heart leapt as she rushed over to it.

'Isla?' she asked, pressing the talk button. 'Are you there? It's Melanie. I'm so sorry for calling round like this, but I've been trying to get hold of you for ages.'

'I know,' Isla replied coolly, the rasp of sleep in her voice letting Melanie know that she had, indeed, woken her. 'I didn't answer, because I don't appreciate being harassed at night, when you know there's nothing I can do for you. Especially when it's the first time I've heard from you in six weeks.'

'I know, and I'm really sorry,' Melanie apologised. 'But this is urgent.'

'There is nothing I can do for you tonight,' Isla repeated firmly. 'I don't have any money in the house, so you'll have to wait until the banks open in the morning.'

'*Please*,' Melanie pleaded. 'I'm begging you. If I don't get two thousand by morning, I'm going to be in serious trouble.'

'I've already told you you'll have to wait,' Isla repeated with strained patience. 'I'll call you tomorrow when I've had a chance to get the money. I've got things to do in the morning, so I can't guarantee what time that will be, but I'll try. Now go home.'

'But that might be too late.'

'I've said I'll help you, and I will. But you need to stop thinking you can dictate the terms when you're the taker and I'm the giver.'

'I know, and I honestly appreciate all the help you've given me,' Melanie conceded. 'But I need to warn you that I'm not the only one in danger. Carl said he'll kill me, you and Jacob if I don't get the money. He's in trouble and—'

'Stop!' Isla barked. 'I haven't been giving you money to help *him* out, and I'm not about to start now. I don't care what trouble he's got himself into, and you shouldn't either. I can't believe you're asking me to bail that thug out after everything I did for you. You should be ashamed of yourself. And, yet again, you haven't even asked how Jacob is. You're an absolute disgrace, Melanie.'

'I know I am,' Melanie sobbed. 'But you don't understand.'

'Oh, but I do,' said Isla. 'You had a choice and you chose him. He's getting nothing from me and, after tomorrow, you won't be getting anything else until you prove you're trying to sort yourself out for your son.'

'I *am* trying. I know I've fucked up and I'd give anything to have a normal life and be a good mum to Jacob. I miss him like crazy.'

Isla released an audible sigh. Then, less harshly, she said, 'Look, I'll call you tomorrow to arrange the drop-off. But, after that, I want proof that you're not living with Carl or I'm going to get legal advice.'

'No, Isla, please don't do that,' Melanie begged.

No reply came, and Melanie swiped at her tears when she realised that Isla had disconnected the intercom. It was a relief to know that she was going to get the money, but she dreaded to think how Carl would react to the news that they were being made to wait for it. It wasn't her fault and she shouldn't have had to come all this way to beg for money to save his stupid arse. But she'd already had a taste of what Wozza was capable of when Carl had been late paying off the first debt, and she couldn't risk that happening again.

At the bedroom window, Isla watched from behind the curtains as Melanie set off in the direction of the village. The woman had sounded really upset and scared, and she felt a little guilty for sending her away with a flea in her ear. But Tia had been right about her only being interested in money, because Melanie had yet again neglected to ask about Jacob without being prompted. That had infuriated Isla, and it had also pissed her off to hear that Melanie was begging for money for Carl. And as for his threat that he was going to kill her, Isla would like to see him try. The village police station was always closed at night, but the sergeant lived directly behind it and emergency calls were routed straight to his phone, so there would be a squad car here before the bastard got anywhere near the front door.

Chapter 27

Melanie was exhausted and frozen stiff when she got home, and her stomach was still cramping sporadically. Luckily, her period hadn't started on the bus, which would have been mortifying, because her jacket wasn't long enough to cover the mess. But it felt like it was going to be a heavy one, so she prayed that Isla wouldn't keep her waiting too long for the money in the morning, or she'd be in no fit state to go out for it.

As she'd predicted, Carl wasn't home when she let herself into the flat. She was actually quite relieved, because it meant that she'd be able to sleep without worrying about him flipping out on her for no reason. When she'd first come home with the money after Isla kicked her out, he'd been really nice to her. But it had all turned to shit when he started taking smack again. If he wasn't high, he'd get moody and start arguments, and then he would storm out and go AWOL for days on end. He had a bad reputation on the Grange and most people gave him a wide berth, so she knew he couldn't be staying with a friend or a neighbour. The only place she could think of was a dosshouse on the next estate over, where addicts, alcoholics and homeless people were known to gather. But she had eventually found out the truth after going through his phone one night when he was asleep. He had been seeing a girl called Kelly. And, going off the date of their first messages, it had started while she had still been staying at Isla's.

That had shocked and deeply hurt her, but she hadn't dared to confront Carl about it for fear of him reacting violently to her going through his phone. It was also sickening to think that he had still been sleeping with her while it was going on. Each time she had slipped home to visit him after Isla had dropped her off at the hospital during that time, he had dragged her straight to bed, and had kept her there all day, as if he'd been starved of sex all week. And, worse, he'd forced her to leave Jacob alone in his room on those days. And if the boy dared to cry – which he inevitably had – Carl would get mad and scream at him to shut up.

That was why she had taken the money and left him with Isla that night: because she had known he would be safer there than at home with Carl.

Stupidly, she had thought it would only be temporary; that Carl would start to miss him as much as she did and tell her to bring him home. But he had loved not having Jacob around. And he'd especially loved knowing that Isla was willing to pay to keep Jacob longer.

In bed, at last, Melanie wondered if she ought to ring Carl and tell him that they would be getting the money tomorrow. Changing her mind, because she wasn't in the mood to speak to him after he'd been so horrible to her earlier that evening, she sent him a quick text message instead. Then, dry-swallowing a painkiller to ease the cramps in her stomach, she curled into a ball and willed herself to sleep.

Carl still wasn't home when Melanie woke the next morning, and he hadn't replied to her text – although he had read it, which told her he was still alive and just being ignorant.

Her stomach was still sore, so she took another painkiller and then got dressed and wandered into the kitchen to make herself a coffee. There was no milk, so she had to have it black, which wasn't nice. But she needed something warm inside her, and that was all there was.

In the living room, she settled in the armchair and spent the rest of the morning checking on her phone every few seconds, waiting for Isla to message or call. As the hours crawled by, she began to get worried that Isla might have changed her mind. She honestly wouldn't blame her, because it had obviously annoyed her to hear that the money was for Carl. But Melanie was the one who would suffer if it didn't come, so she prayed that Isla would stick to her word and come through for her.

The call had finally come in the early afternoon, and Melanie had been directed to meet Isla's friend at the same time and place as the last drop-off. The man hadn't bothered to speak to her this time; he'd merely shaken his head as he handed the money out through the car window before driving away. But that was somehow worse, and Melanie felt nothing but shame as she slinked home with the money in her pocket.

She'd sent Carl another text to let him know that she now had the money, and had half-expected to find him there waiting for it when she got home. The flat was silent, however, so she sat down and counted the money. Surprised and grateful to find that Isla had sent fifty pounds more than she'd asked for, she nipped next door to pay the neighbour back. He didn't answer his door, so she pushed a tenner through the letterbox and then went home and stashed the other forty quid in her underwear drawer to keep Carl from getting his hands on it.

*

Evening crawled into night with still no sign of Carl. Melanie's stomach was still aching and her head was banging after spending the day on edge waiting for Wozza to turn up. Worn out with it all, she turned on the TV in the bedroom and curled up on the bed to try to relax.

She didn't realise she had fallen asleep until a booming sound woke her sometime later, and her heart lurched when she realised that someone was pounding on the front door. She quickly got up and tiptoed out into the hall, reaching the spyhole in time to see Wozza raise his fist to pound on the door again. A movement behind him and to the left caught her eye, and her legs started shaking when she saw three more men standing to the side; all hooded, and all appearing to be holding weapons.

As if he'd realised he was being watched, Wozza suddenly stepped forward and stared straight into the spyhole, and her instincts screamed danger when he gave a sinister smile.

'I know you're there, ya little cunt,' he said softly. 'Now open up before I get angry. 'Cos you know you don't like me when I'm angry.'

If anyone else had spoken those words while grinning like an idiot, Melanie would have laughed. But Warren 'Wozza' Barrett wasn't the kind of man who took kindly to being laughed at, so she covered her mouth with her hand and prayed that he couldn't hear her breathing. If he'd been alone, she would have opened the door and handed the money to him. But those other men brandishing their weapons told her that Wozza wasn't planning on being civil.

'This is your first and final warning,' Wozza went on. 'If this door ain't open in three seconds, it's coming in.'

'What's going on?' another voice, which Melanie recognised as belonging to the new neighbour, demanded.

Still staring at the spyhole, Wozza raised his hand and

gestured for one of his men to deal with it, and Melanie heard a deeper, gruffer voice, say, 'If you know what's good for you, you'll get back inside and turn your telly up, mate. And don't be testing us by calling the cops, 'cos we know where you live. Ya get me?'

The man quickly closed his door, and Melanie's heart sank through the floor. No one else on the block was stupid enough to interfere on her behalf, and she doubted the man would dare to defy the warning and call the police, so she was totally on her own.

'Time's up,' Wozza drawled, holding up three fingers. 'Three … two …'

'OK, I'll open the door,' Melanie cried out in panic. 'But please don't hurt me.'

'Now why on earth would I do that?' Wozza asked innocently, as if he and his boys hadn't laid into her the last time Carl had defaulted on his payments. 'I'm just coming to collect what I'm owed, that's all.'

Melanie quickly unlocked the door, then stumbled backwards into the living room. Wozza strolled in with the other men on his heel and looked around.

'Where is he?'

'I don't know,' Melanie stammered, nervously eyeing the men as she edged towards the sofa with her hands held out in front of her.

Wozza jerked his head at the other men and they went back out into the hall and started searching the other rooms.

'I've got your money,' Melanie said, sliding her hand under the cushion where she'd stashed the money earlier. 'Here …' She pulled out the wad and held it out.

Wozza snatched it from her and quickly flicked through the notes. 'What the fuck's this?' he grunted. 'Where's the rest?'

'W-what do you mean?' Melanie backed up a step. 'Carl said he owed you two grand, and that's what's there. You can count it if you don't believe me.'

'It *was* two grand,' Wozza said. 'But it's late, so now it's gone up to four.'

'It's not late,' Melanie protested. 'You said he had till today.'

'Yeah, and now it's tomorrow.' Wozza tapped his wristwatch pointedly. 'Two minutes past midnight to be precise, which makes it two minutes late. If you'd answered the door when I got here, you'd have been on time. But you kept me waiting, so now you've got to pay the price.'

'I only didn't answer straight away because I was scared,' Melanie whimpered. 'And that's all the money we've got, so please just take it and go.'

'That ain't how this works, sweetheart,' Wozza said, smiling as he stepped closer.

Melanie flinched when he reached out as if to stroke her hair, then yelped in alarm when he grabbed a handful and snapped her head back.

'Where's the rest of my fucking money?'

'I've got another forty you can have now,' she cried. 'But I'll need a few more days to get the rest.'

Wozza pursed his lips as if considering it. Then, shaking his head, he said, 'Nah, time's up,' and drove his fist into her stomach.

She screamed as the pain tore through her body, but no sound came out. Still holding her by the hair, he dragged her back up to her feet when her legs buckled and punched her again.

'Yo, what the fuck,' one of the other men said, grimacing when he came back from searching the bedroom and saw a thick clot of blood on the carpet between her feet.

Wozza followed his gaze and dropped her in disgust. In

agony, she curled into a ball on the floor as the blood saturated her skirt.

'Tell that clown I want the rest of my fucking money by six tonight or you're both dead,' Wozza said, leaning over her. 'You got that?' He waited a second for her to answer and then punched her in the face when she didn't. 'I said have you fucking got that?'

Straightening up when she made a gurgling noise that he took as an affirmative, he jerked his head at the others to follow and then strode out.

Next door with his ear pressed to the wall, Rob Layton heard a door slamming and footsteps passing his door and rushed to the window. A few seconds later, the men he'd confronted in the hallway strolled out through the main door below, and he watched as they hopped into a car parked further down the road and drove away.

He had been out playing pool with some mates earlier that night and hadn't been home long when he'd heard someone pounding on his neighbour's door. When he'd seen a hooded figure in the communal hallway through the spyhole, he had thought it was one of the lads from the gang who hung around the estate causing trouble and had stepped outside to scare him off. That was when he had seen that there were actually four of them out there. And they were men, not boys; all built like brick shithouses.

Rob was no weakling, but he wasn't stupid enough to think he could take on four men and walk away to tell the tale. So when one of them had ordered him to get back inside and keep his mouth shut, he had done just that. The men hadn't looked like they were paying a friendly visit, and he was concerned about the girl. He'd only met her once, but she seemed decent, so he hoped the men hadn't gone there looking for her. Ear to the wall, he had strained to hear what was going on in there. He'd heard voices, but they were too low for him to make out the words. There had also been a couple of muted thuds, but nothing to indicate that anything sinister was going on. And then they had left and now it was quiet again.

Telling himself that it was probably nothing, he pushed it out of his mind and sat back down to finish watching the movie he'd paused.

Chapter 28

After the gloom of the windowless cell in which he'd spent the night, the morning sunlight was harsh on Carl's eyes, and he squinted as he paused to roll a cigarette after being released. In desperate need of nicotine, he took a deep drag and then pulled his hood up over his head before setting off. Every muscle in his body was aching from the kicking he'd received from the security guards at the supermarket near Kelly's after they'd caught him nicking a bottle of vodka the night before. They'd dragged him to the back of the store, out of the range of the cameras so there'd be no proof that they'd done him over when the cops arrived.

Still, as much as that kicking had hurt, it was nothing compared to the one he'd get from Wozza if he didn't get his money. Isla blanking Melanie's calls had left him in a precarious position, so he'd gone to Kelly's to hide out before stupidly getting himself nicked. On his way back there now, he took out his phone to check if the money had come through yet. There were several messages on the screen, most from Kelly, asking where he was and why it was taking him so long to get back from the shop. But it was the one from Melanie letting him know that she had the money that brought a smile to his lips. It had been sent around the same time he was getting arrested, so she would probably have already handed it over to Wozza by now. Relieved to be in the clear, he sent Kelly a quick message telling her to put the kettle on and open the door, and then continued on his way.

As he approached Kelly's block a few minutes later, Carl spotted her standing in the doorway of the communal bin cupboard. She was wearing pyjamas and a dressing gown, and he gave her a questioning look when she waved for him to hurry up and join her.

'What you doing out here dressed like that?' he asked, grinning as he strolled over to her. 'Surely you're not so desperate for a shag that you couldn't wait for me to get up there?'

'Scotty's home,' she whispered, poking her head out to check that no one was around.

'I thought he wasn't due back till Friday?' Carl frowned.

'He wasn't. But one of his mates told him he'd seen a bloke coming round while he was away, so he sneaked in hoping to catch me out.'

'Shit! He doesn't know it's me, does he?'

'No.' Kelly shook her head. 'I told him his mate was lying to get back at me for knocking him back when he tried it on with me. I don't think he believed me, but he hasn't got any proof, so there's nothing he can do. Luckily, my phone was on silent when your message came through just now or there'd have been murder. I couldn't answer it, 'cos he's watching me like a hawk, so I told him I needed to bring the rubbish down so I could warn you.'

'Cheers,' Carl muttered. 'I've already had one kicking, and then I had to sleep on a fucking slab in the cells, so the last thing I need is another fight when I'm already aching like fuck.'

'Oh my God, you've got a black eye,' Kelly said, noticing it for the first time. 'Who did that? And why were you at the station?'

Carl explained what had happened, ending with the goons accusing him of pulling a knife on them.

'Those lying fuckers had better watch their backs,' he spat. ''Cos if I get sent down for this, I'm gonna petrol bomb that place when I get out. With *them* in it.'

'You should be thanking them; they probably saved your life,' said Kelly. 'If Scotty had caught you here, you'd be in that right now, with your throat cut and your dick in your mouth.' She jerked her thumb at the huge bin standing behind her.

'Fuck off. I could easily take him,' Carl sneered. 'He ain't that hard.'

'I wouldn't let *him* hear you saying that,' Kelly snorted, taking another peek around the corner. 'Right, I'd best get back up there before he comes looking for me. I'll call you when he's gone.'

'Yeah, whatever,' Carl said coolly, annoyed that she had implied that he wasn't man enough to tackle her husband.

'What you acting like that for?' she asked. 'This isn't my fault.'

'Never said it was,' he muttered, stuffing his hands into his pockets. 'See you later.'

'No kiss?' she hissed when he started walking away.

He continued on his way without looking back.

Still in a mood about Kelly's insult when he reached his own block ten minutes later, Carl scowled when he walked in through the main door and came face to face with his next-door neighbour coming out of the lift.

Rob Layton saw Carl's black eye and gave a knowing smile. 'Wow, they did a number on you, didn't they? And there was me thinking they were your mates.'

'Fuck off,' Carl muttered, sidling past him to get into the lift.

'I've got to hand it to you for not screaming like the little pussy you are, though,' Rob went on. 'Then again, four big blokes like them coming at you, you probably shit yourself and fainted before the first punch landed.'

'What the *fuck* are you talking about?' Carl asked, looking at him as if he was crazy.

Rob gave a scornful laugh and then turned and walked away.

'Muppet,' Carl spat as the door slid shut.

The TV was on in the bedroom when he let himself into the flat a minute later. Guessing that Melanie must have gone back to bed to sulk about him staying out after paying Wozza that morning, he chucked his jacket over a coat hook and strolled into the room. The curtains were still closed and the only light was coming from the TV, but the bed was empty.

'Mel?' he called out as he walked back out into the hallway. 'Why've you got the telly on if you're not even watching it? D'you know how much leccy that burns?'

No answer came, so he poked his head into the bathroom and then the kitchen before heading into the living room. Cursing Melanie under his breath when he saw that the curtains were closed in there, as well, he marched over to the window and swished them open. Able to see now, he got the shock of his life when he turned and saw Melanie curled up in the middle of the carpet.

'What the fuck are you doing?' he asked, walking over and nudging her thigh with his foot. 'Get up, you daft cow. You nearly gave me a heart attack.'

She didn't move and he grimaced when he saw the dried blood on the back of her skirt. Her legs were also streaked with it, and it had soaked into the carpet beneath her. But worse was the huge clot of blood that was sitting a few inches away from her feet. It had something pale inside it, and he clapped a hand over his mouth to stop himself from throwing up when he realised that it was a tiny, barely formed foetus.

'Oh Christ,' he croaked, stepping away from it in horror and disgust. Melanie hadn't told him she was pregnant, but she clearly wasn't anymore, and he wasn't sure what to do.

He squatted down beside her and touched her shoulder, then immediately snatched his hand back when he felt how cold and almost rubbery her flesh felt. Afraid that she might have taken something to help her with the pain of losing the baby and knocked herself out, he leaned down to check she was still breathing. That was when he saw that her face was also covered in blood, and her black, swollen eyes were partially open and devoid of life.

'*Fuck*!' he squawked, falling backwards in shock. 'Please God, no. This can't be happening. What the *fuck*?'

Shaking like a leaf when his back hit the sofa, he pulled his knees up to his chest and stared at Melanie in horror. There was no way she could have caused those injuries to herself. Somebody had literally beaten her to death. But who and *why*? The front door was the only way in and out, but it wasn't damaged, so it had to be someone they knew or she would never have let them in. But she didn't have any friends, and the neighbours didn't speak to them, so *who*?

Four big blokes…

Pure terror burst inside him when he recalled his neighbour's strange words in the lobby. He'd thought the man was taking the piss because of his black eye, but he now realised that the man must have seen whoever did this. And Wozza was the only man he knew who always walked with a three-man crew and who Melanie would have opened the door to, so he had to have done this. But why kill her when she had the money waiting for him? It didn't make sense.

Tears blurred his vision as he stared at Melanie's destroyed face. 'What the fuck did you do?' he croaked. 'You know what he's like, so why didn't you just give him the money, you stupid, stupid bitch!'

No answer came, but he could feel the blame being directed at him through her unseeing eyes. And it *was* his fault; he knew that. He was the one who'd run up the debt and defaulted on it. But all she'd had to do was open the door and pass the money out to Wozza and that would have been the end of it. Instead, she'd obviously done or said something to piss the man off and this was her punishment. But what now? Was it over, or was Wozza going to come back and do the same to him?

Terrified, he mentally ran through his options. He couldn't grass on Wozza, because the man's soldiers would hunt him down and slaughter him before the day was out. But even if he reported this without naming anyone, the spotlight would automatically fall on him, because the victim's partner was always the prime suspect in every TV murder documentary he'd ever watched. He'd already been arrested and charged with assault on the same day, and possibly close to the same time that Melanie had been killed. To the cops, that would look like he'd done her in and then gone straight to the shops armed with a knife to grab some free booze to drown his sorrows – or even congratulate himself. He could tell them he'd been with Kelly immediately before he got nicked, which gave him an alibi. But he doubted Kelly would back him up for fear of her hubby finding out that she had been cheating on him.

Every which way Carl looked at it, he was fucked. He was sitting here with a dead body – two, if you counted the clot; and if he didn't act soon, the police would eventually descend and it would be game over. And, for all he knew, Wozza could come back at any minute. He needed out of there, and fast. But, first, he needed to get rid of Melanie's body, because the police would put out an immediate warrant for his arrest if someone discovered it.

His best chance would be to get her out of there and leave her in a secluded spot, so it would look like she'd been attacked by a random stranger. But there were ten flats with spyholes on his landing, and if any of his neighbours saw him trying to carry a body-sized item out of there, they were bound to get suspicious. And he didn't have a suitcase or a wheelie bin to stuff her into, so it would be impossible to conceal her. But he could smuggle her out in pieces.

That thought repulsed him, but it seemed like his only option, so he pulled himself up to his feet and went into the kitchen. There were a couple of screwdrivers, a trowel and an old hammer in the cupboard under the sink; none of which were of any use. He needed a saw or a machete, but that would take money, and he'd spent the last of his on a bag of gear the previous night. He'd left it at Kelly's when he went on the booze run, but he'd have given anything to have a hit right then.

Pushing the thought out of his mind so he could concentrate on the job at hand, he pulled the roll of bin bags out from the back of the cupboard and carried them into the living room. He needed time to get everything in place, but he didn't want to have to keep seeing her like that while he was doing it. So, tearing several bags off the roll, he placed the first over her head and her accusing eyes.

Chapter 29

It was almost 6 p.m. when Carl exited the flats that evening with his hood pulled low over his head. He was trying his hardest to act naturally to avoid attracting unwanted attention as he strolled down the road, but it was difficult to even put one foot in front of the other while every nerve in his body was twitching like a live wire. It had been a stressful day, just sitting there waiting for his door to get kicked in at any moment. But he hadn't dared leave the flat while it was light, so he'd had no choice but to sit it out.

One good thing had happened, and that was that, as he'd searched the flat for money, he'd found forty quid in Melanie's underwear drawer. It had initially pissed him off that the sneaky bitch had stashed it there to prevent him getting his hands on it. But then it had occurred to him that the only place she could have got the money was from the two grand Isla had given her. And that, he realised, was probably why Wozza had kicked off at her: for trying to undercut him. She'd probably thought that Wozza wouldn't bother counting it, or that he'd let her off because it was only forty quid. But she obviously didn't know how men like Wozza operated. They enjoyed inflicting pain, and even one penny less than he was owed was one penny too much.

Feeling less guilty after that, he'd unscrewed the bath panel and stuffed her bin-bagged body under the tub before screwing it back into place. He knew he would have to take her out again once he'd bought the right tools. But the thought of someone breaking in while he was out, and the police being there waiting to arrest him when he got back, made it necessary to get her out of sight.

Almost at the shop, he nearly jumped out of his skin when he heard a screech of tyres behind him. Whipping his head round, fully expecting it to be a squad car, his legs turned to water when a car pulled alongside him and Wozza rolled down the passenger-side window.

'Well, looky here,' he drawled, giving Carl a sly grin. 'The very man I was looking for. Hope your girl's feeling better after her little fall last night?'

Carl stared at the man in confusion as the other men in the car laughed. He didn't know if Wozza knew Melanie was dead and was just taking the piss, or if he genuinely thought he'd only hurt her. Either way, it confirmed that he was definitely the one who'd killed her.

'I take it she told you I'd be coming for the rest of my money at six?' Wozza went on. 'That where you're off to now; to get it for me?'

'I, um … yeah,' Carl lied. 'It's at my, um, mate's place.'

'Cool,' Wozza said. 'Hop in; we'll give you a lift.'

Carl's heart started pounding like a jackhammer. If he got into that car, he'd be dead as soon as Wozza realised he'd lied and there was no money. But it wasn't an invitation, it was an order, and there was no way he could refuse. So he turned and legged it down the road, swerving into an alleyway at the end when he heard the car coming after him.

Unable to follow him down there in the car, the men jumped out and ran after him on foot. But Carl was running on pure adrenaline and knew every inch of that area like the back of his hand, so they struggled to keep up as he scrambled over walls and raced through the warren of streets and alleyways like a whippet being chased by a pack of wolves. And he didn't stop running even when the footsteps behind him faded into the far distance and all he could hear was his heartbeat pounding in his ears.

Chapter 30

Isla rapped her fingertips on the steering wheel as the gate slowly slid open. Driving through at speed when the gap was large enough, she parked up, killed the engine, and then quickly lifted Jacob from his safety seat. In the house a moment later, she kicked the door shut and rushed up the stairs. Jacob was fast asleep, so she laid him on his bed and then ran to the bathroom to empty her bursting bladder.

Relieved, she washed her hands and then went back to the bedroom and changed Jacob into his pyjamas before covering him with his duvet. Autumn was coming in fast and the temperature was dropping by the day, but it had been sunny and mild that morning, so she had decided to treat Jacob to what would probably be his last day at the beach for that year. They had been several times throughout summer, and he absolutely loved playing in the sand. Benny had gone with them a few times, but it had just been the two of them today. She was exhausted now and needed a drink after the long drive, so she dropped her sandy clothes into the laundry basket and took a quick shower before pulling on her nightclothes and heading downstairs.

The kitchen door was closed and she frowned when she felt a cold draught coming from under it as she approached. Wondering if she'd left a window open before leaving that morning, she opened it and switched the light on. She immediately saw that the draught was coming through a hole in the glass of the back door, the shards of which were scattered across the floor. Fearing that whoever had broken in might still be in the house, she held her breath in case they heard her and slid her phone out of her dressing gown pocket to call the police.

'I wouldn't do that if I was you,' a deep voice warned.

Almost jumping out of her skin, Isla snapped her head round and saw a man sitting on the sofa in the dark snug. Terrified when he stood up and started to walk towards her, she took a stumbling step back, and croaked, 'I've already called the police and they're on their way, so you'd best get out while you can.'

'No, you haven't,' the man said, stepping into the light. 'And you ain't going to, neither, 'cos I guarantee you'd be dead before they got here.'

Able to see his face now, Isla's heart lurched in her chest. He looked thinner and his face more gaunt that she remembered from the time she'd seen him at a distance through the car window, but his height and dark curly hair told her exactly who he was.

'What do you want?' she demanded, trying not to let her fear leak out in her voice. 'If it's money, I can't help you, because I don't keep any in the house.'

'Well, you'd better find some,' Carl said, looking around. 'You must have something stashed away for emergencies.'

'I gave all the cash I had to Melanie when I asked her to leave,' Isla lied. 'And I've had to go to the bank to withdraw everything I've given her since.'

'Then I guess we'll have to go find a cash machine, won't we?' Carl said. 'Where's your card and car keys.'

'Upstairs in my bag,' Isla told him. 'But I wouldn't be able to get you much. There a daily limit of two hundred and fifty, and I've already used half of that today.'

'That's not enough,' Carl muttered, clawing at his neck as he paced the floor. 'I need way more than that. What time does the bank open?'

'Ten,' Isla said, eyeing him warily. 'Are you in some kind of trouble? Only I gave Melanie money yesterday, and I know it was for you, so why do you need more?'

'None of your fucking business,' he snapped. 'I just *do.* And I ain't leaving till I get it.'

Isla sensed that something really bad must have happened to make him come all the way over here instead of getting Melanie to call her. She already knew he could be violent, but there was a crazed look in his eyes that told her he could blow at any time. Hoping to calm him down before it got to that, she said, 'Would you like a drink? I've got wine and whisky, or I could make you a brew if you prefer?'

'Whisky,' he grunted, clawing at his arms now.

'Do you need anything else?' she asked as she cautiously stepped out from behind the table and walked over to the cupboard to get the whisky. 'I could make you something to eat if you're hungry?'

'Quit acting like we're mates, 'cos we ain't,' he said coldly as he dragged a chair out from under the table and flopped down onto it. 'I'm here for what's mine. When I've got it, I'm gone. Till then, keep it shut.'

Isla nodded her agreement and turned her back so he wouldn't see how badly her hands were shaking as she poured them both a drink.

Carl snatched his glass from her when she carried it over to him, and watched her through narrowed eyes as she made her way to the other end of the table and sat down.

'How do you sleep at night knowing you stole all this shit?' he asked.

'I don't know what you mean.' She gave him a confused look. 'I haven't stolen anything.'

'Oh, really? So you think you *deserve* all this, just 'cos you married the old cunt and fucked him for a few years? This house, them cars out there, the money... You think you've got more right to it than his son?'

'Ah...' Isla murmured, guessing that Melanie must have told him about Jerry being Jacob's real father, and he'd come to stake a claim on the inheritance he believed the boy was owed. 'I know this must be difficult for you,' she said. 'But it hasn't exactly been easy for me, either.'

'Fuck off,' Carl spat. 'You've had it cushy; swanning around in this place like the queen of the fucking castle, while we're living in shit. Playing mammy to *my* kid.'

'I'm not trying to replace Melanie, if that's what you think,' Isla replied evenly. 'I'm just trying to keep him safe until she's well enough to take him back.'

'Safe from who?' Carl roared, slamming his glass down on the table. '*Me*? I'm his fucking *father*, bitch!'

'Please don't shout,' Isla said, casting a nervous glance into the hallway and praying that Jacob wouldn't wake up. 'If I've upset you, I apologise. But we can talk about this without letting it escalate.'

'Don't give me that la-di-da shit,' he sneered, taking another swig of whisky and wiping his mouth with the back of his hand. 'You say you know it must be difficult for me, but you don't know shit. I got dragged up by a junkie whore who couldn't even feed herself half the time, never mind me. Have you any idea what that was like?'

'No.' Isla shook her head. 'And I'm really sorry you went through that.'

'Stick your fake pity up your arse,' Carl snarled. 'Your old man was rolling in it, and now it's all yours. But it shouldn't be. It should be *mine*.' He slapped his chest.

'It doesn't work like that,' Isla said, choosing her words very carefully because she could see and feel that he was coiled as tight as a spring. 'Jerry's will was legally binding and he named me as the sole beneficiary. He was already dead by the time I found out about Melanie and Jacob, and it was too late to change anything by then.'

'But you can change it now,' Carl said. 'It's yours now, so you can sign it over.'

'I've already taken steps to make sure Jacob's looked after in the future,' Isla assured him. 'He's too young to handle any of that for himself right now, obviously, but I'm getting a trustee who can—'

'Are you really that fucking stupid?' Carl cut in.

'I'm just trying to explain what I'm doing, and why,' she said. 'I'm not legally obliged to take care of the child my husband fathered behind my back, but I'm trying to right the wrongs that were done to him. It wasn't his fault that Melanie decided to cut Jerry off and let you bring him up instead. That was wrong of her, and I'm sorry she lied to you. I was lied to, as well, and I could easily have turned my back on them. But Jacob's innocent in all this, and Melanie's really struggling with her chemo, so I couldn't sit back and do nothing.'

'Christ, you're gullible.' Carl gave a scornful laugh. 'When Mel told me you'd swallowed all that shit she fed you, I thought nah, there's no way she really believes it. She's bound to see the holes in her story and pick it apart. But you got proper sucked in, didn't you?'

'What do you mean?' Isla frowned.

'I mean she ain't got cancer,' said Carl.

'Yes, she has. I used to drop her off at the hospital every Friday morning for her appointments. And I watched her go in.'

'Yeah, and she used to wait till you'd gone, then hop on the bus and come home to spend the day with me.'

Isla felt her jaw clench in anger at the thought that anybody could lie about something as serious as cancer. Tia had always had doubts about that and had tried to warn her, and Isla had almost fallen out with her because of it. But she'd been right. Melanie had lied about everything.

'You know what I don't get?' Carl slumped back in his seat and stared at Isla across the table. 'If you reckon you loved Jerry so much, why were you so quick to take a stranger's word and turn against him? Or maybe you didn't really love him, eh? He was way older than you, *and* loaded, so maybe you only married him because you thought he'd pop his clogs in a couple of years and you'd get everything.'

'I did love him,' Isla replied through gritted teeth, angered again by the implication that she had somehow betrayed Jerry, when it was completely the reverse. 'And I didn't automatically take Melanie's word. When she first told me about the affair, I didn't believe a word of it. Then she admitted she'd lied, and I felt sorry for her and decided to try to help her. I only found out the truth after she'd already been here for a while.'

'I *know*,' Carl said mockingly. 'I've been in on it from the start, you fucking idiot. You don't seriously think she came up with all this by herself, do you?'

'In on what?' Isla was confused again. 'I'm sorry, but I'm really struggling to understand any of this. I know Melanie lied to *me*, but are you saying you knew about her and Jerry all along and chose to take Jacob on as your own?'

'He *is* mine.'

'I'm assuming your name's on his birth certificate, which would mean he's legally yours,' said Isla. 'But you're here now trying to claim an inheritance for him on the basis that he's Jerry's. You can't have it both ways, so which is it?'

'You know your problem?' Carl smirked. 'You still haven't worked out what's really going on here.'

'And what's that?' Isla asked.

'You thought your hubby was Mr Perfect,' said Carl. 'And so did my mum,' he added pointedly. 'Remember the story Mel told you, about meeting Jerry in the strip club? Well, that wasn't her. That was my old lady. *She's* the one he fucked then dumped.'

'What are you saying?' Isla frowned. 'That Jacob's your *brother*?'

'Noooo …' Carl shook his head and leaned forward to rest his elbows on the table. 'I've already told you, Jacob's *mine*. And by that, I mean biologically.'

'But I've seen the evidence that Jerry was with Melanie before she got pregnant,' Isla said. 'He was seeing her all the way through, and he was even at the birth.'

'Ah, but was he?' Carl gave a sly grin. 'Or did you just see those pictures we put together for you and believe the worst?'

Isla was more confused than ever and she shook her head as she tried to make sense of what she was hearing.

'That's not possible,' she murmured. 'The photos were on an old phone Jerry lost months ago. And I found it here in the house, so you couldn't possibly have got hold of it.'

'Anything's possible if you put your mind to it.' Carl gave another sly grin and tapped the side of his nose. 'He didn't *lose* that phone, I nicked it off him and used it to blackmail him. And then we planted it for you to find. Although, I've got to say, you took your time with that one.'

'You're talking in riddles and I don't understand a word you're saying,' Isla said. 'First Jerry's Jacob's dad and Melanie's his mum. Now *you're* the dad and your mum is Jacob's mum. How the hell does that work? It's crazy.'

'Nah, it's actually quite simple,' Carl said. 'I *am* Jacob's dad. And Jerry's mine.'

'*What*?' Isla stared at him in disbelief. 'No, this is too much. Jerry didn't have any children when I met him; I know that for a fact. He would have told me.'

'Well, he obviously wasn't as honest as you thought, 'cos here I am,' Carl said, no longer smiling as he swallowed the last of his drink and slid the empty glass across the table to Isla. 'All he had to do was recognise me and we'd have been OK,' he went on when she stood up to get the bottle of whisky off the ledge. 'I told him ... I said I didn't want anything from him, I just wanted him to stop acting like I don't exist and admit he's my father.'

'You spoke to Jerry?' Isla slumped back down onto her chair after handing his refilled glass back to him. 'When?'

'Last time, the day he died,' Carl said. 'But I first tracked him down a while back. I tried to talk to him, man to man, but he didn't want to know. He just kept insisting that I'd got the wrong man; that he'd never met my mum or been to her club. That was a fucking lie, but there was no reasoning with him, so I threatened to tell you. He told me to go ahead; said there was no way you'd believe me. So I took his phone off him and threatened to really fuck him up if he didn't start giving me money. He knew I'd do it, so he had no choice. That was a nice little earner. But then one day, a few months before he pegged it, he stopped paying and told me he was going to get a restraining order if I ever tried to contact him again. He refused to take my calls after that, so I had to pay him a visit. And there we were, right out there in the garden ... Him telling me to fuck off; me threatening to blow his life to pieces. Then, *poof*! His heart goes and he hits the deck like a sack of shit.'

'No…' Isla shook her head. 'I was the one who found him, so I would have seen you if you'd been here.'

'You nearly did see me,' Carl laughed. 'You must have been out when I got here, but you came back just after it happened, 'cos I heard your motor pulling in round the front and had to leg it out of the back gate.'

'Why did you run?' Isla asked. 'If he was dying, why didn't you try to help him?'

'I ain't Jesus,' Carl quipped. 'He was gone, and there was no way he was coming back. So what was I supposed to do? Stand over his dead body and wait for you to walk in and think I'd done him in?'

'You could have told me who you were,' Isla said.

'Yeah, right, 'cos you'd definitely have believed me, wouldn't you?' Carl sneered. 'Just like you believe me now. And don't say you do, because it's written all over your fucking face. But this is the God's honest truth. Jerry had an affair with my mother and I was the result. He promised her the world, then ghosted her as soon as she told him she was pregnant.'

'If this is true, why go to all this trouble to convince me that Jacob was his son and he'd had an affair with Melanie?' Isla asked. 'Why not just tell me the truth?'

'He didn't tell you about me, 'cos he was obviously ashamed,' Carl spat through gritted teeth. 'Rich fucker like him admitting he'd fathered a scruffy twat like me. I saw the disgust in his eyes when he saw me. There was no way he wanted *me* tainting his perfect little life. And then he was dead and I had no way to prove I was his blood, 'cos *you* got him cremated and burned my last chance. But he *owed* me.' He slammed his fist down again. 'So I found another way to get what's mine.'

'By beating up your girlfriend and letting her leave your son with a virtual stranger?' Melanie stared at him in disbelief.

'You knew the little shit by then, so he was fine,' Carl said dismissively.

Shocked to hear him speak about Jacob like that, Isla said, 'If all this is true, why did Melanie tell me she'd had an affair with Jerry, then tell me she'd lied?'

'I don't fucking know,' Carl muttered. 'That was her idea, not mine. I just wanted my money, so I was going to break in after the funeral and force you to hand everything over. Mel talked me out of it, because she reckoned I'd fuck it up and land myself in the nick. She'd spoken to you by then and sussed you for a soft touch, so she came up with the plan to tell you she'd had an affair with Jerry. I told her it'd never work, and it didn't, 'cos you didn't believe her. Then she got beaten up and used it to play on your sympathy. And you fell for it hook, line and sinker. Poor little Mel with her big, bad boyfriend and her needy little brat. Then throw a bit of cancer into the mix and make you feel *really* sorry for her. She was going to string you along for a few more weeks and then ask for money so she could "escape".'

He gave a nasty laugh, and Isla felt like her head was splitting apart as she tried to make sense of the convoluted story.

'OK, so you changed the story to get my sympathy,' she said. 'And I fell for it and let her move in. Then why put those photos on Jerry's phone and turn the story on its head again? And how did you even do that?'

'It's amazing what you can do with AI,' Carl said proudly. 'Fancied himself a bit, didn't he; old Jerry boy? All those photos of him out there on the net for the world to see and admire. It was super easy to grab his image and superimpose Mel and Jacob onto them. It wasn't brilliant and you'd have spotted the mistakes if you'd looked closer. But you were so willing to chuck everything he'd ever done for you in the bin over the word of a stranger, you just accepted it at face value, didn't you?'

'I saw the message Melanie sent him, as well; begging him to leave her alone,' Isla reminded him quietly. 'I'd have been stupid to see all that evidence and think it wasn't real.'

'You should've known him better than that, though, shouldn't you?' spat Carl. '*I* would have had faith in him if he'd given me a chance. But you were probably so eaten up with jealousy that another woman had had his kid when you couldn't, you wanted to think the worst of him? Yeah.' He nodded when Isla visibly flinched. 'Mel told me about you losing yours and how you'd always wanted to be a mam. You'd already bonded with Jacob by then and had practically pushed Mel out of the picture so you could play mummy to him right under her nose. She figured there was no way you'd turn your back on him if we made you think he was Jerry's, so we switched to that plan instead.'

'You didn't *make* me think anything,' Isla bristled. 'I found out the truth when I found Jerry's old phone.'

'Only it wasn't the truth, 'cos we put all that shit on there and planted it for you to find,' said Carl. 'Funny thing is, she honestly thought she'd blown it when you kicked her out. And I've got to say you surprised us both when you went after her and offered her money to leave Jacob behind. It's just a pity you didn't let her stay a bit longer, or she might have given you the brat she just lost as well.'

'Melanie was pregnant?' Isla felt suddenly guilty.

'We ain't talking about her, we're talking about you,' Carl said sharply. 'And look at you now, eh? Setting up a trust fund for a kid who's got nowt to do with you, while *my* old man wouldn't even give me the time of day. That's why we did this: 'cos there's plenty more ways to skin a cat and make a deadbeat pay the price. And now I'm going to get what should have been mine in the first place. All because you were scared I'd hurt my own son.'

'I'd already seen you yelling at him, and I saw the damage you did to Melanie, so, yeah, of course I was scared,' Isla admitted. 'But I didn't give her the money to keep Jacob; I gave it to her because she was ill and I didn't want her to go back to you.'

'She never left me, you stupid bitch.' Carl rolled his eyes. 'And since you obviously missed it the first time round, she *didn't* ... *have* ... *cancer*.'

'So what now?' Isla asked, swallowing her anger as she realised just how gullible she'd been. 'Are you going to take Jacob away after you've forced me to give you the money?'

Carl pursed his lips as if thinking about it and took another swig of his drink. Then, shaking his head, he said, 'It's probably best if I leave him here for now. I need to get myself sorted first.'

'Sorted in what way?' Isla frowned. 'You *are* in trouble, aren't you? But if you're running from someone, what about Melanie? Is she safe?'

'Don't worry about her,' he muttered.

Eyes narrowing when she saw his jaw muscles twitching, Isla said, 'I hope you haven't hurt her again?'

'I never fucking touched her,' he barked, slamming his fist down on the tabletop. 'And stop fucking talking about her.'

'OK.' Isla nervously held up her hands. 'Calm down.'

Carl swallowed the rest of his drink and then scraped his chair back and leapt up.

'What are you doing?' Isla asked, shrinking back in her seat when he walked briskly towards her. 'Please don't do anything stupid. I'm going to get you the money in the morning, but I won't be able to if you hurt me.'

'Oh, you'll be getting it all right,' he sneered, seizing her by the hair and yanking her head right back. 'Now shut your fucking mouth, 'cos I'm sick of hearing you talk down to me like I'm the one who doesn't deserve to be here. By rights, this should all be mine. Every fucking bit of it!'

Crying out when he abruptly let her go and then snatched the whisky bottle off the table, Isla's heart lurched when she heard the creak of the front door slowly opening.

Carl heard it, too, and he dragged her to her feet and put his arm around her throat, hissing, 'Who's that?'

'I don't know,' she whimpered.

'Isla?' a man's voice called out cautiously. 'Are you there?'

'Whoever it is, get rid of him or I'll kill you both,' Carl snarled, pushing her towards the door.

It was too late. Peter was already halfway up the hallway and had seen them.

'Sorry for walking in uninvited,' he apologised, side-eyeing Carl as he entered the kitchen. 'But your gate and front door were both open, and I know how security-conscious you are, so I thought I'd best check that everything's OK.'

'Everything's fine,' Isla lied, acutely conscious of Carl standing behind her with the bottle in his hand. 'What can I do for you?'

'You messaged a while back to ask if I needed the client files Jerry had here, and I was passing, so I thought I'd drop by and pick them up,' Peter said, frowning when he noticed her pale complexion and dilated pupils. He swivelled his gaze to the young man standing behind her, and jerked his chin up. 'May I ask who *you* are?'

'A friend of Isla's,' Carl muttered.

'Really?' Peter raised an eyebrow and gazed down at Isla again. 'You don't seem overly happy to have him here. Would you like me to escort him out?'

'No, it's fine,' Isla said, stepping forward. 'Please just go, Peter. I'm OK, I promise.'

Peter took a step back and then stopped and narrowed his eyes when he noticed the smashed panel in the back door and the glass on the floor.

'Did you do that?' he demanded, staring at Carl with open suspicion. 'What exactly is going on here?'

'Just *go*,' Isla hissed, physically pushing him now.

'Not so fast,' Carl said, leaping forward and slamming the door shut. 'He knows something's up and he'll call the cops, so I can't let him leave.'

'Don't be stupid,' Isla protested. 'You can't keep us both prisoner.'

'Young man, you need to move out of my way right now,' Peter said authoritatively.

'Fuck you,' Carl spat, swinging his arm back with the bottle in his hand.

Peter pre-empted the strike and ducked. Then, head down and roaring like a wild animal, he slammed Carl up against the door, wrapped his arms around him, and then propelled him backwards onto the table, knocking the wind clean out of him. Using his weight to hold him down, Peter wrestled the bottle out of Carl's hand and whacked him across the side of the head with it before seizing him by the hair with both hands and repeatedly smashing his head onto the wood.

'Peter, stop!' Isla cried, trying to pull him off when she saw blood spreading out across the tabletop and dripping onto the floor. 'You're going to kill him!'

Breathing heavily, Peter loosened his grip, straightened up and took a step back as Carl's body slid to the floor.

'He's out cold,' he said. 'Get me something to tie him up, then call the police. *Now*!' he barked when Isla didn't move.

Jumping, she ran into the utility room and came back with a reel of nylon washing-line.

Peter took it from her and knelt down before holding out his hand. 'Scissors?'

Isla grabbed a pair out of the drawer and handed them to him, then watched in horror as he looped the line around Carl's ankles multiple times before tying his hands behind his back and then binding both sets of restraints together.

'Isla, call the police,' he ordered, glancing back at her over his shoulder as he tested that the restraints were secure.

'I can't,' she croaked. 'I'll get in trouble.'

'What?' Peter frowned and dusted off the knees of his trousers as he rose to his feet. 'No, you won't. He broke into your home, so he's the one who'll be in trouble, not you.'

'I've got his baby upstairs,' Isla said quietly. 'I've had him for months, and I'll be in serious trouble if he tells the police I've been paying his girlfriend to let me keep him.'

'What on earth …?' Peter stared down at her in confusion. 'So you know this man?'

'Not really,' Isla sighed. 'It's a long story.'

Peter placed one hand on his hip and ran the other through his receding hair. Then, gesturing to Carl, who was still lying motionless at his feet, he said, 'Is there somewhere safe we can put him while we talk?'

'In there.' Isla pointed to the utility room. 'There's no window and I can lock it from the outside.'

Nodding, Peter leaned down, grabbed Carl by the ankles and dragged him into the small room. Letting out a tense breath when he came back out and Isla had locked the door, he retrieved the upturned whisky bottle off the table and held it up. 'May I?'

'Help yourself,' Isla croaked, shaking all over as she dropped onto her seat. Everything she'd learned and gone through that night was crashing down on her at once, and her head was spinning with the sheer weight of it all.

Peter looked through the cupboards until he found the one where she kept the glasses. Taking two out, he filled both to the halfway mark and handed one to her before sitting next to her.

'It'll help calm you down,' he said when Isla looked like she was going to vomit at the sight of it. 'You've had quite a shock tonight.'

'You can say that again,' she muttered, reluctantly reaching for the glass.

'Are you able to talk about it?' Peter asked, gently stroking her back. Quickly removing his hand when he realised she might take it the wrong way, he said, 'Sorry, that was inappropriate. I was only trying to comfort you.'

'I know; don't worry about it,' Isla gulped. 'I'm just grateful you turned up when you did. He's in some sort of trouble and came to get money, but he was acting crazy and I was scared he was going to really hurt me. If he'd done that, Jacob would have been completely alone.'

'Jacob?'

'The baby,' Isla said. Then, taking a deep breath, she told him the whole story; from seeing Melanie for the first time at Jerry's funeral, to Carl breaking in earlier that night and the crazy story he'd told her.

By the time she reached the end, Peter's face was as pale as hers had been when he arrived, and Isla wondered if he'd overexerted himself when he'd tackled Carl when she saw beads of sweat on his brow.

'Are you OK?' she asked, gazing at him with concern when he took a gulp of whisky. 'You're not having chest pains, are you?'

'No.' Peter shook his head.

'Well, something's obviously wrong,' she pressed. 'Do you want me to call Felicity?'

'*No!*' This time he barked the word out, and Isla saw a flash of panic in his eyes. 'I'm all right,' he assured her, patting her hand after a moment. 'Just needed a moment to gather my thoughts. Thing is …'

'Thing is what?' Isla prompted.

'He's not Jerry's.'

'Sorry?' Isla stared at him. 'How would you know that?'

'Trust me, I just do,' Peter insisted. 'I know I overstepped the mark when … well, you know what I'm talking about. And I do hope you've forgiven me for that.'

'I forgot about it a long time ago,' Isla said, eager for him to get to the point.

'Jerry loved you,' he continued. 'And he would never have entertained another woman. And, believe me, I would have known if he had.'

'I know,' Isla murmured, saddened to think that she had fallen for Melanie's lies and doubted the man she had loved. 'I feel like shit for thinking badly of him now I know the truth. If it's true what Carl said, Jerry wasn't with me when he met Carl's mum, so it's not like he cheated on me. He just should have told me that he had a son.'

'He didn't tell you because the boy wasn't his,' said Peter. 'In fact, he didn't even know about him until last year. And I didn't find out until more recently.'

'So Jerry told you about him?' Isla frowned.

'Mmmm …' Peter nodded. 'He didn't want to, but I could tell something was wrong and forced it out of him. Apparently, Carl turned up one day as Jerry was leaving the office. He told Jerry his mother had been a drug addict throughout his childhood, and had always refused to tell him who his father was; insisting, instead, that he call each of her many boyfriends Daddy. Later in life, she was diagnosed with a terminal illness and, for whatever reason, decided to put him out of his misery and supply him with his father's name. Armed with that, it didn't take him long to track Jerry down.'

'So Jerry *was* his dad?' Isla was confused again.

'No.' Peter shook his head and shifted awkwardly in his seat. 'That was simply the name Carl's mother had been given by the man with whom she'd had a one-night stand while working as an exotic dancer. And I know this, because *I* was that man.'

'*What*?' Isla's mouth fell open. 'Are you serious?'

'I'm not proud of it,' Peter said quietly. 'But it was something we all did back in those days. Apart from Jerry, because he was faithful to Belinda, and then to yourself, of course. But the rest of us weren't so honourable, I'm afraid. We were young and horny and thought we could take our pleasures without our wives ever finding out. We took precautions. But, clearly, they didn't always work.'

'That's terrible,' Isla murmured, shocked that he would betray his best friend like that. 'But if Jerry knew you'd used his name, why didn't he just tell Carl?'

'Because I begged him not to.' Peter sighed, slumped back in his seat and raked his hands through his hair before continuing. 'Many years ago, I was approached by a woman who claimed to be pregnant with my child. She was after money, but I was having none of that, because I thought she was pulling a fast one. I sent her packing and never heard from her again, and over time I forgot all about it. Then Jerry told me about Carl, and as soon as he gave me the details of the boy's mother, where she'd worked and when it had supposedly happened, I knew exactly who he was talking about.'

'So if Jerry knew that *you* were the father, why did he pay Carl to keep his mouth shut?' Isla asked.

'That all happened before Jerry told me about it,' said Peter. 'He'd kept it to himself, thinking that the problem would disappear of its own accord. But Carl wouldn't drop it, and things started to get out of control. By the time Jerry told me, Carl had already been extorting money out of him for a year or so. Apparently he'd been furious that Jerry wouldn't admit to being his father. He'd taken that as a fresh rejection, it seems; after being told all his life that his father had abandoned his mother because of him. Jerry said that Carl had managed to get hold of his phone during an altercation and had threatened to plant graphic child pornography onto it if he didn't start paying him a lump sum each month. Carl had said that he would then hand it over to the police, claiming that he'd found it. Jerry couldn't risk being branded as a paedophile, because that would have killed his reputation stone dead. And that, in turn, would have destroyed the company. So he did what he thought best at the time and agreed to pay the boy.'

Isla frowned as the pieces began to slot together in her mind. 'So when did Jerry tell you all this?' she asked.

'A couple of months before he passed away,' Peter said quietly. 'As I said, as soon as I heard the details, I immediately knew that he'd been targeted because I'd used his name that night. If his mother hadn't approached me years earlier, I would never have known. But it was too much of a coincidence for it not to be me.'

'Did you tell Jerry?'

'Yes.' Peter nodded and guiltily dropped his gaze. 'I thought he would see the funny side and call me a cheeky fucker for using his name, but he was livid. He said he was going to tell Carl and put an end to it once and for all. But my life would have been over if Felicity had found out, so I pleaded with him not to say anything.'

'So you let Jerry die of stress to save your marriage?' Isla was appalled. 'He was supposed to be your best friend. How could you do that to him?'

'I didn't realise how devastating an impact it had already had on him,' Peter admitted. 'It had been going on for a while by then, and had caused him so much stress, he was close to breaking point. If he *had* told Carl, it would have ended there and then. But he was a better friend than I, so he simply cut the boy off without betraying me. I think he was contemplating offering to pay for a DNA test so he could prove to Carl that he wasn't his father. But I guess he didn't get around to it in time.'

'Fuck!' Isla muttered, rubbing her temples to relieve the tension that was building in her head. 'I knew something wasn't right with Jerry. If he'd told me what it was, I could have helped.'

'Please don't blame yourself,' Peter said, reaching out to rub her shoulder again.

'I don't,' Isla said, shrugging his hand off. 'I blame *you*. You let all that go on, even though you *knew* it was making him ill. And then you practically stole his company off him – the company *he* started and allowed you to buy into once he'd got it up and running.'

'He wanted out, and I offered him far more than his shares were worth,' Peter said. 'But Felicity would have demanded to know why I was willing to pay over the odds, and what excuse could I have given her without opening a whole new can of worms? Jerry anticipated that and insisted on selling himself short. Saving me, *again*.'

'Why the hell are you so afraid of Felicity, when it's obvious you two can't stand each other?' Isla snapped. 'She treats you like a walking wallet, and then had the cheek to call *me* a gold-digger.'

Peter shifted in his seat, and Isla could see that she'd hit a nerve when he snatched his glass up and took a swig. Then, releasing a loud breath, he said, 'Felicity is the one with money. If it hadn't been for her, I would never have been able to afford to buy into Jerry's company in the first place. I worked my backside off to help Jerry to raise it to the next level. But she still has her hand in every aspect of it, so it was never really mine. And, *boy*, doesn't she like to remind me of that.'

'If it's always been that bad, why didn't you leave her?' Isla asked.

'And damage her pristine reputation?' Peter gave a bitter laugh. 'I know you and she have never really got along, and that's because you're an astute judge of character, my dear. She's not a very nice person beneath that glamorous mask she wears. And her family have the power to make me suffer for the rest of my life if I were to rock her little showboat world.'

'Wow.' Isla shook her head. 'Looks like I'm not the only one who's been dealt a shit hand. But you *chose* yours. This has all been foisted on me. And what am I supposed to do about *him* when he wakes up and you've wiped your hands of this.' She jerked her thumb towards the utility room. 'I suppose you're expecting me to suck it up like Jerry did and keep my mouth shut?'

'I'll take care of it,' Peter said.

'How?' She stared at him. 'You kept quiet and let Jerry die over it, but now I'm supposed to believe you're suddenly willing to spill the beans for me?'

'God, no!' Peter looked at her as if she was crazy. 'Felicity can never know about this.'

'Where are you going?' Isla asked, panicking when he rose to his feet. 'You're not going to leave him in there, are you? What am I supposed to do when he comes round?'

'Don't worry,' Peter said calmly. 'I'll take care of this.'

'You keep saying that, but *how*?' Isla asked again as she, too, stood up.

'There's one thing I need to ask,' Peter said, peering down

into her eyes. 'If I promise that you'll never see him again, can you assure me that Felicity will never hear of this. That *nobody* will ever hear of it?'

'I guess so,' Isla said cautiously, unnerved by his ominous tone. 'But what about Jacob?'

'What about him?' Peter gave her a blank look.

'I've been looking after him because they told me he was Jerry's son. But if *you're* Carl's father, then Jacob's your grandson.'

'I want no part of him,' Peter replied bluntly. 'I don't care what you choose to do, but my name stays well and truly out of this. Are we agreed?'

Isla nodded.

'Good.' Peter smiled and patted her on the arm. Then, taking his car keys out of his pocket, he handed them to her, saying, 'Would you mind reversing my car up to the steps and unlocking the boot for me, please? Oh, and if you have any bin liners, could you spread some across the carpet. I wouldn't want Felicity seeing the blood and asking questions.'

Unnerved that Peter was speaking as if everything was perfectly normal again and he wasn't about to drive away with Carl in his boot and do God only knew *what* with him, Isla edged past him, grabbed the roll of bin liners out of the drawer and rushed out to his car.

Chapter 31

Peter dragged Carl's body along the hallway by his ankles, leaving a thick smear of blood in his wake. Wincing when she heard the dull clunk of Carl's head bouncing off the concrete as Peter hauled him over the steps and onto the gravel, Isla almost threw up when Peter yanked Carl up to his feet and she caught a glimpse of the open, still-bleeding wound on the back of his head.

'There we go,' Peter whispered, closing the boot quietly after bundling Carl inside. Then, glancing up at the roofline, he said, 'You don't have CCTV cameras, do you?'

'No.' Isla shook her head and hugged herself. 'Jerry never thought we needed them, but I've been meaning to get some now I'm on my own. Just haven't had the time yet.'

'Thank goodness for that,' Peter said. 'This digital age is becoming more dangerous by the day. Never know who's hacking into what and viewing things they have no business seeing, eh?'

Isla forced a tiny smile when he grinned at her. As grateful as she was that he'd helped her out, she'd never seen him act the way he had acted tonight. It certainly wasn't normal for a man of his age and personal standing in the business community to almost beat a man to death and then cart him away in the boot of his car like a gangster from a mafia movie. She dreaded to think what he was planning to do, but Carl was his problem now and she just wanted the pair of them gone.

'Why don't you get yourself inside before you freeze to death,' Peter said, sounding almost fatherly now, Isla thought. 'This is over, I promise you. And you and I shall take our secrets to the grave. Agreed?'

Isla gave a tiny nod and then watched as he climbed into the car and started the engine. Sure that she'd heard him whistling to himself before he'd closed the door, she shuddered as he drove out through the gate. Pressing the fob to close the gate behind him, she rushed inside and locked and bolted the front door, then ran up the stairs to check on Jacob. She had feared that the noise might have woken him and he'd be scared, but he was still sleeping soundly, so she gently kissed his forehead and then made her way back downstairs.

She'd been so desperate to go to the toilet when she arrived home that evening, she had forgotten to lock the gate behind her. And she hadn't thought to check that the front door had properly closed when she'd given it a quick kick before carrying Jacob up the stairs. That had been careless and it scared her to think that anybody could have walked in while she was taking her shower. But, in fact, her carelessness had saved her. Carl had already been in the house, and she thanked God now that she *hadn't* locked up properly, because Peter wouldn't have been able to get in if the gate had been closed. And the thought of what Carl might have done to her and Jacob if Peter hadn't intervened sent shivers down her spine.

Exhausted and still shaking, she felt nervous as she made her way into the kitchen. The silence was deafening now the men and their voices had gone, and she jumped out of her skin at every little creak as the house settled down for the night. The back door was still standing ajar, so she rushed over and locked it. It seemed almost pointless since the panel was missing, and she knew there was no way she would be able to sleep for fear of Carl coming back and breaking in again. He'd been in pretty bad shape when Peter took him away, so she doubted he'd be capable of coming back again tonight. But Peter had refused to tell her what he was going to do with him, so she couldn't trust that he wouldn't just drop him off a few miles away and leave him to find a way back.

There was nothing inside the house that could be used to block the hole in the door. All Jerry's tools and wood were in his shed at the rear of the garden, but there was no way in hell Isla was going to venture out there in the dark after what she'd just been through. So, using all her strength, she dragged the fridge-freezer out of its space and pushed and pulled it across the floor until it was as tightly up against the back door as she could manage. She knew the glass was still under there and that she had probably damaged the floor tiles by dragging the heavy fridge over it. But she was too tired and on edge to care about that right then.

The blood on the table and the floor were a different matter. It was almost midnight and her body was crying out for rest, but she didn't want Jacob to see the mess when she brought him down for breakfast in the morning. She also couldn't risk leaving any traces of Carl's blood here in case he decided to report her and Peter to the police for assaulting him. So, filling a bowl with liquid-soap, bleach and hot water, she pulled on her rubber gloves and scrubbed the floor and the tabletop until they were both gleaming. And then she followed the trail of blood both into and out of the utility room and along the hallway, scrubbing as she went, before forcing herself to go outside to quickly clean the steps.

Satisfied that she'd done as much as she could, but still too wired to even contemplate going to bed, she made herself a cup of strong coffee and sat at the kitchen table as the awful events of the night replayed like a horror movie in her mind.

Visions of Peter smashing Carl's head onto the table and blood seeping out and dripping onto the floor turned her stomach, and she swiped at the tears that suddenly gushed from her eyes as the adrenaline she'd been running on for the last few hours receded and left her feeling empty and cold. She couldn't believe that she had been so stupid for the last few months. Melanie had completely fooled her, and her mind was blown by the lengths the couple had gone to in order to wheedle their way into her life. Even using their child as bait after learning that she had always wanted children of her own. That was evil, and all so Carl could get what he believed was rightfully his. And, the crazy thing was, he didn't even know he had targeted the wrong man.

Peter's confession had shaken Isla to the core. But it had sounded every bit as ludicrous as this entire situation with Carl and Melanie, and she still wasn't entirely sure what to believe. In her heart, she had already accepted that Jacob, with his sweet smile and gentle, playful nature, was Jerry's child; because those were the exact qualities she had loved in her husband. Carl's temperament, however, was the complete opposite, and she found it really hard to accept that he had a single cell in his violent body linking him to Jerry. But Carl's mother had named Jerry as the father, and the man was absolutely convinced that he was his son. It was one big crazy ball of lies, and her head ached just thinking about it.

The sudden ping of a message arriving on her phone shattered the silence, and Isla thought her heart was going to explode with fear. Fully expecting it to be from Peter, telling her that Carl had escaped, her hand was shaking wildly as she reached for her phone. A wave of intense relief washed over her when she opened it and saw that it was a cutesie video Benny had sent. He often did that when he was bored-scrolling through YouTube at night, usually with a little message attached to say good morning, because he assumed she would be sleeping when he sent them. She was still wide awake, but she wasn't in the mood to watch the full video, which was an obvious AI creation. But she knew that Benny would see that she had opened it and would think she was ignoring him if she didn't respond, so she typed: *Thanks, B. Looks fun. Will watch properly in the morning xx*

Almost immediately, Benny replied: *Oops! Sorry. Thought you'd be sleeping. Hope I didn't wake you?* followed by a face-palm emoji and two kisses.

Before she could think of a suitable reply, Benny messaged again, saying: *How come you're up so late? Not like you. Hope all is OK and lil man isn't teething or something?*

No, he's fine, she replied, touched that he'd asked after Jacob, unlike the boy's supposed father.

So what is it then? Benny asked. Immediately followed by: *Oh shit, please don't tell me you've got company and I've disturbed you?* Then: *Sorry angel, I'll leave you to it.*

Shocked that he thought she had a man there, Isla wrote: *I don't have company. Just got a lot on my mind. But I'll be OK.*

Of course Benny wasn't going to leave it at that, and she jumped when her phone immediately started ringing.

'What's going on?' he demanded with a mock-sigh. 'Tell big bro Benny all about it.'

It was so good to hear his voice, Isla immediately burst into tears.

'Hey, what's wrong?' Benny asked. 'Isla, talk to me. What's happened?'

Isla tried to explain, but she was sobbing so hard he couldn't understand her.

'I'm coming over,' he said after a moment.

'No, I'm OK,' she protested, desperately trying to get herself under control. 'Honestly, I'm just feeling a bit down.'

Benny wouldn't take no for an answer, and she heard him grab his keys before ending the call.

Twenty minutes later, Benny's car pulled up at the gate, and Isla pressed the fob to let him in. He leapt out as soon as he'd parked and ran to where she was waiting in the doorway. Her eyes were red and swollen from crying, and she was shivering like a leaf, so he gently pulled her into his arms and held her until he felt her body start to relax. Then, drawing back his head, he lifted her chin with his finger and peered into her eyes.

'Has something happened with Jacob?' he asked softly. 'Has Melanie taken him away?'

'No.' Isla shook her head.

'So what is it?' he probed. 'I've never seen you this upset before. Did something happen at the beach? Were you assaulted or followed?'

'No, nothing like that,' Isla sniffed, drawing away from him when she felt she'd got herself under control again. 'Come in. I'll make you a brew.'

'Sack the brew, I need a stiff one after that drive,' Benny quipped as he followed her along the hallway. 'The speed I was going, thinking I was coming to rescue you from a big bad monster, I'm lucky there were no cops about.'

Hesitating when he entered the kitchen, he drew his head back and gave Isla a questioning look when he saw the fridge-freezer standing in front of the back door.

'Erm, what's this?'

'Sit down while I get you that drink,' Isla sighed, gesturing to a chair. 'You're not going to believe what I'm about to tell you.'

Unable to stomach any more whisky, Isla poured them both a glass of wine and took a seat facing him.

'So what's going on?' Benny asked.

Isla took a deep breath and released it slowly. 'I don't even know where to start.'

'Take your time, sweetheart,' Benny said, reaching his hand across the table to give her hand a reassuring squeeze. 'I've got my toothbrush and PJs in the car, so I've got all night.'

He winked at her and Isla gave him a tiny smile in return; feeling safe for the first time that night.

'Carl was here when I got home,' she began.

'What?' Anger flared in Benny's eyes. '*The* Carl?'

'Yep. He'd broken in, but I didn't realise until I'd put Jacob to bed and taken a shower.'

'He'd better not have fucking touched you,' Benny said, his grip on her hand tightening so much she winced.

'No, he was just sat in there in the dark when I came down.' She nodded towards the snug. 'I saw the back door was open and glass was all over the floor, so I was about to call the police. Then he spoke, and I nearly had a heart attack.'

Benny listened intently without interrupting as she continued with her story. But, unlike Peter, whose face had been deathly white when she'd finished telling him, his face was red with anger, and his eyes were blazing.

'Sick fuck!' he spat. 'Just watch if I ever see him walking round the Grange.'

'I don't know what Peter was intending to do,' Isla sighed. 'But he reckons he's going to sort it and make sure he never comes back.'

'Well, he'd better,' said Benny. 'Because I'm set to make sure the bastard never walks again.'

When Peter had spoken, Isla had felt unnerved, but Benny sounded so protective, it made her shiver with gratitude. She had promised Peter that she wouldn't tell a soul, but she trusted Benny implicitly and knew that he would never betray her confidence.

Just like you believed Jerry implicitly, until Melanie, a total stranger, fed you a pack of lies and you decided to believe her *instead*, she thought guiltily.

'Hey, what's going on in that head of yours?' Benny asked, getting up and walking round the table to sit beside her. 'I hope I haven't stressed you out by getting angry? I'm just mad that this happened to you. I love you and want you to know that I'm here for you. *Always*.'

'Thank you, that means a lot,' Isla murmured, feeling suddenly tearful again as she laid her head on his chest and heard the comforting beat of his heart.

'Isla,' Benny said, so softly she almost didn't hear him.

'Mmmm?' She raised her head and looked into his eyes.

'I can't keep doing this,' he said.

Instantly thinking that she'd got too comfortable and had made him feel awkward, she started to pull away, croaking, 'Sorry.'

'No!' He grabbed her arm to stop her moving. 'I mean I can't keep pretending that this is just friendship. Tell me to shut up if I'm overstepping the mark, but when I said I love you, I meant I *love* you.' He emphasised the word while peering deep into her eyes.

Isla's chin immediately began to wobble, and she whispered, 'I love you, too.'

'For real?' His eyes lit up.

'For real,' she affirmed, barely able to breathe when her own heartbeat started pounding in her ears.

His lips, when he kissed her, were so soft, she felt herself melting into him as the tension of the night evaporated and everything around them faded into insignificance.

Chapter 32

Rob Layton hadn't seen either of his neighbours in weeks. The last time he'd seen the girl was when she'd come round to borrow a tenner. He'd seen the man the following morning when they had bumped into each other in the lift. Since then, there hadn't been a peep from either of them. At first, it had been bliss to have a bit of peace after the constant noise of blaring TVs and arguments. But then he'd noticed a foul smell pervading his flat.

It was strongest in the bathroom, and he immediately called the council out, thinking that there was some kind of blockage and raw sewage might be coming up through the pipes. The council workers had smelled it for themselves as soon as they walked through the door, but they hadn't been able to find anything to explain it. As they were about to leave, Rob had remembered the time he'd reported his neighbour for smoking weed after it seeped though from their flat via the skirting boards, and he asked the men if they could nip round there and take a look at their pipework instead. The men had knocked on the door for several minutes to no avail, and had then thrown up their hands and said there was nothing more they could do.

Unwilling to leave things as they were as the smell continued to stink the place out, Rob knocked on next door several times himself. But when he pushed open the letterbox to yell at them to answer the fucking door, he got a full-on blast of a stench so vile, it sent him reeling.

'You OK, pet?' the old lady who lived opposite asked, poking her head out of her front door and finding him leaning against the wall with his head down, dry-retching. 'Do you need me to call someone?'

'I'll be all right,' he gasped, taking deep breaths to steady himself. 'Can you smell anything?' he asked then.

'Like what?' the lady asked, sniffing the air. 'Oh, yeah.' She scrunched up her nose up when she picked up on a faint, unpleasant odour. 'Where's that coming from?'

'In there.' Rob pointed at his nightmare neighbours' door. 'I've been trying to speak to them and lifted the letterbox, but the stench almost knocked me out.'

'Should've guessed it'd be them.' The old lady rolled her eyes and folded her arms. 'Not the cleanest pair, are they?' she went on in a conspiratorial whisper. 'And the language on *him* is shocking. The council should have put them out years ago.'

'I agree,' Rob muttered, frowning as he looked at the door again when he remembered the hooded men he'd seeing going in there the night before he'd seen the man with a black eye. 'You haven't noticed anyone going in there lately, have you?'

'Not for a while, no.' The old lady shrugged.

A door creaked open at the end of the corridor and a young woman in a two-piece navy uniform with a lanyard around her neck strolled in.

'Morning, Annie,' she smiled at the old woman. 'Who's this, then? Got yourself a toyboy, have you?'

'I should be so lucky,' the old lady cackled. 'This lovely young chap is me neighbour.'

'From across the way,' Rob said, nodding hello.

'Everything all right?' the younger woman asked when she saw the worried expression on his face.

'I'm not sure,' he murmured. 'I don't suppose you could do me a favour and take a whiff in there?' he asked, waving towards the offending door. 'I've got adjoining walls and my place has been stinking like sewage for the last few weeks. Council couldn't find anything wrong, so I've been knocking at theirs to see if it's coming from them. I got no answer, but when I lifted the letterbox, it knocked me sick. Just want to make sure I'm not imagining it.'

'Ooh, this sounds like one of them true crime things,' the woman grinned. 'The mail had been piling up for weeks, yer honour, then I smelled summat bad and just *knew* there was a body in there.' Grin slipping when Rob's expression grew more grim, she said, 'Sorry. I've got a dark sense of humour. This door, you say?'

Rob nodded, then stepped back to avoid getting another blast when she leaned down and raised the letterbox.

'Oh, fucking hell,' she gasped, spluttering as she stumbled back. 'Sorry, Annie,' she apologised. 'But that's not normal.'

'I think I need to call the police,' Rob said.

'I agree,' said the woman. 'Best get our lovely Annie out of the way, in case, eh?' she added quietly, giving him a knowing look. 'I'll be here for half an hour if you need me.'

'Cheers, love,' Rob said gratefully, pulling out his phone as she hustled the old lady indoors.

Chapter 33

Isla felt happier than she had in months as she watched Benny playing with Jacob outside while she cooked dinner. Jacob was totally steady on his feet now, and Benny had recently taught him how to kick a football. They were racing around out there like a pair of lunatics now as the sun went down behind them, and she smiled when Benny suddenly yelled, 'Goal!' and lifted the giggling boy into the air before doing a lap of honour with him.

Benny hadn't officially moved in, but he'd barely been back to his own house since driving over here the night Carl broke in. The scent of aftershave hovered in the air of her bedroom again, but now it was Benny's delicious scent that made her stomach tingle whenever she walked in there. He treated her like an absolute queen, and she loved falling asleep in his arms and waking up to his sexy smile.

Jacob loved having him there, too, and his delight at seeing Benny on the morning after that awful night had been beautiful to see. The only cloud that still lingered over Isla's head as far as the boy was concerned was that Melanie could ask for him back at any time.

She hadn't heard from her at all after Carl's unwelcome visit, and she did sometimes worry about her silence, given that she had been relying on Isla's money. She had thought about reaching out to her, but couldn't bring herself to do it in case she knew about Carl coming round and started asking awkward questions. There had been no word from Peter, either, but Carl hadn't shown his face again since. Which was just as well, because he'd have had Benny to deal with if he ever dared to try.

When she'd told Tia about Carl breaking in and revealing that Jacob was biologically his, her friend had reasoned that Melanie probably assumed that he'd taken Jacob and done a runner that night and that she had probably decided it wasn't worth the trouble of trying to track them down and get dragged back into a life of violence. She'd gone on to say that Melanie obviously hadn't cared all that much about Jacob, considering she'd been happy to leave him with Isla for so long; so Isla should put it out of her mind and deal with it if and when Melanie ever decided to get in touch again. And Tia was usually right – as she had been about Melanie from the start. So Isla had stopped thinking about Melanie *and* Carl, and had concentrated on giving Jacob the best time while he was still with her, while also building a new life with Benny – something else that Tia had been dead right about.

Later that evening, after they had all eaten and Jacob had been bathed and put to bed, Isla and Benny sat out on the patio to drink wine and watch the stars under the patio heater. Snuggled up to Benny as they chatted about their day, Isla excused herself and sat forward to reach for her phone when it started ringing on the table.

It was Tia, and she blurted out, 'Open the gate!' when Isla answered.

'Is something wrong?' Isla asked, jumping up and rushing into the kitchen to get the fob as Benny followed behind.

'Just open it; I'll tell you in a sec,' Tia said, hanging up.

On the doorstep, with Benny standing beside her, Isla gave her friend a questioning smile when she leapt out of her car. 'What's going on?'

'This!' Tia shoved her phone under their noses. 'Watch!'

It was a video of a newsreader speaking into the cameras as the lights of numerous police vehicles and ambulances strobed the walls of a block of flats behind her.

'Is that the Grange?' Benny squinted to see more clearly.

Tia shushed him and pointed at the screen, ordering them to carry on watching.

Isla couldn't really hear what the newsreader was saying, but her stomach almost dropped through the floor when another image suddenly popped up. It was fairly old, obviously taken some years earlier. But it was unmistakeably Melanie.

That shot disappeared after a few seconds and a second one appeared; this one of Carl in his younger years.

'What's going on?' Isla gasped when the story switched to the weather report. 'What was she saying?'

'Sorry, I should have let you watch it inside so you could hear it properly,' Tia apologised. 'But as soon as I saw it, I leapt in the car to come and show you in case you hadn't seen it.'

'So what's it about?' Benny asked, closing the door as they all walked inside. 'Have they been arrested?'

'No.' Tia shook her head and gave them a grave look. 'She's been murdered and the police think *he* did it. They're looking for him now, and they've told the public not to approach him if they spot him, because he could be armed.'

'Holy shit,' Benny muttered, putting his arm around Isla when he saw that she was shaking. 'You OK, sweetheart?'

Sniffing back tears, she nodded. Then, to Tia, she asked, 'Do you know what he did to her, and when it happened?'

'They haven't given any specific details yet, and probably won't at their stage,' Tia replied. 'They usually have to wait for autopsy results after a murder. Unless it was really obvious, like a shooting, or something. They did say they think it happened about three weeks ago, because none of the neighbours have seen either of them in that long.'

'Probably the night he came here,' Isla said as the pieces started to fall into place. 'That must be why he was in such a state and got mad every time I mentioned her that night. And, come to think of it, he had a black eye and kept scratching himself, so she must have tried to fight back.'

'Well, good for her if she did,' Tia said approvingly. 'Not that either of them deserve pity for what they put you through, but at least they're gone now so they can't bother you again.'

'Carl might, if he gets desperate enough,' Isla murmured. 'Maybe I should speak to Peter and ask what happened that night.'

'I wouldn't do that right now,' Tia cautioned. 'It might spook him if he's seen the news.'

'Did they mention Jacob?' Isla asked fearfully.

'Yeah, they think Carl's taken him and gone on the run. So, if he doesn't get found, they'll eventually stop looking for Jacob as well.'

'Do you think I should call the police and tell them he's here?'

'Why? All they'll do is take him into care, or send him to Melanie's folks. And they refused to have anything to do with her, even though they knew she had him, so they don't sound much better than her.'

'But what if the police find out I've had him all this time and didn't say anything?' Isla asked.

'Melanie told you he was Jerry's son,' Tia reminded her. 'And she left him with you because she knew you'd keep him safer and give him a better life than she could.'

'Yeah, but that was all lies. He's not related to Jerry, so I've got no rights to him.'

'*We* know that, but nobody else does. Only Carl, who didn't even want to take him that night when he had the chance. And now he's on the run, there's no chance of him turning up for him in the future.'

'Peter knows, as well,' Isla said.

'He's already said he wants nothing to do with him, so he's not an issue,' said Tia. 'You've got all the evidence on Jerry's phone that he was the dad, so stick to that. And you won't get into trouble for not going to the police. You haven't heard from Melanie in months, and you never watch TV, so how would you have even known that she was dead?'

'I guess,' Isla murmured.

'I think Tia's right,' Benny interjected. 'If the police ever find out he's here, you could plead ignorance on the grounds that you weren't in touch with her anymore. No one will ever find out that you gave Melanie that money now she's gone and he's on the run, so you're safe in that respect. And Jacob's already been here for ages, so I doubt he'd be taken away from you if the authorities did get involved. All they'd see is a happy little boy whose stepmum has been taking great care of him.'

'I agree,' said Tia. 'But save that for if and when you actually need it. Jacob's the important one here, and you don't want to throw his fate to the wind by alerting the authorities and risk having them dig into this and decide that you shouldn't keep him.'

Isla nodded slowly as she digested the advice they had both given her. She had always known that his mother or father might come for him, but the thought of Jacob being placed with strangers when he had a perfectly good life here was unbearable.

'OK, I'm not going to do anything,' she said. 'I'll wait to see what happens.'

'We've got your back,' Tia assured her. Then, sticking out her pinkie finger, she said, 'Sisters for life.'

Isla smiled and linked pinkies with her, then laughed when Tia raised her eyebrows at Benny, saying, 'This is the pinkie pledge of allegiance, so why aren't you joining in?'

'Er, 'cos I'm not a girl,' he quipped.

'Could've fooled me,' Tia snorted. 'All that prancing around in tights back in the day.'

'I'll have you know they were skinny jeans,' Benny said, puffing up his chest. 'And I think you'll find your friend here knows different now.'

Blushing when he winked at her, Isla grinned at Tia when he tutted and rolled his eyes before hooking his pinkie around theirs.

'Sisters for life,' they all chanted, Benny making them roar with laughter when he did it in a girly voice.

Epilogue

It was a crisp but bright day, and the stained-glass windows of the tiny, ancient crematorium twinkled as Isla, Benny, Tia and Sam made the short walk from the car park. Isla had wanted to bring Jacob along as she'd thought it right that he should be there, even if he wouldn't have understood what was happening. Tia had talked her out of it, warning her that someone might recognise him and start asking questions, so she had agreed to let Sam's sister, Elaine, look after him for the day.

It was the same chapel where Jerry's funeral service had been held. It had been packed out on that day, but there was only one solemn-faced man, an old lady and a younger woman in a carer's uniform standing outside today. Isla went over and introduced herself as Melanie's girlhood friend and chatted to them briefly as they awaited the arrival of the hearse.

The man, who introduced himself as Rob, turned out to be the one who had raised the alarm, leading to the discovery of Melanie's body; wrapped in bin liners and already decomposing enough to stink out both her flat *and* his. He told Isla that he hadn't really known her, but had felt it his duty to pay his respects because he'd heard how badly Carl had treated her.

'Pardon my French,' he'd gone on quietly. 'But I hope they throw the absolute book at that bastard when they catch him.

The things I heard through my wall, I wouldn't wish on my worst enemy. And to beat the baby out of her like that…' He'd stopped at that and had shaken his head in absolute disgust.

Annie, the old lady, hadn't held back with *her* vociferous condemnation of Carl, and Isla had been saddened to learn that nobody on their block had really known Melanie, because 'that filthy little scumbag with evil eyes' had practically held her prisoner in their flat. The carer had a quiet word with Annie after she said that, and Isla had been amused when the old lady apologised if she'd caused any offence.

'Don't worry, I think everyone shares your opinion,' Isla had assured her. 'I didn't know the man, but if he could do that to the mother of his child, he's beyond redemption.'

The hearse arrived, and Isla felt a little tearful as she watched the wicker coffin being lifted out. She'd paid for a beautiful flower spray for the top of it, consisting of all the colourful flowers Melanie had used to admire in her garden and the wild ones she'd excitedly told Isla about after taking her walks in the woods.

The police had never reached out to Isla, because they hadn't known about her recent involvement with Melanie. But she hadn't been able to get the woman out of her mind after hearing what Carl had done, so she'd made discreet enquiries, claiming to be an old friend who had known Melanie on the estate but had lost touch with her after she married Jerry and moved away. When she'd found out that Melanie had been listed for a council funeral because her family had refused to bury her, it had broken her heart and made her think of the way her own mum had cut her off and made no effort to reach out since. Given everything Melanie had done to her, Isla could only imagine that she must have done worse to her family to make them keep their backs turned to her even after finding out she'd been murdered.

That aside, Isla still felt a little guilty for kicking Melanie out, giving her no real option but to go back to Carl. And it saddened her to think of the woman taking her final journey with nobody to send her on her way and celebrate her life. So she had offered to pay for the funeral.

A notice had been listed in the local paper, detailing the time and date, but, apart from the neighbours and the carer, nobody else had bothered to turn up. Isla wondered if she'd made a mistake by arranging to have Melanie cremated at the village church, because it was an hour's bus ride away from Manchester, which might have made it inaccessible for a lot of the people who had lived around her. But, however much Melanie might have lied to her about everything else, Isla knew that Melanie had loved her time in the village, so she'd chosen to do it here so that Melanie could rest in the place where she had spent those few short months of absolute peace. And she would also be close to Jacob, which had felt important.

Unlike Jerry's wake, which she'd held at the house, Isla had decided to invite the other mourners to join them in the village pub for drinks and snacks. The neighbours only stayed for a short time, and Isla and her friends drove over to Elaine's place to pick up Jacob before heading back to the house.

Jacob was wide awake and wanted to play, so Benny and Sam took him into the garden to play football, while Isla and Tia sipped wine on the patio and giggled about how perfect their men were.

'Did you ever imagine you'd end up with Benny?' Tia asked.

'Not in a million years,' Isla replied truthfully. 'I thought me and Jerry would be together forever.'

'I know how much you loved him,' Tia said softly. 'And I'm

really sorry Melanie put you through all that shit and made you think badly of him.'

'Me too,' Isla sighed. 'She made me question everything I thought I knew about him. Don't get me wrong, he had his faults,' she went on. 'I didn't really notice at the time, because I was happy. But, in hindsight, I guess he was a bit controlling at times. Nothing nasty, obviously; he just liked to be in charge. And I went along with it because I knew it came from a good place; that he was just trying to be a caring husband. But I do feel like I lost a bit of myself along the way, so it's been nice to make my own decisions again without worrying what Jerry would think of it.'

'I know you loved him, and I genuinely think he adored you, too,' said Tia. 'But he was a lot older than you, and he was your boss when you got together, so it probably felt natural to him to keep a level of control after you got married. I'm not knocking him for that, because he gave you a great life. But even when we were kids, I always knew you and Benny were the perfect match.'

'No, you didn't,' Isla said amusedly. 'You thought he was gay.'

'That's his fault for acting camp,' Tia chuckled. 'And you've got to admit he was too damn cute to be straight.'

'Oh, so I'm assuming you must think the same about Sam?' Isla raised an eyebrow. ''Cos he's pretty cute too.'

'He's all right, I suppose,' Tia said mock-grudgingly. Then, grinning, she added, 'But, seriously, how fit do they both look right now? We're lucky girls.'

'We certainly are,' Isla agreed.

'Only one thing left to do now.' Tia nudged her. 'When do I get to plan the wedding?'

'*You're* not even married yet, and you've been with Sam for way longer than I've been with Benny,' Isla reminded her.

'I'm the planner, not the bride,' Tia said flatly. 'And me and

Sam are just fine as we are, thank you. But you and Benny are a different kettle of fish; especially now you've got lil man depending on you both. So, I'll ask again. When do I get to plan the wedding?'

'If it ever gets to that, you'll be the first to know,' Isla murmured, feeling the usual tingle in her stomach when Benny saw her watching him and winked at her. 'But for now, let's just enjoy the view.'

'Amen to that, sister,' Tia said, raising her glass and blowing a kiss to Sam when he glanced over at her. 'Amen to *that*.'

Acknowledgements

All my love, as ever, to Win, Michael, Andrew, Azzura, Marissa, Lariah, Antonio, Marlowe, Lorenzo, Ava, Amber, Martin, Jade, Reece, Kyro, Diaz, Azariah, Auntie Doreen, Pete, Lorna, Cliff, Chris, Glen, Toni, Natalie, Dan, Rayne, Amari, Zi, River, Silvia, Marvin, Lee, Ell, Val, Norman, Richie, Julie and co, and the rest of my clan.

Huge thanks to my agent, Sheila Crowley; my editor, Louisa Cusworth, and all at Orion.

Much love to Betty and Ronnie Schwartz, Kimbo, Wayne Brookes, Leodora Darlington, Jeanna Polley, Ian Martin, Katy and John, Jayne and Nev, Laney, Tasha, Rik, Chris and Allan, Jo and Dom, Brian and Jac, Louis Emerick, Jodie Prenger, Steve Evets, Joe Gill.

Love to my old mates in Warrington and Hulme, and to my readers and friends on FB, X and Insta.

Special thanks to my witches, Liz and Tracy Whitwell, for all your help.

Heavenly love to my dad, and all the loved ones who are no longer here. RIP x

Credits

Mandasue Heller and Orion Fiction would like to thank everyone at Orion who worked on the publication of *The Child*.

Editor
Charlotte Mursell
Louisa Cusworth

Copy-editor
Jade Craddock

Proofreader
Alex Davis

Editorial Management
Niyati Naudiyal
Jane Hughes
Charlie Panayiotou
Lucy Bilton
Patrice Nelson

Marketing
Hennah Sandhu

Audio
Paul Stark
Louise Richardson
Georgina Cutler-Ross

Contracts
Rachel Monte
Ellie Bowker
Phoebe Miller

Design
Tomás Almeida
Nick Shah
Deborah Francois
Helen Ewing

Photo Shoots & Image Research
Natalie Dawkins

Finance
Nick Gibson
Jasdip Nandra
Sue Baker
Tom Costello

Inventory
Jo Jacobs
Erika Andrejuskinaite

Sales
Dave Murphy
Victoria Laws
Sammy Luton
Group Sales teams across Digital, Field, International and Non-Trade

Production
Ruth Sharvell
Katie Horrocks

Publicity
Sian Baldwin

Operations
Group Sales Operations team

Rights
Rebecca Folland
Tara Hiatt
Ruth Case-Green
Maddie Stephenson
Ruth Blakemore
Marie Matuschka

A killer stalks the [illegible] of [illegible]. Will she be the next victim?

[illegible]

A killer stalks the streets of Manchester.
Will she be his next victim?

Lisa lives too close for comfort to Westy Lane. Too many women have been murdered on that road, each left with a tiny blue flower on their bodies. She can't help but wonder if her mother might be next. After all, people don't care if women like her mother go missing. There's no one to protect them.

And then everything changes . . .

One night, **Benny** arrives in Lisa's life. He's tall, dark, and the most gorgeous man she's ever seen. But he is not all as he seems. While Lisa savours true love, Benny wants more from her than she will ever know . . .

If you loved *The Child* - don't miss *The Family!*

Since her mother died of an overdose, kind-hearted Cheryl's always had to look out for herself. **Until Dale Moran walks into her life.**

Dale and his family have just bought the house across the street, and within a day, he's chased off the violent thugs who've been threatening Cheryl for her ex-boyfriend's debts.

Dale is devastatingly handsome and a fierce protector. It's no wonder Cheryl falls fast and hard. But when Cheryl finally meets the family; when she notices that they go quiet as she enters rooms; **when she hears gunshots in the middle of the night on their estate, she has to wonder whether her new romance has taken her out of the frying pan and into the fire . . .**

Cheryl's not sure how wrapped up Dale is in his family's secrets. But she's certain of one thing: The Morans are hiding something. **And unfortunately for Cheryl, finding the truth could mean losing her life . . .**

Turn the page for the first chapter of *The Family*.

Prologue

The air in the room was icy, but her body felt like it was on fire. She could hear her friend talking to the older woman who had arrived a few minutes earlier, but she was in too much pain to make sense of their words.

'Help her!' the girl's friend pleaded when she cried out. 'She's losing too much blood.'

'Stay here and keep an eye on her,' the woman ordered. 'I'll fetch the doctor.'

'That will take too long. The baby is coming already. Please . . . you have to help her.'

'Shut up before somebody hears you. I'll be back as soon as I can.'

Terrified when the older woman rushed from the room, the younger one hugged herself as she gazed down at her friend. Her skin was slick with sweat, but the colour had completely drained from her face, making the red stain on the sheet beneath her stand out all the more starkly. Her friend suddenly screamed and arched her back before flopping silently against the pillows, and she stared in horror at the bloody mess that had slithered out from between her legs. Realising that she needed to do something when she saw that the baby wasn't moving or making a sound, she ran to the bathroom and grabbed a towel and a pair of nail scissors before rushing back to the bed.

Her friend was still breathing, albeit weakly, so she concentrated on the baby, using the towel to ease it the rest of the way out before cutting the umbilical cord, as she'd seen the village midwife do when her mother had given birth to her baby brother. Tears scorched her cheeks when she gazed at its tiny face after wiping away the blood and the mucus, and her voice faltered as she whispered a prayer before wrapping it inside the towel and gently rocking it in her arms.

Chapter 1

It had been a busy day at The Bluebell Café, but the takings didn't reflect that when Cheryl Taylor cashed up after showing her last customer out. Most of her regulars were elderly, and she knew they came for the companionship and warmth; but them nursing a single cup of tea for hours on end wasn't good business, and the owner was already hinting that he might have to shut up shop if things didn't improve. A lot of the other units had already closed, and the once vibrant market hall was beginning to feel like a ghost town as customers deserted it in favour of the newly renovated Arndale Centre. But she hadn't lost her job yet, and she didn't want to add the worry of that to her existing list of woes, so she pushed it out of her mind and got on with cleaning up before heading home.

It was dark and bitterly cold when Cheryl stepped off the bus after a hellish ride through rush-hour traffic, and she kept her head down and her hand firmly on the strap of her bag as she hurried past the high-rise flats that lined the perimeter of the Langley estate. She'd lived there for ten years, but this particular part had too many hiding places where muggers were known to lie in wait, so she was always cautious about walking through there at night.

Relieved to reach her own road on the more well-lit side of

the estate, she glanced over at the derelict house on the corner when she noticed that the *For Sale* sign that had been standing in the jungle-like front garden was gone. The sole survivor of the privately owned Victorian villas that had once dominated the area, it had been left to rot following the death of its elderly owner three years earlier, and a gang of youths had been using it as a hang-out for the last few months, causing havoc for the residents as they raced around on stolen motorbikes at all hours – and threatening anyone who dared to confront them.

Hoping that someone had bought the place and the trouble-makers would be cleared out, Cheryl walked on to her next-door neighbour Bob Baker's house. His front door swung open as soon as she touched it and she shook her head in despair as she stepped inside. She was forever telling him to keep it locked, especially now it was getting dark so much earlier; but the stubborn old bugger seemed to think he was still young and fit enough to fight off potential intruders.

Bob was sitting in his battered armchair next to the blazing fire when she popped her head around the living room door. His mangy old cat, Cyril, was curled up on his lap, and the TV was blaring.

'Bloody hell, Bob!' She covered her ears with her hands. 'That's deafening!'

'Sorry, love.' He grabbed the remote and quickly muted the TV. 'A load of workmen have been in Edna's place making a racket, so I had to turn it up.'

'Yeah, I noticed the sign was gone. Has it been sold, then?'

'Looks like it, aye. A couple turned up this afternoon and took a look around.'

'What were they like?'

'No idea, but they had a lovely motor.'

'Trust you to notice the car but not the people.' Cheryl tutted. 'Typical man.'

'Couldn't help it; it was a beauty,' Bob chuckled. 'So, how's your day been?'

'Not great. But that's good for you, 'cos there were loads of butties left over.'

'Thanks, love. What do I owe you?'

It was the same question he asked every day, and Cheryl gave the same answer as always in return: 'Nothing. They'd only have gone in the bin if I hadn't brought them home.'

'There's more than usual,' Bob remarked, raking through the contents of the bag. 'It'll take me a week to get through this lot.'

'I'm sure Cyril will help you,' Cheryl said, watching as the cat sniffed the air before stiffly standing up.

'What would we do without you, eh?' Bob said, pulling a chunk of tuna out of one of the sandwiches and feeding it to Cyril.

'It's my pleasure,' Cheryl replied, patting his bony shoulder when she saw the gratitude in his eyes. He'd been an active man when she first moved in, always out and about doing odd jobs for the neighbours and looking in on the older ones. In his seventies now, with his health in decline, he rarely ventured past the doorstep, and she knew he probably wouldn't speak to another human for days on end if she didn't call in on him each evening. Making a snap decision to stay a little longer than usual, she said, 'Fancy a brew, Bob?'

'I'd love one,' he said. 'But I don't want to keep you if you need to get home to Chris.'

'We split up six months ago,' she reminded him as she slipped her coat off.

'Did you?' He frowned. 'I could have sworn I saw him going into yours earlier.'

'I doubt that, seeing as I took his keys off him when I kicked him out,' Cheryl muttered, her jaw clenching at the memory of the day she had arrived home early from work and caught her boyfriend of four years screwing one of her so-called friends. A lot more had come out after that, and she'd been shocked to learn that he had not only cheated several other times, but had also been helping himself to her money and taking out loans in her name – some of which she was paying off even now.

Still furious with herself for ignoring the red flags that she would have seen in a heartbeat if it had been one of her friends' boyfriends acting the way Chris had, Cheryl determinedly pushed him out of her mind and laid her coat over the back of the sofa before heading to the kitchen. It was the same layout as her own, with the same beige units and cheap council lino; but that was where any similarity ended, and she stared around in shock after switching the light on. The ledges were barely visible beneath mounds of rubbish, the dishes in the sink were immersed in a pool of slimy liquid, and there were so many bin bags piled up behind the back door, it would be impossible to escape if there was a fire at the front of the house.

Bob was a proud man and she didn't want to offend him by offering to clean up, but it was obvious he needed help, and she wondered if she ought to ring social services and ask them to send somebody over to check on him. Or, better still, she could track down his waste-of-space daughter and tell *her* to do something. The selfish cow lived nearby, but she only ever showed her face when she wanted a handout – and she was always in and out within seconds, so she never spent any quality time with him.

'You OK in there, love?' Bob called out from the living room, breaking into her thoughts.

'I'm fine,' Cheryl called back. 'Won't be a tick.'

Sighing, she swallowed her revulsion and gingerly plucked two cups out of the swamp.

Bob had been in a talkative mood and his voice was still ringing in Cheryl's head when she got home an hour later. Her house was freezing, but she was already dreading her next gas bill, so she decided to watch TV in bed rather than put the heating on.

The doorbell rang as she was about to make her way upstairs, and she was surprised to see her best friend, Anna Johnson, standing outside when she peeped through the spyhole.

'What are you doing here?' Cheryl asked, opening the door. 'I thought you were going out with Sean tonight?'

'He's dumped me,' Anna said, bringing a blast of icy air in with her when she stepped inside.

'Why?' Cheryl ushered her into the living room and switched the light on. 'I thought it was going well between you.'

'So did I, but he obviously thought different,' Anna said, flopping onto the sofa.

'What happened?' Cheryl perched beside her.

'He was supposed to meet me in town, but he didn't turn up,' Anna explained. 'His phone kept going to voicemail when I tried to ring him, and I started to get worried that he might have had a crash or something. But just as I was about to ring round the hospitals, he texted saying he wasn't coming 'cos everything's moving too fast and he thinks we need a break.'

'I'm sorry, babe,' Cheryl sympathised, reaching out to squeeze her hand. 'But at least he hasn't finished it completely, so there's still a chance he'll change his mind.'

'I just don't get what I did wrong,' Anna replied miserably. 'Why do the nice ones always end up ghosting me? I'm not that bad, am I?'

'Of course not,' Cheryl assured her. 'And Sean hasn't ghosted you, so don't write him off. I'm sure he'll get in touch when he's had a chance to think things over.'

'Well, he'd best not take too long about it, or he might find I've moved on,' Anna huffed. 'I could walk into any club in town right now and have at least ten guys' numbers by closing time.'

'But they're not the type of men you want,' said Cheryl. 'And if you went with someone to get back at Sean, I guarantee you'd regret it.'

'I know,' Anna conceded, sighing as she reached into her bag and pulled out a bottle of vodka. 'Oh well, there's nothing I can do about it tonight 'cos he's turned his phone off, so go get some glasses and let's get hammered.'

'I'll get one for you, but I'm having tea,' Cheryl said. 'I've got work in the morning.'

'One shot won't kill you,' Anna insisted. 'And you can't let me drink alone at a time like this.'

'OK, I'll have one,' Cheryl agreed. 'But then I'm going to bed.'

'We'll see,' Anna said, grinning as she twisted the lid off the bottle and raised it to her lips.

RAISING READERS

Books Build Bright Futures

Dear Reader,

We'd love your attention for one more page to tell you about the crisis in children's reading, and what we can all do.

Studies have shown that reading for fun is the **single biggest predictor of a child's future life chances** – more than family circumstance, parents' educational background or income. It improves academic results, mental health, wealth, communication skills, ambition and happiness.[1]

The number of children reading for fun is in rapid decline. Young people have a lot of competition for their time. In 2024, 1 in 10 children and young people in the UK aged 5 to 18 did not own a single book at home.[2]

Hachette works extensively with schools, libraries and literacy charities, but here are some ways we can all raise more readers:

- Reading to children for just 10 minutes a day makes a difference
- Don't give up if children aren't regular readers – there will be books for them!
- Visit bookshops and libraries to get recommendations
- Encourage them to listen to audiobooks
- Support school libraries
- Give books as gifts

There's a lot more information about how to encourage children to read on our website: **www.RaisingReaders.co.uk**

Thank you for reading.

hachette UK

---

[1] OECD, '21st-Century Readers: Developing Literacy Skills in a Digital World', 2021, https://www.oecd.org/en/publications/21st-century-readers_a83d84cb-en.html

[2] National Literacy Trust, 'Book Ownership in 2024', November 2024, https://literacytrust.org.uk/research-services/research-reports/book-ownership-in-2024